CIVIL LI

CIVIL LINES 6

Edited by

Mukul Kesavan, Kai Friese and
Achal Prabhala

HarperCollins *Publishers* India
a joint venture with
THE INDIA TODAY GROUP
New Delhi

First published in India in 2011 by
HarperCollins *Publishers* India
a joint venture with
The India Today Group

Anthology copyright © Civil Lines

Individual copyright in individual pieces vests with the respective editors.

ISBN: 978-93-5029-098-9

2 4 6 8 10 9 7 5 3 1

The contributors assert the moral right to be identified as
the authors of this work.

All rights reserved. No part of this publication may be reproduced,
stored in a retrieval system, or transmitted, in any form or by any means, electronic,
mechanical, photocopying, recording or otherwise,
without the prior permission of the publishers.

HarperCollins *Publishers*
A-53, Sector 57, Noida 201301, India
77-85 Fulham Palace Road, London W6 8JB, United Kingdom
Hazelton Lanes, 55 Avenue Road, Suite 2900, Toronto, Ontario M5R 3L2
and 1995 Markham Road, Scarborough, Ontario M1B 5M8, Canada
25 Ryde Road, Pymble, Sydney, NSW 2073, Australia
31 View Road, Glenfield, Auckland 10, New Zealand
10 East 53rd Street, New York NY 10022, USA

Typeset in 10.5/13.7 Scala at
SŪRYA

Printed and bound at
Thomson Press (India) Ltd.

CONTENTS

Editors' Note vii

GREAT EASTERN HOTEL 1
Ruchir Joshi

FLIGHT 36
Itu Chaudhuri

SCHEHERAZADE 46
Itu Chaudhuri

ERAZEX 62
Achal Prabhala

THE REMEMBERED VILLAGE 81
U.R. Ananthamurthy

THE ARCHIVIST 86
Ananya Vajpeyi

EXIT THE GULF 102
Shougat Dasgupta

SKELETONS 113
Naresh Fernandes

BUILDING BRIDGES   124
   Manu Herbstein

THE MUSE OF FAILURE   167
   Anand Balakrishnan

THE ADVENTURES OF IDI AMIN DADA   179
   Binyavanga Wainaina

MOBIUS   188
   Rimli Sengupta

NEST   189
   Rimli Sengupta

SUGARCANE   190
   Nilanjana Roy

RAAGTIME   200
   Benjamin Siegel

NIZAMUDDIN AT NIGHT   227
   Gauri Gill

CONTRIBUTORS   246

EDITORS' NOTE

Civil Lines went to bed in 2001 and rose a decade later in an unrecognizable world. Rip Van Winkle slept twice as long but woke up less disoriented. Time moves faster in Googleworld than it did in the Catskills in the late eighteenth century. One of the early contributors to this issue (we have them carbon dated now) moved from initial impatience to a mature curiosity about our editorial methods. 'You know,' she said, 'since you accepted my stuff I've lived in three continents, done a Ph.D and changed jobs. So what's been happening with you?'

We want to say that we have been letting things breathe and get better, but if cleverness has a sell-by date, ten years and counting is well past that time. So the best explanation for the elephantine gestation of *Civil Lines 6* is the truth: unsure of our editorial judgement we waited for the submissions to pass the test of time. And the book you hold in your hands is a collection of the pieces that survived that gruelling test: only the best and cleanest A4 manuscripts survived.

Civil Lines was conceived of not as a literary magazine, but as a literary miscellany. This sixth issue is the first collection that surfaces in a world where writing and publishing and editing and all the judgements associated with them have been systematically remade or subverted by the Web. Large questions have been raised about the role of literary gatekeepers in a world where one's every thought can be published in 140-character instalments without intermediaries. Magazines, literary and otherwise, wrestle with the economics of publishing in a world where netizens have become accustomed to downloading 'content' free.

A technologically au fait friend asked us if we had a website, if we planned to have one, and if we did, what fraction of each issue we planned to post online. These were interesting questions but luckily they seemed to connect to a prior something called a business model, which we did not have, so we ignored them and concentrated on our main business, collecting and publishing work that had been written for ever.

For us at *Civil Lines*, the advent of the World Wide Web is rather less significant than the deaths of the two people who were responsible for *Civil Lines*' intermittent existence. Dharma Kumar, whose idea *Civil Lines* was, died in 2001, the year that the last issue before this one appeared. Then Ravi Dayal, who published the first four issues, died in 2006. Dharma and Ravi would have approved, we think, of the contents of *Civil Lines 6*. This issue is dedicated to their memory.

GREAT EASTERN HOTEL

Ruchir Joshi FROM A NOVEL IN PROGRESS

Calcutta, 1944

So, yes, let's do this to jazz: the percussion sound of bone-crack, not full crack, just the light crunch of skeleton upon skeleton, the long trombone of the 9 o'clock siren, the long whimper of the truck engine dying down, good old Bedford 4-stroke bass, the bone-beat still going, the scat of morning dogs about to be left hungry, their food being trucked away like a tune being pulled on them, but, but, but, just before the half-number ends the horn yowl of 'maaaaago, O! maaaaago', some poor dame's voice shiny as if through brass rubbed paper-thin, but still full, all the timbre of life, not clear if she's going high for some husbandman's face she's seen on a body drumming into the morning transport, or if it's just her own face she sees there tomorrow, or her third or fifth's baby's, or her old mama she's just seen going down.

In grand and meaningless memory, hey man, let's put the sharpest cook-knife into the carcass of jazz, between the luscious dead meat and the marrow-rich bone, between the smooth score and the maverick high-hat, between the slothful, slumberous, deep sax – bar-y-tone, since you akse – and the hopped-up guitar strangling its own strings, between the LieutCol's white-ass double-bass, who does the motherfucking-motherfucker fucking think he is, Motzart? and the mewling of the rear-gunner's clarinet, hope for his crew's sake he shoot sharper than he blow, hope for all of them a quick and early death, a clean wipe-out, unlike the *bone-bags being shuffled here in front of my sad and sorry eyes, a clean go a mile above the whitest mountains on earth, maybe as many as five seconds, ten, maximum fifteen, of knowing that this is your end, your big hello to Hell-heaven, and then you'se goooooone, either the record-finish scratch of nothing-type eternity or, or, or, or floating in that ocean of air like one of these statues these people love to float into the river after their carnival, floating and knowing you managed to take a few slant-eyes with you, who knows whether foe or friend, Jap or Chink, but knowing for sure the flak can't touch you no more, knowing the shell-puffs is now like some sort of celebrationary send-off to you, your life, who you used to be.*

But not like this, not like this, not like this card-pack shuffle of bodies, filthy with the ghost of a shit they managed to pass before their passing, their stomachs still craving, empty as a beer-barrel on Monday morning. Even after death, their eyes looking for food, their mouths looking for a taste they was unlucky enough to have when they was kids. Sound of an ungrown kid all of this rattling, sound of a mass kid that never grew up, sound of something that learned to dream too damn early for its own good, like a bunch of mosquitoes trying to write poetry, like a band of cockroach trying to follow a tune-sheet.

It's like someone drop a big slow bomb on these fuckers, a bomb bigger than God, that spreads and spreads and spreads, something like the Universe, big four, eight, twelve-engine silver bird dropping a big piece of resonance, and you know what? It's gonna come down the old Mississippi one day, just like it come down this here delta wearin the face of hell. But what hell, where in hell is hell except right here, right in front of my burning eyes, and maybe I shouldn't feel so bad for them, at least not for them that's dead because they done got away, the whole daily stack of them. Hell maybe gets carried away to the river every morning, in three camouflage-green trucks, the backs filled to the top, and baby there's nothing you did-could give me, nothing you can take away, that plays any tune with this. So, let's do this to sound, let's do this to jazz, let's just do it.

Something stands firm behind Byron's head, doesn't swim and slide like everything else around him, and he realizes it's the wall he's been leaning on. As he stares, trying hard to stop his eyes from prancing, the men pull down the tarpaulins, curtaining the packed corpses. One by one, the Bedfords growl into life, their exhaust pipes blasting out in sequence, first one, then the other, then two together, then all three going at once in smoky agreement. The scraping of the horn rim against the wall comes to Byron much after he finds himself tottering in the middle of the lane, much after he has pushed himself away from the support and walked right into the exhaust fumes. As the first weary lorry creaks away from the narrow pavement, he looks down and sees: without any permission from him, his feet have spread themselves into playing position. *That's right,* he thinks, *let's do this.*

As the trucks nudge themselves into line and head towards New Market, Byron brings up his cornet and presses the mouthpiece to his lips, not too hard, just so. He breathes in everything, the smoke, the morning air on Kyd Street, the whole dirty blue sky above him. Then he narrows it down to his instrument and lets go of it all.

7 August 1941

1.

The Poet's House

Her first thought is a bomb. A street full of houses wiped out. She turns her head, this way and that, looking for accompanying rubble, but the buildings seem intact. Next thought, shoals of fish washed ashore, thousands of little fish smashed out of their water by some infuriated sea. But that doesn't fit either. She needs to turn another doorknob, open another story.

There are binoculars. Being sensible, and having come expecting a distant spectacle, she has brought binoculars. They swing from her neck, knocking gently against her chest, reminding her that they are there to be used. But there is no distance here to pin down, what's there is all around her, and she looks down at the brown case and feels stupid – caught carrying a lacrosse stick on a golf course.

Slippers, she thinks, but not slippers really, what's the word? Chop-something. Choppol. Her teacher is from the north of the country and he has made many jokes about how the local people cannot pronounce a flat 'a' without turning it into an 'aww'. He would call them 'chuppull', spelt c-h-a-p-p-a-l, not c-h-o-p-p-o-l, but the meaning was the same – those things they walk around in. What they wear on their feet.

She has even tried on a pair once, when she went to Bentinck Street to one of the Chinese shoe shops. 'Madam, you have large size ... I don't have your size, but if you want, I make you.' She remembers the odd double feeling of constriction and freedom, her big toes trapped by the tight hoops of leather, the rest of her toes naked to the air, her insteps too snug, too intimate with the strap, and her heels sticking out a mile, scraping the cool floor as she walked around the shop, and her mother saying 'Darling, surely ...' the voice stained with panic, trying to stop her wild daughter from jumping out of an aeroplane.

A thick carpet of slippers, chappals, sandals, covering the road, everywhere, left ones and right ones, all mixed up, as if they had rained down from the sky in a hailstorm of leather. And she feels as though she too has dropped from somewhere, parachuted down, no memory of falling, just landing, and now walking in this alien landscape, on this strange dirty street sprouting thousands of absent feet.

Among the chappals and odd scatterings of flowers there are a few shoes as well, and she recognizes them – familiar faces in a crowd of foreigners. There's a lone one, black and shiny, a man's shoe, leaning right side up against a wall with its inner sole pulled out like the tongue of a recently slaughtered animal. Even in the vortex of her bewilderment, she feels for it as one does for one's own kin.

She can now see there are layers and layers of them, pulling away from her, turning the corner of the street and catching sunlight, as if a giant with millions of small feet has rushed off to a party. It's not what she has been expecting. She has come because she is taken by an idea of literature, but this is not how she had imagined it before setting off. The death of a poet should have been something gentler, smaller, more within the rhyme and metre of propriety, not marked by this detritus of a stampede.

As she wades through the small dunes of leather she notices two urchins picking through the piles, trying to find matching pairs. They play in this vast jigsaw puzzle, their hair caked with dust, their grey-brown rags fluttering around them, both the boy and the girl slapping about in chappals that are far too big for them. Their brown bodies are thin, alive with excitement, and they shout triumphantly to each other even though they are no more than five feet apart. The little girl has found a jute sack and she carefully puts two pairs of chappals into it. The boy hitches up his shorts and moves over to peer into the sack, examining the booty. Then they squat down the way only natives can – she has never seen a European managing to fold himself up like this – and get back to their sifting.

After a while, the boy comes across a small pile of marigold flowers and he picks an orange ball up and throws it at the girl. The girl squeals out a laugh. Then he throws another, which she manages to catch and fling back at him. Suddenly their collection of chappals is forgotten and they are up, tripping and stumbling, showering each other with flowers. The boy throws one hard at the girl and it misses and flies towards Imogen who tries to catch it. Her hands close too late and the flower explodes on her binocular case, shrapnelling her with petals. The kids petrify into statues, staring at the memshaheb.

The girl is the first to recover and she whips around, looking for her sack. The boy's legs jerk, about to start sprinting, but his slippers are trapped in the debris. This gives Imogen enough time to smile at them and pull out her binoculars. She puts them to her eyes and cranes her neck forward, pretending to look through them. The children pause, now not sure whether they need to run. Imogen puts away the binoculars and smiles again, desperately trying to remember the phrase for 'It's all right.' But her toddling Hindi has lurched out of reach, so she calls it out in English. Then she pats a hand in the air, trying to indicate both 'sit down' and 'don't worry', acutely aware of how foolish she must look.

The boy gets it, and he cups his hands around his eyes, mimicking her, and he tilts his head left and right, a grin shining on his face again. The girl puts down the sack and copies the boy. Imogen mimics them back, tilting her head this way and that, and then they all laugh and it's fine.

Imogen waves goodbye and moves away, leaving them to their business. As she looks around, her eyes now able to stray from the ground, she sees that she is right before the entrance of the famous mansion. The big iron gates are smashed open, one barely hanging on a hinge, the other ripped completely off, lying flat on the ground. Beyond the entrance the trees droop, mourning in the muggy air. The tree-lined drive leads her eyes to the doors and windows of the house which are open, as if the place has just been evacuated before an approaching army. Obviously there is nothing left to steal. Or, perhaps, even the thieves have gone to the cremation.

The Beautiful Boy

Gopal marks the pretty one about three-quarters of an hour before he strikes. He picks him out of the crowd while they are still on Cornwallis Street, a full forty minutes before he gets him.

Then he goes and manages three others, minor, all the while keeping the beautiful boy in the side of his eye, keeping him as his main prize. He could be wrong, but no. Just something in the way the head is held, something loose and careless about the kurta, and the way the hands swim away from his body, pushing people, pushing away push, making even more contact because he's trying to avoid the touch of other bodies.

Since the news of the death spread across the city, Gopal has been warned that the procession would be big. But this crowd is huge, bigger than anything Gopal has ever seen in his twenty years, washing right up against the walls of buildings on either side of the road. The incredible crush of people is good, perfect beyond dreams, but still it's not quite right.

What bothers Gopal is the singing. He realizes that day – his last one on the job though he doesn't know it yet – how much he depends on sound. The clang of the tram stopping, the little argument about standing room, about whose foot is on whose chappal, or maybe the sudden attack of a baby wailing, or some idiot hero striking a match, lighting a cigarette in the middle of a crowd or, sometimes, a big car going paa-paa-paa, trying to shove past the bus, the noise horning into passengers' heads, making them angry and careless. Like the best of them, Gopal works to the kick of sudden noise, uses it as one of his tools, but this singing is not like that, and it feels like it's set up against him.

It is an awful, slow chorusing but people seem more aware of each other because of it, all these wet-eyed fools caught in the web of some soft and stupid grief. The singing is loudest around the lorry carrying the body. Even though the old man is dead it seems as if these voices are coming out of him. Him, stretched out, wrapped in flowers, like a fish in banana leaves which has suddenly sprouted white hair. Every now and then someone lobs more flowers onto the bier and some of them roll off in a small landslide of yellow and white, leaving a trailing paste of squashed buds in the procession's long wake.

Gopal looks up at the sky. Near the Jorasanko house there had been a bit of mild sunlight but here it is overcast, and Gopal greedily prays for rain. A bit of water and mud underfoot would help, people slipping a bit as they walk, so many of them barefoot, further distracted by sliding and needing to concentrate on their balance. But there is to be no rain that day and he pushes the thought aside. He doesn't really need it, he tells himself, there's already enough to work with.

Sure enough, in a few minutes Gopal has used the push and pull of the crowd to work himself close to the pretty boy. A little behind him and a little to his left, because Gopal's experience tells him that most people of that class carry it in their left pockets and not the right, the same side as they wear their watch.

With the clunky inevitability of a carriage manoeuvring to hook up with an engine in the Howrah sidings, Gopal now comes up right behind his quarry. Once in position, he stays there, the right side of his body pressed into the left side of his beauteousness, pressed right up against him, building familiarity, normalcy, conveying an apologetic 'What to do bhai? What a crowd, no?' through his partial embrace. 'Never hurry,' his Ustad has drilled into him a long time ago, 'the ones who hurry get caught.' And Gopal is now a champion at biding his time.

Joined like Siamese twins, Gopal and the pretty boy float with the procession for what seems like a long time. As they move, Gopal notices things: the roofs and balconies of the houses on Grey Street are overflowing with people, all craning their necks to catch sight of the action; he wonders if someone will fall, adding to the death toll of the day like a small drop after a big torrent. On one roof, he sees a man with a cinema machine, a black cloth covering his head and the top of the machine, moving the apparatus left to right on the stand, following the truck; in a second-floor window he sees a few sadhus, their orange showing out of the shadows, their kartals clanging out a completely different rhythm to the slow song of the crowd, one of them moving a smoking aaroti in a circle, his lips fluttering out a silent shloke. Overhead he sees a small aeroplane, banking and circling, flying quite low, obviously some military shahebs wanting the best view; he doesn't need to look at the pretty boy, he needs to feel him properly and this he does – the bony shoulder, the slim body under the dhoti-kurta, the slight bump of his small buttocks, a pleasurable mound of muscle, pity there is no way to both do the job and get in front of him to feel his – and then, yes, sure enough, on the side of the hip, in the left kurta pocket the bulge of what can only be a loaded wallet.

While maintaining contact, Gopal is careful not to stay on the wallet too long. He moves his hip away as soon as he confirms its presence; his hands have stayed away from the pocket area throughout; they will only come into play at the last moment and it's crucial not to give the victim any advance notice of their presence.

Ocean of Peace

Kedar suddenly starts to feel as if he's being carried in the wrong direction by a strong current. He knows why he is here, he is sure of that, he knows how he got here, he knows how he came to be barefoot on this dirty, slimy avenue, how his chappals were torn off in the crush at the gates of Jorasanko, he even knows his own name, but he no longer knows why he is carrying on.

There are banana fronds tied to the back of the driver's cabin and he can see them waving gently over the great man's body as the truck inches its way forward. There are people sitting on the truck and they constantly wave incense sticks in circles, wiping away tears, swiping away flies and choking as they try to find voices to join the chorus:

> *There's sorrow, there's death,*
> *The fire of separation burns,*
> *Still, there's peace, there's joy,*
> *Still the eternal awakes.*

As he pushes against the wall of bodies Kedar can see some people smiling through their tears, one woman with the end of her sari clutched hard against her mouth trying to stifle her sobbing, two small children sitting on their parents' shoulders, flowers in their hands, looking around at the endless spread of heads below them, no tears and no smiles, just pure wonderment on their small, clean faces.

One song ends and another begins: *Aanondolokey, mongolalokey, beee-raaa-jo ... In the blissful land, in the blessed land, may you rule* – it's too much, and the old man was never about too much, there was always a holding back, even in his storms and tempests. Even at his most powerful, he never rained on you. His genius was that he broke open your own monsoon inside you, and this sweaty, crowded death was not right for him. Unavoidable, perhaps. But not right.

Another thought attaches itself to that one, and Kedar realizes it's time for him to get out. But, just as he thinks this, a surge in the crowd makes other people push up even harder against him. It's as if other bodies have pasted themselves to him and he can't unglue himself. The harder he tries to move sideways and out of the flow the more he is caught in its forward-moving crush. The more he tries to breathe in clean air the more he can smell the body odours, the smoke from the dhoop, the engine fumes from the slow-gearing truck. He tries to calm himself down and he succeeds at the exact moment the commotion breaks out.

Kedar is not very tall and, at first, he can't see much but he can hear it. Suddenly there is shouting, then a woman screaming over the raised voices, and then a huge current of violent jostling that pulses through the crowd. Kedar feels himself actually being lifted up from the ground and, for a brief moment, he gets a completely clear view of the truck. Two men are wrestling with a thin, dark man who is trying to do something to the dead body. The men grab the thin man's hands and pull them away from the poet's face. Then they try to prise open the man's fingers, trying to get at something clutched in his fist. A policeman leaps onto the truck and, as he is brought back to the ground, Kedar can see the police baton go up and swing down hard. He can hear the man's cry of pain and then people shouting 'Hair!', 'Hair!', 'He was trying to snatch some of Gurudev's hair!', 'He pulled at the beard!'

By the time the full understanding of the incident sinks in, Kedar finds himself far from the centre of the procession. It's as if someone much bigger has heard him and begun to take him out of the throng. Slowly spun him around and sent him bobbing in another direction. For a brief while he's caught again in a tight knot of people, a stick of sugarcane being squeezed through a juice mill, and then he is out of it, stumbling along a side lane, trying to control his numb legs.

As he moves away, he can hear the next hymn. Someone with a strong voice leads the song Tagore wrote specifically to be sung at this, his own funeral –

The ocean of peace lies in front,
Launch the boat, O helmsman ...

Kedar shudders, sloughing off the feel of other bodies. As he walks further, his limbs accrue back to him and he begins to enjoy the naked feel of the rough asphalt under his feet.

In a few minutes, he is in another world. A quiet maze of north Calcutta galis, strangely empty. The only sound is that of loitering crows, then a rattle of kitchen metal, pots and pans being washed in an unseen courtyard, and then, from some other house, the news crawling out of a radio. The newsreader's voice is faint at first, then louder as he passes under the window, then faint again –
'... and in the North African theatre, the seige of Tobruk continues as the small number of gallant troops still defy the might of Rommel's Afrika Korps. In Cairo, the commander of the Commonwealth forces, General Auchinleck said yesterday that ...'

Kedar cuts out what Auchinleck said by starting to hum a song. *Jodi tor daak shuney keu naa aashey tobey ekla cholo re ... If no one heeds your call, if no one comes along, then walk alone ...*

Walk alone, walk alone, walk alone, my friend, walk alone, walk alone, he's still humming the same tune, his heart now a lot lighter, when he reaches Esplanade and feels the warm metal of the tramline under his feet. He sees a tram that will take him home and jumps on without waiting for it to stop. The conductor shouts at him, irritated at this young fool for trying to get killed on his shift. Kedar smiles, tilts his head in an apology, and reaches into the pocket of his kurta to pull out his wallet.

2.

The Girl in the Mirror

This evening it's not so much the house as her mother's voice that is foreign. The sharp climb of the 'Darling!' and then the next pokey-peak at 'crowd' in the 'Darling! You didn't get mixed up with the *crowd*, darling, did you?'

Did you? The didjyu hanging there like an old anxiety, a family heirloom, out of its tissue paper again.

She has noticed it since she was a child – the trick going somewhere new plays on you. This tricky business of going somewhere new and then coming back home. When you leave home, home is home, it's as you know it. Then you go into another world, a strange corner of the city perhaps, north of Euston Station perhaps, or maybe somewhere country. And then, just when you return, then, just as you turn into the street that leads home, or perhaps the crossing that's two corners away from home ... suddenly everything feels different because of where you've just been. This strange place where you've just been comes padding back right behind you and infects your house, your whatyouknow, and turns it into a strange place too.

The layout of the house allows Imogen to go to her own rooms without actually passing her mother. She reaches there, flinging a voice up the stairs, 'It's fine, Mummy! I'm fine, it's all right, really!', her own voice now a sketch of her mother's and the sentence a toll she pays as she quickly crosses the hall to her door.

Her shoulders sink as soon as she shuts the door. She switches on the fan and then just stands there, recovering, looking around this strange room she knows so well. Her clothes feel heavy and it's not just the sweat. You'd think by now they'd be used to people who looked like her, but it seems not. Two hundred years of memshahebs making not a jot of difference, and it often feels as if she's the very first.

Today, as she has walked and wandered, her body has picked up the looks of natives, lookings, starings, like molluscs adhering to a ship, like crows on a cow's back. A hardening of eyes here, a lecherous half-smile there, a bunch of women on a passing tram pointing at her and laughing rudely, and then the two old beggar women with their muddy corneas, staring not so much at Imogen as at some half-sensed ghost standing next to her. Today, she has caught all these eyes and carried them with her, been forced to accumulate each gaze like unwanted shopping, each encounter making her more wooden, each contact pushing into her body, the small of her back and the cross of her neck becoming stiffer and stiffer.

Every day is not this bad, though. On some days, in fact, the exchange can be mysterious. Exciting. And, though she dare not say it to people around her, nourishing, yes, nourishing in a strange, guilt-simmered sort of way, secretly helping her keep head above water.

As she tosses her hat on the bed and takes off her binoculars, Imogen suddenly remembers the boy and the girl sifting their shoe-treasure. Yes, like those two for instance. Her heart lifting, she steps out of her shoes and curls her toes, flexing her calf muscles by moving her ankles up and down. She checks her watch: still two hours before Andrew arrives to take her to the party. She makes sure the thin curtains are drawn and hooks an arm behind her, reaching for the buttons of her dress.

The sticky cotton print peeling off her body exposes her skin to the fan circling above and gives her new energy. She attacks the rest of her garments ruthlessly. Got you, sock! Off! And, here's your partner ... thumbs in, pull it down, throw. Moe-zaa, singular for sock, moe-zey, plural, jaao mozey, bhaago! Get thee, the pair of you, to a laundry basket! Her brassiere is captured next. It puts up a struggle, but it's wrestled with, unhooked, vanquished, and then sent flying to lie wet and dead on top of the socks. No word in Hindi for that yet, nor for the camiknickers that she unbuttons and wriggles out of, dancing now, trying to snake her waist and hips like the little shoe-girl. Nothing saucy about this, no trace of Paris nightclub, just the sheer pleasure of moving freely, of catching the air as it spins down on her hot body. Pick up knickers, start to bring them up to nose for the smell, a habit from back home where there wasn't-and-will-be no dobby-woman to wash memshaheb foundationals. Hmm, this not England, very hot weather, no point smelling, best to dispatch – off! Jaao!

She pauses, having run out of hosiery, and catches a glimpse of herself in the long mirror at the other end of the room. The late afternoon light dramatizes her, but she is no Diana, no Aphrodite, no Rodin voluptress.

Freckles. She can see them being cheeky from across the room. And a precise patchwork of dark and light skin, the lines chopping off her upper arms exactly like an old Greek statue, and again in a sharp semicircle around her neck, where the territory of cloth has ended and the sun had its full play. The freckles romp across these colour frontiers, ever there, loyal companions that have stayed with her wherever she has travelled – Butlins, Folies Bergeres, Jungfrau, Southampton-Cape Town-Bombay and now here, in this subtropical hellhole ... no ... not fair. Honestly, quite a nice hellhole, except for Mummy and Daddy and this monsoon clamminess. Truth to tell, the freckles have rarely been happier.

Her glance traps itself in the mirror again and this time she can't stop herself. Legs spread wide, hair a frightful brown-blonde shipwreck, naked as the day she was born except, now, much taller than the mother she came out of, perhaps, surely, perhaps she's imagining it, but her downstairs hair now growing quite wild, like an untended, triangular allotment; her eyes a mad, out-of-place blue that she often wishes she could send back to the suppliers in a box marked: *Unsatisfactory for this region. Please replace with a darkish brown,* and now this lunatic smile hopscotching all over her face. She stops trying to stop herself and sends a signal to her knees to squat down like a native. They obey her the best they can, and she suddenly finds herself suspended like a discus thrower, arms stretched out for balance, thighs frozen in protest, her buttocks jutting out, but no closer to the floor than three feet. As she looks at the mirror again, the bothersome laughter welling up in her empty stomach does nothing to alleviate the cramp.

Promotion

The boats tell him the river is good today. Just from the way they nudge each other gently, playing with their mooring ropes like village grandmothers tugging crib-cords, he can tell it's a good day to go out on the water. Not that he needs to. All he has to do is jump from one tethered boat to another for about seven boats, step onto the rusty barge, cross over the top to the side facing the river and go down the steps to where the small launch sits at its usual early evening berth.

As Gopal steps off the mud bank on to the first boat, he nods to the two boatmen squatting just outside the curve of its covering. 'Tsaa khaaba na ki?' one of them asks him, fanning the fire in the guts of a small chulha he has lit on the wooden deck. Gopal raises a hand – no time for tea just now – and skips on to the next boat. The launch too has a chulha and there will be tea, tea with much more milk than the boatmen can afford, but it remains to be seen whether he is offered any today. Given the weight of the day's take bulging in his pockets, his best day yet as a pocketmaar, he suspects he may even get something to eat, but life has already taught Gopal never to take anything for granted.

A sluggish breeze comes off the river, but even that feels cool after the grinding crowd. For several minutes after twisting his way out of the thick snake of people, Gopal felt like a mulch of spices ground by a crazy masalchi. It took him a while to transform himself from a wet mess back into a human being, and then it took all his self-control not to break into a triumphant run. On a nearly empty Strand Road he pulled himself back, forcing himself into a slow walk till his wits returned to him. Moving south and away from the huge mass of mourners heading to the cremation ghat, he worked out a plan. The plan led him to a quiet corner of the Victoria Memorial gardens where he spent some time organizing himself. Now he is calm and ready to face his Ustad.

Being quietly fond of his own life and the idea of continuing it, Gopal has rehearsed a few times what will happen once he reaches the launch:

'Hm! Gogai! Come here!'
'Ustad.'
'Everything all right? No trouble with the police? People tell me many cockroaches were in plainclothes today.'
'No, Ustad, no problems. Uniform-mamas too busy looking after VIP types. And I kept looking out for plainclothes. Some fool tried to snatch hair from the dead body and the mamas nearly killed him, but otherwise ...'
'Hm. Show me.'

From the secret pockets inside his trousers Gopal will pull out the remaining purses and wallets, the three watches, one heavy golden key-chain, everything except the wallet he took off the pretty boy, and lay it all on the floor of the cabin. Ustad will nod approvingly, sifting through the stuff, sorting out paper money, small change, the other bits and pieces people always nest away with their money. Then the old man will contemplate the takings for a while, his eyes journeying elsewhere, as if lost in deep religious thought. The bigger the booty, the longer, usually, the contemplation. After which he will sort out the share, playing slow chess with the money and the objects.

It was usually during this game that the Ustad caught people out. Once, Gopal had seen him suddenly wipe aside another boy's takings with a sweep of his arm and, with the return of the same arm, smash the boy's face, breaking his jaw. Ustad had then turned the whimpering thing over, ripped his pants down and yanked out a sack the poor fucker had tied between his legs, just between his balls and his backhole. What followed with the boy's testicles still turned Gopal cold with fear. On another occasion, Ustad had finished his chess game, looked up at the girl who had brought in the take, and unleashed his teeth in a smile. 'You know Ustad doesn't like to hit girls, don't you ma? But if you're ripe enough to steal from Ustad then perhaps you're ripe enough to go to work in Banshibadi, yes?' As the understanding crept up around her neck, the girl stared back like a madwoman, Banshibadi being the worst of the brothels Ustad controlled, the place near the docks where the lowest dirt from the visiting ships took their pleasure.

Others had taken the calculated risk of hiding their loot elsewhere, and they too had paid a price for their mistake. Neither Gopal nor any of the other pocketmaars had yet figured out how Ustad always managed to smell things out from people's heads, but he did.

Gopal is aware of all this, but still, today, for the first time, he is about to try and do what he always advises the others never to even dream about. Maybe the craziness of the crowd has got to him, maybe it's the heady contact with the aroma of real money, maybe just the feel of the pretty boy's body against his own, but today he is going to try and put one over Ustad.

Like a good actor, he throws away the husk of his rehearsals as he climbs on to the barge and works his way through rotting ropes and pylons to the other side. As he's about to jump across the small gap between the barge and the launch, he sees Aurangzeb standing on the deck and he falters. His nerve nearly goes. The launch suddenly feels like a toy boat that a grown-up has decided to take over. One stamp of a foot and the thing will break in two and sink, one wrong elbow and the cabin will go flying into the water, decapitated, one ... Aurangzeb brings his huge head up in a stare and Gopal feels his heart rubber-ball up and down. What is the big sisterfucker doing here?

Another body peels out of Aurangzeb as Gourango steps out from behind the larger man. Both of them here together. Gopal feels his toes lock up and his knees starting to turn him around, every part of his being getting ready to send his body leaping back across the barge and away from these two as fast as he can go. For the second time that day Gopal stops himself from running. He slows everything down – his legs, his breathing, his eyes. He nods to the two who are now looking at him, jumps across, and moves to go down into the cabin. He even finds the courage to bring his voice in, half grunt, half squeak, nodding at the dark cave of the cabin, 'Ustad bhetorey?' and, somehow, everything holds while Gourango takes his time before jerking his head in a yes.

'Eijey Gogai!' The familiar ratchet sound snakes up to the deck. 'Where are you thinking of running to? Don't tell me you're scared of these two!' The voice leaks barely contained mirth but that does nothing to lessen Gopal's thudding heartbeat. 'Come here, come here, Ustad will protect you from these bad men!' As Gopal ducks in through the low door, the old man is chortling. 'Come here and show me what you've got.'

'Ustad,' says Gopal, nodding his head in salute before starting to reach into his many pockets. As he puts the stuff down in a pile, Ustad grins at him, reaches out a hand and puts it lovingly under Gopal's chin. 'Oh-ho. Looks like you're the king today, Gogaibabu. Was it hard work?'

Before Gopal can reply, Ustad calls out for some tea. Suddenly, everything is back in tune with what Gopal has imagined, the questions about the police-mamas and the plainclothes, the pauses, the looks, almost everything. A difference – when he mentions the man trying to pull hair from the dead body – 'Ah! Now see! Now that poor bokachoda had the right idea. One or two of those hairs might have been worth a hundred times what you've got here!' More guffaws, a cursory flicking through the take piled up before him, and then a subtle shift. A going quiet that Gopal knows all too well.

Gopal realizes the tea is next to his knee on the floor and he reaches for it. Ustad waits till the hot cup is right against Gopal's mouth before asking.

'All this, very good Gogai. But what did you bury in the Memorial gardens?'

Gopal takes a swig of the tea before replying. He hasn't rehearsed this one but he is surprised at how little shock he feels at the question. He puts the tea down, controlling the surprise he shows, calibrating its flow like you do water coming out of a tap. Not enough awe at the old man's ownership of the world and he would be suspicious. Too much fear and he would know. But today is Gopal's day for playing everything right and he handles it perfectly. A slow lowering of the cup, with eyes widening more in admiration than in fear, and then a grin, looking straight back at the man who is the closest thing he has to a father.

'There were too many purses and things Ustad, I was afraid the bulk was showing even under my shirt, so I got rid of a lot of useless ... I can go and get it all back ... there's nothing valuable ... but, how did you ...'

The old man rummages through his beard, trying to stuff his triumphant smile back into his head. 'Eijey! Aurangzeb!' he calls out. 'Shunchhish? Did you hear? Our boy is now old enough to decide what is valuable and what is a horse's egg!'

There is no response from Aurangzeb. Gopal fights the urge to turn around and ward off the sure knife about to plunge into his back. A long horn echoes across the riverside and a wave punches the launch gently as a big boat passes. Gopal absorbs the sideways movement under him. Calm yourself now. No knife. You would have heard anyone coming down into the cabin.

'Don't worry, kono bepaar nahi.' Ustad is now scratching the skin just outside his left eye, a sign that he is thinking how to say something important, 'I already checked what you buried and you did right, there was nothing valuable there.' Gopal looks down to see a fly nosing around above his teacup and suddenly he is relaxed enough to snap it up. He lets it buzz inside his fist for a moment and then crushes it dead. The old man notices this but leaves it unremarked. He clears his throat.

'Gogai, you know that I don't do all that garbage, about how you've been like a son to me, how I feel like a father to you, and all that time-waste.'

This is not anywhere within the furthest spread of Gopal's anticipation. He feels his gut tighten, but he keeps his face blank. 'No, Ustad.'

'I am lucky you are not my son and you are very lucky I am not your father. Yes?'

Gopal has no idea how to respond to this, so he pays out the smallest nod he can.

'But you could say I brought you up. Made you into human.'

This is true, and Gopal can now nod a vigorous yes, but his mouth is completely dry.

'Now, listen.' Ustad loses his hesitation. 'If I were a selfish man, I could let you do this pocketmaari business for as long as you like, you're one of the best I have ever taught and, look at today, you bring in a lot.'

'Yes, Ustad.'

'But if I am to keep bringing you up properly, I have to give you a chance to be something more than just a pocketmaar. Do you understand what I mean?'

Gopal keeps quiet. He knows he is not supposed to understand.

'Pro-mo-shon,' pronounces Ustad, rolling the word in his mouth as if parting with a secret prayer. 'Promoshon. Do you know what that is?'

Gopal shakes his head in a no, a stubborn corner of him still wondering if this is a death sentence.

'Like, when a mama does well, he is moved up from a constable to a havaldar. And then from havaldar to sergeant. Like that. It's called "promoshon" in English.'

Gopal nods without trying to convey too much understanding.

'So, if the cockroaches can have their promoshon, why not us?' Ustad takes out a cigarette, taps it against the tin and lights it, not expecting any interruption. He takes a long drag and looks hard at Gopal.

'It's different kind of work, but it would mean more money, a lot more. Sometimes easy work, sometimes very hard. And working with Aurangzeb and Gourango. You have to be ready for that. But I've been watching you and I think ... yes, you would be good at it.'

Gopal delivers the nod of gratitude that is expected, still saying nothing, his body now tense in a different kind of way, his earlier fears forgotten, replaced by an excitement that he is unable to name.

In the future, whenever he thinks of this moment, Gopal will find the words gone. The actual substance of what was said will always teeter on the verge of evaporating. Strongest in him will be the memory of smell, the river, the waft of many different kinds of water, the sandpaper whiff of Ustad's cigarette mixing with the smoke from the overworked factories on the other shore, in Howrah, and then the ineradicable tickle of something frying on the chulha outside, onion filluries or fish in batter, he will never be sure, and the smell of fresh kashundi chutney playing hide and seek with the monsoon air.

'Anything else, Gogai?'

When Ustad's voice finally pulls up at the expected station, Gopal knows not to jump off. His answer is natural, neutral, one that comes from total belief in what he is saying. At that moment Gopal has forgotten about his hidden wallet and, as he replies, he has no reason to doubt that he will be believed. The launch moves under him as his stomach moves under his heart.

'No, Ustad,' says Gopal, suddenly feeling very hungry, 'nothing else.'

A Banana from Paanchpukur

If he looks down, he can fool himself that his feet have released a lake of blood. No, not blood, the floor is both too beautiful and too normal for that. A rich, dark red stretching away, gleaming with forty years of constant footfalls, it's too calm, and the black border too neat. It's too much a part of his sanctuary, his home, to have anything to do with something as crude and fresh as blood. In any case, to paint it he would need to mix a deep maroon, quite different from the scarlet of blood.

The garden next to the verandah presents quite different problems to a painter. The grass is now an intense green, a green loaded by rain and, in this coy evening light, made even more gaudy by the white pillars which frame it at regular intervals. Paul Gauguin is the only one he can think of, among them all, who could approach it. And Gauguin did not, strictly speaking, even belong to that particular 'them', but he is the one who would have come closest. Perhaps Van Gogh too. And after the two of them,

Matisse, Picasso, et cetera, but none of the main people. Not Monet, not Pisarro, not even Cezanne. From what he knows of it, none of them except Gauguin ever saw this light, none of those stay-at-homes ever experienced what humidity and cloud could do to their normal supply of sun. They had snow, of course, which Kedar has never seen at close hand, and he knows that a European winter puts up a very different kind of obstacle course for the painter but still, it's very different from a subtropical garden in August. Not that he'd mind a bit of snow under his feet at this moment, though the cool floor feels good as well.

Sitting on the verandah, Kedar hikes up his crumpled dhoti a bit further and stretches his legs as he waits for Raskolnikov to bring him his sandwiches. Though he hasn't shed any blood at all, it does feel as though his energy has leaked out of his battered soles. A loss that needs to be replenished by an immediate infusion of meat, which is why his first demand after coming home has been ham sandwiches.

With clear instructions. Because Raskolnikov, while far from being a dullard, always needs clear instructions. In fact, it is precisely because Rasko is not stupid, precisely in order to stop him from exercising his billiard-ball of a brain, that clear instructions always need to be given.

In this case: the good bread from Nahoum & Co and not foul slices from the bread-walla's morning delivery, the ham from Empire Provisions behind New Market and not the stuff Kaku procures from the Anglo-Indian fellow in Elliot Road and proper English mustard, which means not that kashundi stuff Rasko makes in the kitchen, proper mustard, *lightly* spread. And tea. As in proper Darjeeling made from the Benkabari Spring Tips and not that sawdust from Dooars. 'Bring me the good tea, Rasko, without boiling the water too much, If you bring me any of that other nonsense I will kill you, bujhechho?' 'Yes, Dada Babu, understood.'

Kedar is not sure why death makes people hungry but he has seen it time and time again, the violent gorging people immerse themselves in after the cremations and shraddhos of loved ones. Some do this shamefacedly but others are not so discreet, quite openly gluttonous – in fact, trying to affirm life, scrambling to put up a kind of food wall against the steamroller of mortality. Kedar is sure, though, that his current famishment is not of that ilk. It's just that he has walked barefoot all the way across the city, from Harrison Road and Portuguese Church to Sunny Park in Ballygunje, which is not something he has ever done before. Not that he isn't fit, not that, but playing a few sets of tennis, twice or thrice a week, is quite different from struggling through the massive crowd and then walking, what? maybe four miles? with his feet getting cut by tiny stones, glass, and all the other unnameable whatnots with which the roads of the city are mined. The whole thing today has demanded the use of different muscles from the ones his body normally deploys, and needed different muscles, he realizes, from his brain as well.

'Different muscles of the brain'. He mulls the phrase over, absently, not really thinking, more, just sleepwalking through the events since news of the great man's passing came, just after one this afternoon.

The sense of loss the news brought, of time suddenly carving a different shape out of the fixed sculpture of their lives, is now diminished: something rare – his mother crying openly, bent over the ebony holder shaking in her hand, her cigarette managing to catch some falling tears, the wasp-hiss of the dying tip; his father folding and unfolding his arms behind his back, as if in callisthenics, before finally reaching up into a bookcase for a copy of *Chaar Odhhaay* inscribed for him by Gurudeb himself; then Borun Kaku, his father's younger brother, striding off into the garden as if he had been personally mauled by fate; and last but never the least, Raskolnikov, standing behind Ma with the tea tray.

A tall, thin ghost doing aaroti with a tilted tea cosy hatching the handle of a tea-pot. Garlanded by the steam being emitted, Rasko, eyes afire, suddenly intoning the words of the song he had been taught by Borun Kaku – *Je raatey mor duaar guli bhaanglo jhorey* ...

getting out the first line in a reverential drone before Ma whirled on him and snatched away the tray, snapping at him through her sniffles to go back into the kitchen at once. Yes ... nothing worse than having your servant reciting a love song at the wrong moment.

Kedar remembers Borun Kaku, a few years ago, trying to teach Raskolnikov English, trying to use the song as a platform upon which to build. 'That night, *Rasko, dhyan daao!*, that night when the storm, storm *maaney jhor, pay attention*! that night when the storm broke open my doors!' At the time, the boy had scratched his head, and shaken it in complete fuddlement – what was Kaku Babu saying? But, this morning Kedar could have sworn he heard him muttering the English words under his breath as he beat a defiant retreat to the kitchen, 'That naaiit. Whuen tha eshtorm. Borokopen. Maii dhores.'

Raskolnikov's name began from Kedar's father calling him 'rascal' when he first arrived to work in the house, a boy between eleven and fourteen years of age, something like that, but a little older than Kedar and much, much, taller. A few years later, Borun Kaku, avid reader, changed rascal to Raskolnikov – 'Na, na, o bhishon complex character, o'r onek parts achhey, jemon in Dostoevsky.' The boy's alleged complex character with many parts and facets did not impress Kedar's mother. 'That's all we need,' she said tartly, 'one fine night for him to come up the stairs and murder me.'

'But Boudi! You are looking at the obvious! Banal! Surface!' Borun Kaku exploded as much as he could with his older brother's wife. 'Do you think Raskolnikov to be a mere murderer of older women?'

The 'older women' was a bad mistake. When recounting the incident to Kedar's father, Borun Kaku censored it to 'older ladies', and he got away with it, at least for that moment. But 'Boudi' being a higher rank and carrying more weight in this particular house than 'Kaku', despite Borun Kaku's protests, a typical family compromise was distilled over the next few weeks. The name had stuck, and so it stayed – officially, Raskolnikov – but to appease Kedar's mother it was shortened to 'Rasko', which is what everyone now calls him.

Not once in all of this was Romon, from Village Paanchpukur, Thana Badalghat, District Midnapur, asked what he wanted to be called. And neither did he ever say. But, as he grew up, it became clear that Rasko was the last person in the household who would murder Kedar's mother. Despite her daily insults and snappings, Rasko was completely devoted to Boudi. 'Like a dachshund with legs,' as Borun Kaku put it. Around sixteen, when Kedar was in his detective novel phase, he would work out elaborate plots centred around the murdered corpse of his mother, with the imbecile police inspector always making Rasko the chief suspect, and Holmes or Hercule Poirot or Miss Marple or Inspector Maigret inevitably demonstrating that the murderer was someone else: Kedar's grandmother, Kedar's father, Borun Kaku always a favourite, the meat-man, the fish-man, the bread-man, the maali and, once or twice when the story got away from him, even Kedar himself.

Kedar's mind goes back to his evaporated wallet and the tiny surgeon's slit at the end of his kurta pocket which confirms that he hasn't dropped it. There is still a phantom presence where it used to live. Walking back from Badabazaar, where the conductor – relishing the rare moment of power over an obvious bodolok rich boy – triumphantly ordered him off the tram, Kedar has repeatedly gone over what he has lost with the wallet. Some money, thirty rupees, not a lot in his mind, though he is aware that to someone else it would be a small fortune, a couple of visiting cards he's been given at the tennis club, no great loss, a receipt from Salamatally Tailors for his new summer suit, not a problem, they know him well, a couple of other bills and things, again, no great loss, and a tiny reproduction of Cezanne's *Jug and Peaches* which he'd cut out from a book and put in the photo window. A pity, that one, a painting he really loves, he'd put it in the wallet to remind himself that one day he would reach the Louvre and see the original, so, yes, a loss but not a great one. The main thing is the wallet itself, worth far more than what it contained today. That is *loss*.

Bulldog Kaku, his father's first cousin, younger than his father by a couple of years, had given it to him on his twenty-first birthday. 'Eijey, young Kedar! This is for you! Finest pigskin from Chalk and Boxall, best leather-goods suppliers for gentlemen in London. Quality-ta appreciate korbey! You will not find a better wallet anywhere in the world.' And then, with his fat Lahiri nose frying in the oil of its own humour, 'Also, Kedar, now that you are of age, we expect you not only to not lose it, but also to do some work towards filling it! Hah, hah, hah!' This accompanied by a breath-destroying slap on Kedar's back from a heavy, artillery major's hand.

Major 'Bulldog' Lahiri is currently serving in North Africa, commanding his batteries, and there is little chance of his returning soon to question Kedar about his wallet. There hasn't been a letter for a while, but – the German not yet being born who can actually kill him – sooner or later he will be back. And then he is bound to ask, the sound exploding out of his chest, the mouth a mere barrel, 'Kedar! Fellow-me-lad! Show me! How full is that wallet I gave you? And was any honest sweat involved at all?'

War's not going well over there so maybe he's been killed, Kedar thinks, and immediately reprimands himself for such a thought. He doesn't want the loudmouth to actually die, though, in the deepest cellar of his heart he knows he would much rather Bulldog Kaku stayed alive giving the Germans a headache than himself or his family. 'Only a major, kintu thinks he's a Field Marshal. And we are jemon his foot soldiers,' Borun Kaku likes to say.

Again conscious of his aching feet, Kedar wonders whether there will be any dancing at the party tonight. It seems wrong, somehow, with the whole city in mourning, but that is unlikely to affect the English – their parties will go on regardless of minor events such as the death of the greatest writer India has ever produced.

Kedar catches himself in two minds, three, actually, if the state of his feet is to be taken into account. On the one hand, tonight of all nights, he has no desire to join revelry, especially the kind of desperate thing that passes for jollity nowadays, with all sorts of strange, newly-arrived army types, both gora and native, going about as if every drink, every dance and every flirtation is their last, pretending to be heroic-posthumous, many of them well before they have seen any action. On the other hand, he's had his fill of mourning today, a surfeit of damp, romantic gloominess – the juggernaut of tears and quavery song has inexorably pushed his own ability to feel anything into a roadside ditch.

He knows he will mourn Rabindranath's passing and remember it for the rest of his life, but this evening there are enough people across the city doing the expected thing, and he is sure it will make no difference to the great man's spirit whether he goes to a party or not. Then again, he has his feet to think of – the match is set for this Saturday, and he has no wish to give that snooty Cardu Motherwalla a walkover because he can't walk.

'Dada Babu. Samwhuich.' Rasko stands over him with a tray.

'Hmh.' Kedar grunts, nodding in the direction of the side table. Rasko arranges the tray and gestures to the tea-pot, asking if he should pour.

'No, leave it.' Kedar lunges forward to grab a sandwich, the upward angle of his crippled feet making him do all the work from his abdomen. Rasko notices Kedar's awkwardness.

'What's happened to your feet, Dada Babu?'

'Feet ... haan ... feet,' says Kedar, not paying attention, his eyes wandering over the garden as he bites into the ham and bread. Maybe walking on the lawn would be good for them.

'Mustard,' Rasko assures him, 'I've put mustard like you asked.'

'Mustard, yes, good.' Kedar dismisses him, still not looking up. Rasko turns to leave.

'Oh, Rasko.' Kedar has a thought.

'Haan, Dada Babu.'

'Listen, bring me a bucket of hot water with lots of salt in it.'

Rasko's look asks the question.

'For my feet, Rasko. Large bucket. Hot water. Salt.' Kedar semaphores the words through a mouthful of sandwich.

'What happened? Where are your chappals?'
'Gone. The crowd ate them.'
'Oh-ho ... was there a big crowd, Dada Babu?'
Kedar nods as he chews and then he swallows, which allows him to speak clearly. 'Crowd? Yes, big crowd. Huge. Thousands and thousands of people.'
'Were people crying?' Rasko is now a tall tree curving with curiosity, wanting to know about this great circus he has only heard about. In exchange, he drops small bits of information. 'All the shops are shut. And people crying here all day. Boudi. Kaku Babu. Not joking, even Bodo Babu, for two minutes, even he shed tears. And then –'
'Rasko! Bucket. Hot water. Salt. Go!'
As Rasko hurries off, Kedar's feet communicate something upwards and he works some of the new muscles in his brain.
'Rasko!'
'Haan, Dada Babu?' Rasko stops as if he has been yanked by a Meccano hook.
'Come back with the bucket, then I'll tell you all about it. My wallet got pickpocketed.'
Rasko turns around, looking aghast, wanting to engage with this new piece of news, but then he remembers the bucket.
'I'll be right back, Dada Babu. Back at once.' He heads to the kitchen, the white of his bearer's uniform washed yellow by the setting sun, his bare feet pattering urgently across the verandah floor.
Kedar keeps listening to the sound of the feet long after Rasko has gone. The sound briefly sends him into a poetic detour. Rasko: the first man in the universe walking on the first piece of ground which is, somehow, a long verandah with white pillars and a polished red floor that opens out on to a large garden. A garden that is still being formed by the Cosmic Gardener.
Still the eternal awakes. Behind all its other traffic, Kedar's mind has been trying to understand what came over him at the funeral procession. His friend Rudro, older than Kedar by about four

years, keeps insisting that Kedar has a delicate and oversensitive flower at the core of his soul. Kedar knows this to be one of Rudro's jovial insults, but it's one of the more irritating ones precisely because it's so demonstrably untrue. 'Kedu Moshai, the madding crowd is to you what the ocean is to a fine freshwater fish from a small pond! Too big, too open, too salty, and too full of too many nasty creatures. You are as equipped to deal with this vast nastiyota as Red Riding Pomfret is to deal with a pack of wolves!' Rudro said this in the presence of Kedar's other tormentor, Borun Kaku, who, for once, jumped to Kedar's defence or, rather, into gleeful attack against Rudro. 'A pomfret, my dear knowledgeable fellow, is first of all a sea fish. And I daresay a pomfret dealing with wolves in mid-ocean might even manage to drown them and survive.' Which then took the duel away from Kedar into the uncharted territory of whether and how far wolves could swim out to sea.

It has been the same since Kedar was a child, Borun Kaku and Rudro ganging up on him, in cricket, or chess, or quoting from the Encyclopedia Brittanica. From an early age Kedar has watched them play things out in their respective styles – Rudro using ten words where three would do, and Borun Kaku the opposite, preferring, at least in matters to do with Kedar and Rudro, to be extremely economical. The ruthless straight drive past the bowler's feet as opposed to Rudro's ornate verbal cuts and deflections. Because of this battering from two directions Kedar sees himself as quite a tough character, not easily shaken by the tricks and turns of life. But today, strictly between him and himself, he is forced to invite Rudro's jibe into the analysis.

Absolutely Red Riding Pomfret. Gasping for air in a bit of crowd. Managing to lose his precious wallet to some grizzled old street thief with a rusty razor blade. Bloody idiot. What a moment to get an attack of 'sensitivity', almost swooning, almost like some Victorian memshaheb. Oh, my handkerchief! An utterly girlish panic. Kedar feels a sudden anger welling up at himself, coupled with a mad urge to go back into the crowd, back to the point – though he cannot put his finger on the exact moment – when the pocketmaar struck, and back before that to – should he have stayed the course till Nimtolla Ghat? Gone all the way and stood there through the cremation?

No. Out of the question. This is not something he can convince himself about. Just as the anger has risen, a counter-tide of memory, of the sense of freedom once he had torn himself out of the procession, comes surging back to drown the feeling of having been soiled by his own inadequacy. What the devil could one have done? Jaak ge, gelo toh gelo, forget about it. Don't let it happen again. He looks up from his cup of Darjeeling and sees that the light in the garden has slid from rich to soft, from a Gauguin extreme to something well within the range of someone like Monet.

Not to say that Monet didn't have range, never, never, never that. In fact, though he doesn't have any of the skill, patience or application, Kedar has often wanted to paint the changing light in the garden the way Monet painted his haystacks. The high English hedge, the square squadrons of dahlias, the unruly, celebratory sprawl of the gulmohar tree, he has watched them all like a hunter watching delicious prey but, somehow, never been able to move in for the kill. His excuse is a flimsy one – that the light changes too quickly – and Borun Kaku's riposte to this is a smash to his weak lob: 'People who are not artists have excuses. Genuine artists have none. They are as if at war. And in a war you don't talk, you just do!'

The pickpocket had obviously understood this: don't talk, just do. Did that make him an artist as well? An infinitely lesser one than the dead man being carried to his cremation but, unlike Kedar, somehow belonging to the same species as the poet?

The light on the cremation procession has already shifted in his mind. And, though the going of the wallet hurts, it's not so much the material loss as the cut of realization that it opens. Bengal. Bengalis. Calcutta-Kolkata-Kolikata. Lok. Jonota. People. These are words he has taken for granted, as he has the vast districts of meaning they represent, but today, he feels he has made his first real journey into the actual territories, and the trip has jolted him.

The thing that began drenched in the hazily innocent sadness of a clean morning is now illuminated by the soiled rays of a sinking sun – the last rays of the last sunset ever to light the earth, now washing the wall behind Rasko's face as he bends down before him.

Kedar looks at the steaming bucket at his feet. He looks up at Rasko, who nods encouragement. He puts his feet in and does nothing to stop the scream that escapes from his throat. Rasko links his thick eyebrows, the same two that Borun Kaku has named Ribbentrop and Molotov, and looks both concerned and satisfied at the same time.

'Dada Babu, you had asked for hot, isn't that right?'

His breath now skipping somewhere far out across the lawn, Kedar manages nothing more than a thin gasp. Rasko takes this to be a sound expressing gratitude.

'You ask me for something, Dada Babu, you know I'll do it.' Seeing long-term profit on the horizon, Rasko pushes further. 'The samwhuich was good?'

Rudro's old nonsense slides its way in through the lattice of pain that stretches from Kedar's feet and legs up into his middle. 'Samwhuich? Yes! Capital! Bhery gooood! And also the Samwhuere! But more importantly, Rasko, Samhow? And even more crucially, Rasko Ustad, Shomrat of Philosophy, Sam*why*?' Rudro's voice slips into Kedar's own ongoing mimicry of Banglish – O Death! Whuere is thaai steeng? Death, thy sting, it is where? It is heaar, at the bhery base of my feet. Or, as in Billy Bunter, the achingness of my blessed feet is, alas, splendidly excruational.

Slowly, his body overcomes the shock, and the palliative properties of heat and salt begin to take effect. Rasko watches with interest as Kedar's grimace relaxes into almost an ecstatic expression, the eyeballs now moving slowly under closed lids. He goes around to the side table, lifts the lid of the teapot to check whether the tea is finished and takes the tray away.

Kedar hears his footsteps recede and, to his surprise, soon

return. He hears Rasko put something down next to him. A plate, perhaps.

'Ki?' he asks, attempting to be testy but not quite managing.

'Niin. Fruit khaan.' Here, have some fruit.

'Fruit?' Kedar opens his eyes and looks down at the table. On it is a white china plate upon which curves a luridly ripe yellow-and-black thing. 'What's this? You know I hate bananas.'

'This is not just any banana. My aunt, Shombhu's Ma, sent a basket all the way from my village, from Paanchpukur. I've been hiding them from the other servants. In fact, I didn't even tell Boudi and, please, don't you tell her either.'

'Rasko. I hate bananas whether they are from Paanchpukur, Jhaarbagan or Jamaica. Take it away and eat it yourself. Quietly, if it's so precious!'

'Oh-ho. You are not understanding. These bananas from our village are special. They have many powers. You have had a hard day. This will help bring your strength back.'

'Strength? Special powers? What strength? What's all this nonsense?'

'Not nonsense, Dada Babu, eating one of these keeps a man strong for a day and a night.'

'Night? People sleep at night. Why do I have to be strong at night?'

Rasko hesitates before answering. Ribbentrop and Molotov twitch briefly towards each other. His black eyes shine under them with sincerity as he speaks.

'I'm not saying anything, nothing like that, but these bananas are very good for when, sometimes, you know, for when people don't sleep at night. But also very good after you've had a hard day's labour.'

It takes Kedar a moment or two to understand this, but when he looks back at Rasko he doesn't show any sign of having understood. 'Hm. Thik achhe. Now go and see that my DJ is ready, and ask Bahadur to ask the driver if there is petrol in my car.'

'Are you going out again?'

'Yes. Why sleep when you've eaten a Paanchpukur banana?'
'Dinner here?'
'What's for dinner?'
'Vegetarian only. You know ... because of Gurudeb's passing ...'
'Hm. Keep a little aside in the pantry. Not a lot. And quietly.'
'Should I tell Boudi when she comes back?'
'Tell nobody anything. If anybody asks, just say Dada Babu went out. And don't say I was wearing a suit.'

Rasko nods and moves away. 'Eat the banana, Dada Babu, don't forget,' he calls over his shoulder before disappearing into the kitchen.

Kedar sits there, thinking. 'For when people don't sleep at night ...' Was Rasko reading his mind? Not that he expects life to yield up all its pleasures so soon, not that at all, but perhaps a first step could be ... no, do not get carried away. All she had said was 'I hope I shall see you at the party.' And that was a nothing, a mere pleasantry from a Mem girl. This was not a heroine from a Tagore novel but a European, and what was said was exactly what was meant – she hoped she would see him. At the party.

His feet still planted in the bucket, Kedar looks around surreptitiously to make sure none of the gardening staff are looking; for reasons not clear to himself, he doesn't want servants to see him eating an aphrodisiacal banana. Having made sure he is unobserved, Kedar reaches for the champion fruit of Paanchpukur, peels it and takes a small bite. He closes his eyes, chews briefly, swallows. Then he takes a bigger bite.

FLIGHT
Itu Chaudhuri

I

The thing is, you see, I really can *fly*.

Not, you understand, anything as ambitious as the soaring flight of large birds, the precise swoops of crows I remember from the prison-grey hostel courtyard at school, grabbing the bits of soft buns we'd throw up at them; not the lazy circling of eagles up up up there, little dots in a carousel, now an aerial arabesque, now a dog-and-bone game, Biggles and the Red Baron on LSD. That's schoolboy daydreaming stuff.

This is adult flight, and not a flight of the mind. Adult, because it's doable and *real*. Not real like those dole-fattened Germans, Dutchmen or Brits you've seen on the Discovery channel, soft accents confessing to watering their pathetic fantasies in secret, sneaking into garages to stick chicken feathers to cardboard wings – because this time, surely this time, the flight must last one second more than the last. See them make yet another sorry jump off some disused bridge or rooftop, landing with a soft plop on a haystack. There might be a little audience, cheering the poor man on: Break a leg! (And he often will.) Dotty in Dortmund, that's what I call it. Next sequence: Dr Somebody, MD, white lab coat, goatee, tells you what Hermann or Basil suffers from: a convincing three-worder, a properly studied name, as if nomenclature could cure. That's not me either.

Some evenings, I jog in a forest, and I build in long jumps as a part of the routine. I'd been an enthusiastic jumper at school, never as successful as the faster, bigger boys, but decent enough for what I'd been given by way of a frame, and enthusiastically coached. We'd charge at full pelt into the sandpit, vests wet with effort, straining for every last bit of distance, until the coach entered our lives, and taught us to aim for *height*. He'd hang a white handkerchief from a makeshift bamboo pole, at a calculated height, so that an outstretched arm held high up would just touch the muddy white rag – at the very peak of the jump. The results were amazing, adding several feet to the distance. At the end of my first session, I was too excited with this insight to be able to think of anything else. I ate dinner without registering it. Afterwards, I lay awake in the darkness, on the concrete dorm bed, thinking, unwashed, as though the sand from the pit were needed to rub the lesson home. Calves contracting involuntarily, and up, lifting off, right arm stretched towards the sky, eyes fixed on coach's kerchief. Playing in my head, again, the voice coming out of the track suit: jemp for height, woanly then you can jemp good dishtens. *Height is everything.*

Thirty years later, I still jump this way during my jog. I make sure that I am alone in the government-run forest I like to use (Keep the Nature Clean, No Spitting, No Playing of Transistor Radios), almost perfectly silent save for the sound of distant traffic, now fading as I run deeper into the park's woodiest parts, the sun dipping behind the kikar bush, the canopy of trees cutting off the sky's light just enough to deliver the comfort of darkness and privacy, yet leaving the uneven, eroded ground visible. My jumps were not long, perhaps eight or ten feet at best. Smooth glides in the air, and then, in a triple jumper's action, there'd be another leap, and so on. What happened next I haven't yet worked out, but I found one day that if I tucked my legs under me, like they'd taught, I could will myself to stay in the air for longer than I'd thought was possible, and then a little longer still.

And then I'd *remember*. Remember – that's the closest I can get to explaining how it works, since I have always known it in some buried part of me. Remember, as I was saying, how to get my mind to suspend the moment of landing. This needs a decisive intervention in one's thought-machine, at the peak of the jump. I do not deny, as you will see, that this first part *is* a jump, powered by muscles. And the Nikes I wear, with their rubber soles curving up from beneath, and wrapping around onto the upper, a giant retroflexing tongue of pimpled polymer, or the toe pad of a jumping reptile, evolved over aeons. When I first saw the shoes one truant afternoon in the halogen glow of the store window, it was like someone winking at me, someone who *knew* my secret and delighted in it. A secret I was relieved not to have to tell a human, while enjoying the release that admission brings.

But after the gentle effort of lifting off (which, note again, I do not underrate) what happens isn't about the gross strength of muscle, tendon or shoe. This is about *feeling* for the precise moment when the jump is peaking; do not try to calculate it, put all trajectories and parabolas out of your mind. I virtually think in diagrams, so this is not easy. Thought is the enemy here: the thought-machine must stall mid-air, its fuel pipe smartly yanked off, quick and smooth. Hear it gasp, choke silently in vacuum. (In war movies, the propeller spins to a stop.) When I time it right, my undercarriage will retract fully, *all by itself*, the pimply rubber nearly touching my buttocks. Recent knee surgery, which you will hear more of later, does not allow complete retraction nowadays, for a few weeks anyway, but the lift is unaffected, as also becomes clear soon. Then, the thrill of the flight, never quite being sure where you'll land, the delicious suspense of it all. Twenty feet, thirty, seventy, or a couple of hundred feet? Easy, depends on the correct synching of the jump's peak to the squeezing off of the thought-machine. *Cogitus interruptus.* How high? A foot or three, who knows? Never measure, never even look back. This is flying, floating, not jumping.

II

This evening, though, things are different: I'm at home, recovering from surgery. Not usual for me, at home evening after evening. No jogging, ever since I tore a piece of cartilage in my knee three weeks ago. It's been operated on, and my walk is less of a hobble now ('More ambulatory,' Dr Uberoi says), free of pain, but far from properly functional. Bits and pieces of the knee mechanism are in need of strength, and others have forgotten how to work in tandem, having lost all but the most basic vocabulary in the language of movement ('Proprioception', Dr Uberoi calls it). Movement must now be learnt, one lesson at a time. The whole of the movement will only be internalized when its parts are forgotten. Like the body in flight, every bit of my knee has its own thought-machines: bits of nerve and muscle that need to be taught to think again, laboriously, like a tour guide teaching Hindi words to an American tourist. Pair seedha karo. Ab usey kaso. Wazan daalo. Bahut achchhe. Phirse. For the thought-machines must work before they can be switched off.

Kavi and BJ have come over to see me, a mix of a getwellsoon and an itsbeenages evening. My knee will play host, it loves the fuss. I really like Kavi and BJ too. Kavi is a part of Delhi's art crowd, a critic and curator. She is an effortlessly visual person, and her writing has a light touch that makes you feel clever. She is pertly attractive, and so without the self-consciousness that goes with official beauty. Her compassion is instinctive yet calibrated; it emits both reassuring clucks of sympathy and words of real concern, but pulls short of highlighting frailty. BJ, on the other sofa, is silent and leonine, a thick greying beard and mane giving him a chunky, solid presence. BJ is a hugely and eclectically read geologist with a bewilderingly large set of interests – and abilities. His concern is of the quiet kind, somewhat professorial, a caring fringed with casual scholarship. BJ knows nearly everything, I am sometimes certain: The Brain, with soft-toy appeal thrown in.

They occupy a sofa each, two largish, newly upholstered three-seaters at right angles to each other. A large woven dhurrie marks the rectangle defined by the sofas. I sit opposite them, facing the corner of the room on a dining chair that lets me extend my leg comfortably. It's a warm scene: thick candles are alight, and the old living room hasn't looked this way in what, years? Shaded table lamps light up the gorgeous lilies and yellow roses Kavi has brought me: now, do you have a vase, or are we going to use a water jug? In response, I bustle about trying to make my apartment appear better provisioned than it is, like a bird fluffing itself up for volume. Limping smartly between bar, kitchen and sofas with drinks and refills, dragging my left knee behind me.

It is during one of those trips back from the kitchen (do have more ice, there's lots to go around) that I start to notice the buoyancy again. The left foot taking just that bit longer to descend to the ground, coming down onto the woven dhurrie with a cushion of air underneath. Perhaps a reaction to the forced inactivity of the machines in past weeks, a little electric mutiny of muscle and nerve? I try to ignore it, but can't help looking down at my feet. I don't even have the Nikes on, these are a ten-year-old pair of Hush Puppies, very worn, my tribute to fashionable scruffiness. I look at my friends, have they noticed? I've never done this in company, dear God, tell me they didn't see it. Kavi, beatific and pulling on a cigarette, lost, I hope, in the Mozart that's playing, looking straight into my face. 'A twitch,' I find myself explaining (what was the need?). 'Galvani saheb,' says BJ, his gaze straight, the voice serious and ironic at once. I need to sit down. Get some rum inside me, face them squarely, recover, and then the mutiny must be put down.

I begin with damage assessment. Assuming they have noticed, there will be requests to do it again. If – if, for this is not a certainty – they can face the truth, it will be a terrible burden keeping it quiet, but a necessity; and questions I can't answer: from the basic 'How?' to the 'Do you feel the breeze?' I'd tell them if I knew, but I don't: when flight happens, it is all I know. Sometimes I am tempted to come out with it, go public. This I cannot countenance: there will be questions, serious questions, questions of unthinkable inanity. About how long I can really jump if I tried. Why I didn't report the discovery (to whom?). The IITs. The ministries of God-knows-what (civil aviation?). God-men on television: this is merely (!) an ancient siddhi, described in the ancient Vedas, routine in ancient times; I will perform this on the night of the next new moon. The newspapers, testingly empty-headed: do I flap my arms? Why don't I just fly to work? Or teach flight to poor children? Would I fly a few feet with a small payload (a five-year-old girl due to die of leukaemia any month now)? In any case, the stress of exposure would surely kill my chances of suspending the thought-machines, and then of course I'd be the 'Fraud that Flew'. No, do not even consider this for a second. Concentrate.

Considering that flight is elusive (the mind does not always allow it) I ought to be grateful for each involuntary *whoosh* I'm having this evening. Flight is the subtlest of the mind's skills, but this evening, staying grounded is proving harder, and harder still with each trip to the kitchen. I enter the living room, ice box or water jug in hand. At the corner of the dhurrie, I helplessly feel the calves tensing, and that familiar lift. Now! Push in a thought, a sticky one, any thought. Think *weight*. Think physics: unpowered human flight is impossible. Think of the surgery, three holes in the knee, three black nylon stitches with their knotted ends crisply upright, a butch fashion accessory; think impossibly contorted sex, anything. Ground the machine! By round three, the floating stride has become embarrassingly long, and I can get Kavi's glass to her from the bar at the far edge of the dhurrie in one nine-foot glide. It spills once, despite the feather cushion landing. She doesn't notice, thanks me and tells me I really really *mustn't* bustle so much. My face is flushed: do I look guilty? BJ looks straight ahead. Neither seems to have noticed; or they'd rather not; or they can sense I don't want to be confronted. Odds one in three each, look for a clue, a plan.

No help at all. I am now getting to my chair from the living-room door in a single step, eight feet as the crow flies, longer with the airy pirouettes I am having to do to avoid landing on the Kavi lap (would not do, you understand); hips hiked in hula-hoop fashion and settling softly on the chair seat. By the simple up-and-away standards of my forest flights, this is awesome aerobatics, but I need another kind of expertness now. After a few minutes on the chair, I reach a decision. I will tell them. These are intelligent, evolved, kind people; they have travelled around the mind and around the world. They will face the truth, they will switch on the agnostic modules in their belief machines. They'll never make me feel a freak, and they will spare me the word 'Power'. They'd anticipate the difficulty less open-minded people would have with it, fed as they are on simple rationality or worse, occult beliefs – and so will surely keep the secret. They *must*.

I pay no attention now to the words I use, and they rush out with diarrhoeic intensity. I cannot explain why I feel a little ashamed, rather than proud, of telling them; is guilt the dark face of relief, is this coming out a confessional of sorts? Perhaps there is an unspoken taboo surrounding abnormal ability, lifted only when the owner's duty to place it in the public domain is fulfilled. This is why walkers-on-water invoke the shield of religious practice, or penance, as if to expiate in advance the sin of extraordinary power. This is my crime. Flight, enjoyed in secrecy, not attributed to a higher source, just to the withdrawal of mind. I will not obey these laws, Kavi and BJ will respect this. I talk for fifteen minutes, ignoring my tiring throat. Gesturing, feeling a little silly about my hand instinctively forming an aircraft, thumb extended, palms facing earth, trying to show them just what happens. Share the secret, draw them into the circle, earn their complicity.

Through my rant, Kavi's entire seated posture has been rotated to face me, to let me know that she is listening to me, her kind face looking directly at me. When I lift my eyes to look at her for relief, I know at once that I am destroyed. Her face has a pious, I-am-there-for-you look, as luminous and as real as a greeting card bought at an all-night petrol bunk. It is her professional mask, reserved for tragedies that cannot be comprehended or for first-time writers seeking advice. The voice automatically gives out hmms, very much the editor marking up the words I am spewing out. One hmm, insert a paragraph break; two short ones, nudge the pace along. There are tiny glances at BJ, still tinier ones aimed to miss my face. She is distancing herself to allow herself to widen her belief system, or to avoid judging what she is hearing. Kavi and BJ, dear friends and cherished sources of support. Kavi, human, sensible, a taster of imagination and expression. BJ, a sherpa of the the rational world, so rooted. Neither can hide this: they are having none of it, and while their patience is intact, it is being tested.

'From what I saw, it didn't look, you know, that it was anything out of the ordinary,' says Kavi, the voice gentle but level. 'Standard jump,' says BJ, teeth just starting to show, a smile forming but being held back. A chess master looking smugly at a middle game, knowing he can push this into a won ending.

Enough. I am committed to a course of action, and if desperation calls for desperation, so be it. I clear the chairs and move the corner table from its position between the two sofas. BJ looks with interest, to his credit. Kavi is still empathizing: she must be ignored. Time to show them how it is done, crash-land on their incredulity.

The first effort takes me from the far corner of the dhurrie to the wall opposite. It is worth about fifteen feet in measurement terms, and my feet *settle* on the wall about a foot above the ground. I leave them there a moment, and allow an image of a tape measure to restart the thought-machines and interrupt the flight.

'So you have learnt to jump into a wall,' says BJ, 'but it's still a jump.'

'*Ooh* that must *hurt*,' come the Kavi two-bits. Even a child can see it's my *right* leg that takes off, not the one with the injured knee, but pointing that out would only focus on what she wants to see.

'Didn't you see me land, so softly on the wall? Stay there for several seconds? And if it was *just* a jump, how long do you think it would have been if the wall hadn't been there? Thirty, forty feet?' I shoot back.

'I suppose one could do the precise calculations using a standard gunnery chart,' he goes on. 'You have to know the distance from the gun position to the peak of the arc. With the altitude known, and one does have to factor in wind speed of course, but in this room, I suppose you can hush that. I mean, Napoleon's lower command did have access to the Prussians' artillery tables which didn't take wind factors into account, and so ...'

My second effort reaches the wall at a spot fully three feet above the first, or four feet above the ground. I am halfway up to the ceiling now, and I suspend myself in place like a rock climber. I twist around to get a glance at BJ and Kavi, risking losing flight. I think one of them does glance up at me, but for the most part they just sit there, uninterested and polite, as though waiting for an off-key elder to finish singing his pet song. I allow irritation to enter and let myself down.

'I suppose you didn't see that either. A hop and a step, what do the charts say?'

Kavi: 'Are you sure that knee of yours will hold up? I'd hate for you to hurt it, you know?' The slightly angled face with large black eyes. Compassionate, pained, and uncomprehending.

'But of course it hurts. Can't you tell?' I spit the words out.

And just as her stoic expression is giving way to hurt, I launch into flight three. Diffuse anger rises in the thought-machine, but luckily no thought crystallizes. For a tiny part of a moment, I see Coach's white hanky in the twilight and I reach for it instinctively. I float up to the corner of the room, my head approaching the ceiling. Twisting around, I settle down with the back of my head snugly nestling in the ceiling's curved cornice. I am looking down on them now from the ceiling a good ten feet up. It is surprisingly little effort to stay there. This is even better than flight, but every now and then anger threatens to lower me from my perch. I must steer clear of forming arguments – think, and flight ends, such are the Laws of Flight. I am determined to stay there till they can ignore me no more.

BJ is looking at Kavi, who is looking glassily at the floor, trying to deal with hurt and embarrassment. BJ wants to come to his wife's aid, but retaliation would muddy the image of the objective investigator he needs to believe in: his defence against the Dark Arts.

'I think it's time to go, shona. Deadlines tomorrow, and his knee, too, needs some rest.' Good move: return to the everyday, the quotidian. I watch Kavi gather her bag, arrange her hair, dragging out the departure to communicate her hurt to me, I suppose.

For my part, I am determined to make myself comfortable and let them know that the evening is over for me, too; I will play the tired convalescent, but remain suspended against their disbelief.

I rest the side of my head on the crook of my arm, my body's side against the vertical wall. I even make a few fidgeting movements, my clothes rubbing against the whitewash, all clean and cool and white, a sleepy body fidgeting for that perfect position. I take a quick look at my guests, I'd like them to see how utterly at ease I am, see the sleep filling my eyes. They are letting themselves out. Neither make a move to say goodbye. I wish them goodnight anyway. When I hear the harsh diesel engine of their taxi starting up, I know I am alone again, as I should always have been.

Ten feet below me, I can see melted wax gather in pools on top of the wide, white candles, reflecting the burning wicks, a double-flame illusion. The lilies look unfamiliar and alight, catching the rays of the table lamps with textured brilliance. The dusty tops of the light bulbs mar the view. Do not plan any cleaning now, or the flight machine will stutter.

I contemplate in-flight sleep, wondering if it is provided for in the Laws. Probably not.

III

The vertical surface of the wall feels both reassuringly normal and exquisitely comfortable. My side rests against it, putting *weight* on it; it's as if the walls are horizontal, somehow. My arm feels pliant and cottony and softly registers the impress of my head. I cannot feel with any certainty the Hush Puppies on my feet, which are hidden under the waves of the whitewash of soft fabric still cool with the night's air. And when I look down, the light in the room is not from the candles, more a broad mass of luminosity with no visible source. It is in the Laws: the flight is over.

SCHEHERAZADE

Itu Chaudhuri

I

'No way you're going anywhere, okay?'

A vast hand, beefy and white, slams down on the tabletop, pinning my forearm to it with laughing ease. It is a moderate weight, one that I could shake off with a little effort, except that when I try to, its mass increases with infinite speed, seeming to transform it into the black grinding stone in my father's mother's kitchen, her batta, the one it takes two cooks to operate. My arm, of course, is the piece of ginger to be ground on the thick black faux-granite top of the cafe table we are occupying. I fall back onto my chair, facing the old square piazza, so that the arm pinning mine down can only be seen by turning my head to face its owner.

I look at the street, with its surfaces of medieval stone with balconies and arches, the precise geometric cobbling filling the square behind the cathedral in the city's centrum. This could be one of many cities in Europe, though there is an especially severe grandness to the old Flemish walls of Brugge. I take my time turning around to face Pietr, leaving him at the very periphery of my vision before beginning a super-slow turn of the head. The deliberate gyration is intended to mask the panic, and the annoyance I feel, a bit of both. I let, therefore, my gaze take in the buskers performing their turns, civilly competing for custom from the clusters of tourists strolling Brugge in the yellowing afternoon light. Where the old buildings cast shadows on the piazza, an Indian magician in a lemon-yellow kurta stands, extracting ball after ball, iron spheres larger than golf balls, from his mouth. It is accompanied by fearsome bellows of expectoration, *ho-o-oawkk!'* mimicking the pain and effort of regurgitation, but whose real purpose, I am sure, is slapstick distraction, magician's patter in a universal tongue. An assistant prepares the turban he will pass around, while his eyes try to draw a busload of Japanese into his audience in time to add some euros to the takings, for this is the last stop before dark.

But finally, I must face the owner of the arm. His face is friendly, really, and the stopmeifyoudare expression appears purely for effect, but I have got to know Pietr Jurgen too well in the last three days to believe that.

Pietr and Max have been my shadows on the road, hitch-hiking acquaintances first sharing nods at places where backpackers lurk together. And then information, food and destinations. Pietr is at least six feet eight, immensely strong, his enormous fleshy bulk well proportioned, so that every part of him seems uniformly scaled, a body with a huge magnifying lens permanently attached. A black baseball cap with an IBM logo shades kind green eyes capable of suddenly conveying detached recklessness, the kind that makes murderers look scary. Pietr is kind (has pulled me out of trouble more than once) and intimidating in turns, and smells *foul* always. Pink people eating pink meat/Soon become what they eat, my vegan grandma, addicted to rhyme and repelled by the phirangee, would chant; her polemic on pork is the family favourite. It could also be his feet: those black basketball shoes surely haven't been taken off in weeks, their laces tied around the loose rings of filthy black denim that gather at his ankles, so you can hardly tell where the jeans end or where the shoes begin. The wrist holding mine down wears a thick leather strap with conical steel studs, like the collar on a prize Rotweiler. Pietr is gay: his companion Max sits timidly next to him, and is his bodily opposite number in every detail. Pietr is American, despite the name; Max is Austrian, short and wiry, clean, wears colours and smells of talc. Theirs is an unequal relationship; last night Pietr made a half-serious advance at me while Max watched. A massive fist squeezing my crotch hard, yellow teeth laughing into my face, then releasing its grip with surprising tenderness.

'So where to, huh, in all that hurry?' Pietr demands. 'I have to pee,' I say truthfully. We've been at the local beers all morning. 'Take a leak. Piss. P-i-s-s.' I spell it out to show my irritation. 'Pass water. Spend a penny,' I add, the out-of-date Brit expressions my private, useless taunt at the American.

'Watering your horse, you mean,' he counters. 'Well, sweetheart, tell me what the hurry is, I'll bet you have a pretty story to tell. Start now, and the sultan lets you go if he's happy, right?' Pietr's grin is broad. He looks down slowly at my stomach, and I pray he will not see humour in giving my full bladder a sharp jab; there is nothing subtle about Pietr.

I have been monitoring the lavatory door in the cafe. It is pushed open by the first of three Japanese men, who have travelled half the earth's circumference to a place unusually rich in heritage of beer, to drink Kirrin or Sapporo, something even Pietr puzzles over, though he respects the quantities they've been quaffing. They walk with urgency, in single file, disappearing behind the white door. My bladder, already feeling the darts of sensation, freezes at the disappointment. Then follows the familiar feeling of suspended animation: the urgency of urination stops abruptly, though the pressure can be felt strongly. It is like the long-distance runner's second wind, when he has run through and past the first frontier of pain and can postpone agony till the next checkpoint. Panic ceases.

'I don't feel like it any more,' I report smugly to Pietr. I test his persistence by trying to free my arm. One hundred per cent traction, no give at all. 'I can go any time, so you may as well let go my arm before it goes to sleep.'

'How come? Some kinda Yoga self-control crap?' Pietr's deep suspicion of things Asian, reluctantly lifted for me, is antimatter to my grandmother's visceral rejection of all humans who eat higher up the food chain, especially whiteskins unschooled in the wisdoms of the ages. *Shiva shiva shiva.*

'It is a story that begins two whole continents ago,' I begin, shamelessly watching the interested expression on his face. 'Let go now.' Time to press a little.

'Always wins, the *bass*-tard.' Pietr relents, now smiling. Max looks pleased.

The grip eases, the stone batta lifts, and I can feel normalcy rush past my wrist into the veins at the back of my hand. It is release, of a sort.

II

Before we go any further, I tell Pietr and Max, you must understand that we Indians are a people who have spent millenniums constructing elaborate taboos around the most routine of tasks, but yet our males are unrestrained urinators. We piss in the open, not in the secluded openness of fields and forests, but when I say open you must try to visualize what I am telling you. By open I mean, for instance: on the side wall of a cinema theatre, twenty feet from where people are queuing up (not necessarily in the linear manner you understand) to buy tickets; on a street wall plastered with layers of film or election posters, the citizen's roving critique, perhaps, on politics and cinema; or on a wall, standing on broken earth in a narrow corridor formed by two buildings, so narrow that the urinator arches his body to let a cow squeeze past, a Matador without audience. Nothing stops him: not people, not food sellers, he is exercising a right, a communion with his inner self, at once personal and public; just like the quick folding of hands in devotion when he bicycles past a temple, handlebars momentarily free, balanced by God.

It's not that there are no taboos surrounding public urination, and I will admit that you will not see quite as much of it in the better quarters, the more urbanized parts. But in an Indian town or city, the better and poorer quarters snake around each other. You could go from one kind to the other and back merely by turning around the corner of a building, in a matter of yards. Even the most urbanized of us, like me, know that at a pinch, a piss site is never far. You foreigners wouldn't manage that easily, though; you need our trained eye to pick out spots, though your noses might serve you better than ours, inured as they are to the most ubiquitous of odours in India.

It starts when you're a kid. I went to a residential school, miles from the nearest town, a generously wooded paradise with a collection of trees and plants as good as a botanical park, imposed on an arid, rocky landscape of low hills and brush, by will and a £60,000 donation. For a ten-year-old boy at school, opportunities for alfresco pissing were everywhere; the penis was a toy, charged with water every few hours. We'd stand, Aroon and I, competing to see who could 1) piss farther 2) aim better 3) last longer. The third of these contests was often conducted as a mock fencing match. *En garde!* we'd shout. Épées flashing, silvery arcs of water waved about to catch the sunlight, now intersecting, now cunningly withdrawn, though the one who lasted got to shout: Touché! By adolescence, when the toy awakes to its second purpose, urination games had become acts of subversion, played at night. We'd leave the hostel at midnight, three or four mujahideen wrapped in grey bedcovers, and roam the campus in perfect darkness. The agenda on a night might be: carefully rehanging the founder's portrait in the staff room upside down, or it might be a piss target. Tick them off: watering the good length spots on the cricket pitch the night before a match, never mind the matting that would undo the good work; blessing the music room where the drums and string instruments lay, the domain, by day, of the orthodox tyrant who taught music. The next morning, the loudest intifada would complain of the stench, and the damp in the music room carpet, demanding the class be cancelled; another hand-picked boy would interrupt a staff meeting to point out the inverted portrait to the headmaster (I was just passing by Sir, couldn't help noticing, Sir). No American fraternity has anything on this.

I am telling you this at such length because your cultures have nothing like it. Yes, I saw Manneken-Pis in Brussels, last month. It is a beautiful bronze sculpture, green with patina, of a cherubic child, pretty parabola of water issuing forth from his spigot into a stone pond. It is, of course, a fountain in a public square. It is witty, all right, but twee, its continuous supply of water symbolic of state, suggestive of bonsai dissent, humoured, even cultivated: how cute to see/a little boy pee! gran might have said. On our subcontinent, urination is a *private* good, a private act, so what if it is performed in public? It is an act of volition, stopped or started anywhere, any time. Each male secedes when the urge strikes him, the state riven by half a billion mutinies.

III

I was twenty years old, and in love. Mandira lit up any room she entered with promise, humour and beauty.

Six months ago, my parents, both scientists, had left to teach at a university in Tanzania. The early promise of professional satisfaction on a good salary had disappeared, and they planned to pay their way out of their contract. There was, however, a sliver of compensation: the contract provided for an air ticket for one child under the age of twenty-one to visit them. If I caught the flight just as my college semester ended, they suggested, I could manage a short trip, and make it back just before my twenty-first birthday.

This wasn't an easy decision; the semester break was the perfect time to accelerate matters with Mandira. Our relationship had moved beyond simple friendship, and I was straining to guide it past nowhereland in the direction of an affair. But I understood the sacrifices my parents were making: they were going to spend a chunk of their savings to host me for a fortnight, and a bigger chunk to buy travel packages to the game parks in Tanzania, the finest (and most expensive) in the world. The only Indians who travelled abroad on leisure were the very rich, so this was a coming-of-age present of continental proportions, an act of love and profligacy. I said an uncertain goodbye to Mandira, and landed in

Dar one warm morning. A few days later, we took off to see Tanzania's forest reserves.

Tanzania has several great game parks, each with some unique feature, all superbly run and regulated with great sensitivity. To get there, you must share a long ten-seater van; in ours the other seven seats were occupied by a mix of westerners and Japanese couples. You grind bumpily along the (German-made) roads, once proud strips of tar and asphalt, the tyres of the Volkswagen van falling in and out of the rippled ruts that are the signature of armoured tanks. This is a poor country scarred by a decade of war, and you drive through towns that commerce seems to have passed by.

But when the journey ends, there is Ngorongoro.

We arrived at a spectacular lodge, finished all in wood, and were taken to individual cottages; taken, because it was getting dark, when water buffalo roam the resort. Not even lionesses mess with water buffalo, so no tip-sucking bellhop will do; a forest ranger is a must. Once settled in, we went across to the main lodge building, and looked down, past an almost sheer drop, on a panoramic view of the park, nearly half a mile below us. I realized why, even before I had sighted a single lion, all game parks must pale before Ngorongoro.

It is a dramatic formation: a flat circle of land, sixteen kilometres across, walled in by a steep rim six hundred metres high, a crater of a long extinct volcano presenting man with a game park without fencing. Evening haze obscured the horizon, but there was still enough sun to see a vast glowing sheet of pink, miles away so we could only guess at its size: several thousand flamingo, we learnt, flocking in the shallows of a saltwater lake in the crater.

We rose before dawn, my parents and I, to change into another ten-seater (a purpose-built Ford) for the journey into the crater. Only authorized four-wheel-drive vehicles are allowed, the drivers are strictly trained to observe park protocol, and in any case few others would manage the drive down the rim. The idea was to escape the post-breakfast hordes who, as we had experienced in the past week, would descend in groups and form circles of ten wagons around a solitary lion. Look, Myrtle, look at him get his workout! Do you think the Goldbergs have a better view?

Steven, a greying Tanzanian who had driven vehicles in this park for fifteen years, smiled as we ended the bone-shaking ride down the rim, a test of man and machine. His knowledge of the animals was formidable, the commentary delivered in a bass voice commanding respect from everyone. We were in the crater just after first light, great plains of yellow dry grass backed by curtains of green: low, wide, trees, adapted to present the smallest surface to the wind. I shall not describe the beauty of the scene, you have seen it on television. The van had a sky roof so you could stand and look over the roof of the vehicle. The sky roof was hogged by Kurosawa, the name I gave the Japanese with a perpetually whirring movie camera, and by the elderly American in khakis and dark glasses, who was, of course, General MacArthur.

We were looking at our most remarkable sight of the morning, a family of lions feasting on a fresh kill. The lion lay drowsily on the grass, full to the brim. The lioness had also eaten her share, we could tell from her swaying, heavy belly, and was supervising her cubs, soaked in blood up to their bony shoulders, burrowing their heads deep into the side of a gazelle. That's when I realized that our early start had left my bladder full – and the cups of coffee my father doled out from his flask hadn't helped. I wanted to pee.

The General and Akira competed for the sky roof, letting in the fine savannah dust, now lit up with the low rays of the early sun. My mother pulled her scarf over her hair and mouth, eyes wide and staring hard at the meal. My father watched in a reverie, making mental notes. Mrs Mac and Mrs Kurosawa looked at their watches. Tourists nine and ten took pictures. Steven was watchful but silent: commentary was unnecessary, this was kill number three of the morning, better to preserve the moment. It was clearly a bad time to speak up.

Steven started up the engine after an age, and we took off along the trails worn by automobiles. I considered the situation. First, there was the matter of etiquette. In India, I would simply and quite casually walk across to the driver and request (nearly command) a stop if one was not imminent. From what I have told you, you can guess the rest. No infantile euphemism is necessary. A male bond is established with a knowing nod, impersonal but friendly. He will find a suitable spot to stop, and his judgement is good, or at any rate, final. You get off, and reappear when you are ready. No one complains about the stop, for you are a sovereign country.

Steven, however, was not an Indian bus driver who was one with his passengers, however removed their social class. Nothing could have prepared Steven for this: to lead mzungu groups in an automobile, clad in a dark crisp uniform and a peaked hat. In any case, how did one broach the subject in his society? No, surely Steven operated by his professional culture, taught by white teachers, hadn't he been a driver since the days of the white rulers? The West ruled here, within the six doors of the Ford, and the West has rules. Stopping the van meant letting one individual show disrespect for the time and space of the group. Mrs Mac and Mrs Kurosawa were already looking at their watches. Fight, said my bladder, think quickly.

Twenty minutes later, I knew that I was running out of time. I would have to ask Steven to stop, but to do it discreetly, I would need the seat next to his, which Mrs Tourist Ten occupied. Luck struck: a herd of giraffe decided to pass by our van, really close for these shy animals. We are very lucky today, pronounced Steven, cutting off the engine. The General stood at attention through the sky roof and inspected the march past, Kurosawa whirred away, the wives squealed. Inspiration: my mother's camera, a plastic box absurdly moulded into Mickey Mouse hanging from her neck. I grabbed it and asked tourist ten if I might shoot some pictures for my mother from his window, which had a better view. I pressed the shutter (Mickey's ear) several times, squeak™! squeak™!, even though I couldn't see the tiny viewfinder and I didn't care. Keep shooting till the van starts or you lose the seat, said the crisis manager, Preserve film. Two frames left, said Mickey. Fake it then, said the crisis manager. Get off the van, said my bladder.

The giraffes passed. We watched them until they became a phalanx of rumps, heads barely visible above the dust. Steven fired up the Ford engine and started off again. I decided to wait until everyone busied themselves in their thoughts or simply looked into the distance. Steven described a tree with unique survival properties, greatly valued among the Masai, but soon sensed that after the fresh kill and the giraffes, act three was not a thriller and best kept brief. General MacArthur sat back relaxed in his seat, the now bright savannah reflected like a movie in his aviator-style dark glasses. Kurosawa reloaded film, his lenses on the only empty seat, all concentration on his hands, feeling for camera and reel inside a black leather bag. Tourist nine and girlfriend decided to mark this special moment by kissing softly. My parents watched with indulgence. The wives conversed as though they'd been neighbours for years. What are you waiting for now? screamed the bladder.

I negotiated the shooting pains of fullness and tried to gain control over my mind. Etiquette was to be discarded, civil society could wait. In any case, Mr Steven Matondo was an operator of a motor vehicle, paid for in part by my parents; we were a parliament of bladders, one seat, one vote, full bladders get veto rights.

'Mr Matondo,' I began. 'Mr Matondo, may I speak with you for a minute?'

Silence. Steven turned to face me, eyebrows raised.

'Mr Matondo, I need you to stop somewhere for a minute,' I said urgently. 'I need, you see, well we've been driving two hours, right, so I need to relieve myself.'

'From what?' came his first words to a single person, the voice soft and rich.

'I need to take a leak, to piss, urinate,' I said, hoping one of them would do.

'I am not permitted to stop and let you go away from the vehicle, so you should have gone to the toilet back at the lodge.' This was a blow I hadn't bargained for, and the bladder pressed harder and sharper, each message more searing.

'Steven. Please. If you find the right place, right near those trees, I will only ...'

'I cannot deviate from the trails, it is not allowed,' he cut in. 'When we get back, only an hour or so more.'

An hour! Patience, I told my bladder, quiet while I find a way past this idiot. I will give up this minute if you can't, it replied. I will have to control you, I said, with my mind. I will rob you of all movement, all sensation, I threatened it. You will lose, it shouted back hysterically.

'In ten minutes, not an hour, Mr Matondo, I will wet the van. The floor, the seats, whatever.' The words left my mouth before I could consider them. Steven looked at me again. I met his eyes, let him see the panic on my face.

'Okay, let me see what I can do.'

Steven guided the van towards a clump of trees. We were in a dusty part of the crater. When they show you the savannah on television, they keep the dust from you. It swirled around the van, and Steven turned the wheel, this way and that, charging boldly into the clouds of dust, confident in his knowledge of the crater's every trail. And then he braked to a halt! He stopped the van! I felt a rush of relief, and my bladder, sensing an end, almost gave up the fight. Don't wreck it all *now*, I pleaded.

'There is a fine, if you are caught here, of $600 for stopping here,' boomed Steven, for the benefit of everyone. My parents tried to look worried, but they let me handle it, and I was grateful for that. Everyone stared. Some clucks from the back, some suppressed grunts of irritation. Akira looked non-committal, the General livid, though I couldn't see his eyes.

'And how would anyone know?' I demanded of Steven, victory making me a tad cocky.

Steven pointed grandly at the crater's rim, tracing its periphery, brandishing a long finger like Excalibur. 'There are fourteen telescopes, of 100x power, all around the rim.' Steven warned, contempt edging the bass warning. 'They are manned by the wardens. First violation, all of you share the fine with me. Second, a three-month suspension and $1000; third time, the driver is banned. For ever. Go quickly now, you have about three minutes.'

I got out of the van carefully, the steps precise and tentative, as though I was carrying a teacup filled to the very brim. Every pair of eyes bored into the back of my neck. There was muffled conversation. He's hardly a damn kid, for Chrissakes (the General). You take it easy now, right, honey? (Mrs Mac). As my steps became longer, the dust began to go down, and I took in the scene. Soon it was clear.

Do you remember I told you about how the poorer and the better parts of towns are intertwined, in India? Well, it's exactly like that with the yellow of the dry grass and the green woody sections in Ngorongoro. As the dust settled, I realized that Steven had, in the fraction of a minute that we were in the dust, steered us to the middle of an immense flat of grassland stretching as far as the eye could see.

After I had walked about a minute, the nakedness of my position hit me.

There was nothing, absolutely nothing around. There was me, and there was, well, space. It was a clear, lovely day, and the sun lit up the grassland with perfect visibility. I could see to my left perhaps two miles away. A green line suggested a wooded section. To my right, more woods, with a mile or more of dry grass between us. In front of me, the horizon: its line obscured by a herd of perhaps a thousand wildebeest, raising a wavefront of dust, seemingly stationary. I turned around to look behind me. Not a tree, nor a bush not a stump, nothing. Only the van, faces pressed against each window.

There was nowhere to hide. However far I walked, there was no corner, no obstruction. We need, you see, an object to urinate *against,* a wall, a tree, even a mound or berm, as a counterpart in the process of communion. So what? I was part of a proud tradition of the free, schooled in public watering, a urinating commando, not a pissless white. I was at a decent distance from the van, so I unzipped my fly, clutching its brass handle between trembling fingers and tugging downwards breaths short and fevered fumbling desperately to lower my underpants and free myself feeling the tension that comes just before the thrill of release, and—

Everything just stopped. Stopped. The trees. The wildebeest froze, all thousand, mid-stride. The grass was still. The van, engine idling. Steven angry, tense; Kurosawa, the General, tourists nine and ten, the wives, waiting, watching, lining the van's windows, like spectacles for a ten-eyed beast; the wardens with 100x telescopes high up on the crater's rim.

Relax, let go, I said, let the eyelids drop gently, breathe long and deep. Inhaled air dusted the tops of my lungs and left. My bladder froze into a solid block of pain, its manic chatter shocked into silence. Nothing. Not a drop. A tiny wisp of breeze started up, and I realized that sweat that had formed on my face. I waited, but soon realized that I would have to fake the motions of urination. I did, and began the walk back to the van.

Walk unrepentant, walk tall, I commanded myself, it is time for another long battle with the body. Divide it in two fronts of war: the facial muscles, which must be mastered, and those at the lower regions of the trunk, which must deal with their own tensions.

The hour passed quicker than expected. I remember very little of it. The agony stayed, sensible, but oddly dulled and muted. Steven droned on and on about something. We saw the flamingo up close, tens of hundreds, rising vertically and settling down again into the water, a Mexican wave in pink. My father, son of his mother, quoted Wordsworth (Ten thousand saw I at a glance/Tossing their sprightly heads in dance), completely baffling General MacArthur. My mother winked at me and smiled. I don't think it was my father's unaccustomed burst of verse: I think she knew.

Back at the lodge, I rushed to the cottage, unescorted (it was day, no water buffalo) and took a long, relieved, leak. I smiled, reflecting that while I had manoeuvred myself out of an awkward situation in the van, I had lost to a most unexpected enemy; ten-time Wimbledon champion loses final to unknown outsider. A one-off.

Ngorongoro was the last, climactic stop of my tour of game

parks, and two days later, I caught the flight back to India, a day before I turned twenty-one.

IV

I called Mandira as soon as I landed at Delhi, although it was two in the morning. She sounded happy. We agreed to meet the next day, catch a movie, while away the rest of the day. Despite the fatigue of travel, I could barely sleep and counted the hours before my noon meeting with Mandira at the cinema.

Noon came. Mandira appeared! I saw her before she saw me, threading her way through the matinee crowd, and I allowed myself a few moments to just look. She wore a flaming orange kurta over jeans, hair hanging black and straight, face brown and glowing. I waved at her, she smiled, waved back. What joy! Hi! So how was Africa? Africa? Aah yes, Africa, great, I missed you so much, I've already forgotten! I held both her wrists in my hands, my eyes looking to lock into hers. Then I felt her wrists pull away ever so gently, and the eyes looking, for just a second, over her shoulder. 'Hi! This is Rohit. He's with me in college. Rohit, this is my best friend, he's just back from Africa! You've got the tickets? Great!'

The movie started, and I made sure I sat between Mandira and her new friend. I tried to be polite to him, and watched the movie with only half my attention. Mandira ate popcorn, drank cola, and generally stayed fixed on the movie, a smile tossed my way from time to time. At the break, the lights came on, and I excused myself to take a leak. I'd make sure I was back quickly.

Delhi was still in the last days of cool weather, and so the men's was busy. There were long queues, one behind each urinal stall. I took my place behind what seemed to be the shortest one. I stood, uncomfortable, and thought about tactics. Head back to Mandira? No, too painful, why show desperation? Besides, it doesn't seem right to leave a queue, it seems irresponsible and fickle: didn't you know this is a lavatory, not a tickets counter? This Rohit business – but look, the queue is moving along, wait it out.

Finally, my turn. Ten whole minutes of waiting! I prepared to piss, inhaling while I undid whatever I was wearing, my exhalation primed to synchronize with the moment of release, and—

It happened again. I seized up, stiff and unproductive. Behind me, ten men, and men everywhere around. Waiting, fidgeting, just like I'd been: shoe soles rubbing audibly against the lavatory floor, feigning patience and civility, but each hiding a beast within.

I could feel the urge desperately, but, here, in a room created especially for the act, I could have been in Ngorongoro. I faked the motions again, exaggerating them, for there was no panoramic savannah between my back and the relentless eyes behind me.

Outside in the foyer, the crowds of people milling around the concessions stands had begun to thin. Just as I approached the heavy swinging door of the theatre, the bell sounded to announce the second half. The first half of the film had ended on an intriguing note, full of prurient possibility, would the leading guy score? The bell brought the droves, some clutching cola bottles, everyone generally making a charge for the door, pushing, jostling, as only crowds in Delhi do. This would be a good moment to head back to the toilets. Like a salmon swimming upstream, I fought my way back to the men's. Just as I'd hoped, it only had a straggler or two and rows of unoccupied stalls. I waited a while, just to be safe, and soon I had it all to myself. Thank God. When I got back, Mandira's new friend had moved to the centre seat. I sat through the rest of the film, wondering what the score was, was that his denim jacket on his lap, its empty sleeve snaking up to the armrest they shared, or was there a hand in it?

Mandira never called me after that. I called her a couple of times, but soon learnt not to.

My bladder never spoke to me either, not ever; I went to every toilet alone, or not at all. I've been that way ever since.

V

'You really lost your girl, just like that?' Pietr is disbelieving and sorry. I say nothing. Max is moved and aghast. I say nothing.

Four Germans, jolly, red, and singing some kind of drinking song, file past the door to the men's and swing it shut. It shuts after several swings from side to side. They're happy.

'Come with me, now,' says Pietr. He grabs my arm and rises, pulling me to my feet. He strides to the lavatory, Max following earnestly. 'Wait here a minute. Max, come with me.'

I don't know whether it is little Max's polite speech or the six feet eight inch giant standing behind him, arms folded across his chest, who backs Max's each word with silent menace, but the Germans file out of the toilet, uncomprehending and a little cowed; they're not going to sing any time soon. It's a coup.

'Go now, it's all yours,' says Pietr, emerging. 'All yours,' echoes Max, all pride and pleasure, delighted with his role.

I pull my headphones and music player off my neck and put them around Pietr's. Grandma would approve; listening to sitar in the loo would defile Saraswati, the goddess of music.

I enter the men's room, with its row of gleaming urinals, the solitude a most unexpected gift. Even though my guardians (what else can I call them?) wait outside, I find release, pure and simple.

VI

I come out, refreshed. Pietr and Max have been standing by the door, ensuring my solitude. The Germans have regrouped, sullenly waiting like a deposed cabal waits for the new king to die. Pietr looks unconcerned, as though this is his job. He is listening to my music player with absorption.

'This is the worst crap I've heard in my whole life,' he declares. 'And this ... Rah-vi Shank-car,' he growls, reading the name off the little music player's screen, 'He can't play for shit!'

Outside, it's dark. Brugge's old walls are lit up in a sodium glow, their softness mingling with gleaming ATMs, painting the streets with colour, thrilling and precise. We step outside into the cool evening, friends for another night.

ERAZEX

Achal Prabhala

'Our students are simply the wrong kind. Look at the other schools. They get directors' children, corporate people from Delhi. And our boys? They're from ...' Mrs Mehra paused dramatically, as though marshalling inner strength to say the name aloud – '*Raebareli*'. We were at morning assembly. As head of English, I suppose Mrs Mehra's hysteria was somewhat justified. Raebareli was shorthand for mufassil towns all across the cow belt, for feudalism, crime, and corruption – and a distinct lack of English skills.

I had decided to spend a year coaching squash at an all-boys' boarding school in Dehradun. It was an easy job to get: I knew the principal was looking for young instructors who might bring with them a somewhat more contemporary world view than usually available in the school. And there is little competition for short-term school jobs. Once upon a time, elite hill schools produced prime ministers and captains of industry; today, they thrash for life in a muddy puddle of nostalgia, mediocrity, and brutality.

My prior acquaintance with the town of Dehradun had been brief, limited in fact to a two-day stay in its outskirts, at the weekend home of a friend. I knew nothing of the place beyond its beautiful boundaries. I saw the school for a few hours one afternoon, when I went over to meet the principal. It was one of three prominent boarding schools in the area, and the other two – unfortunately – had superior reputations. He asked me to eat lunch with the students in their refectory. I did. It was a lacklustre affair. The dining hall stank and the potatoes were uncooked. Conversation was banal. I remember wondering how I would survive.

But my reasons for wanting the job were convoluted – and personal. No matter how stilted the talk or dull the students, I was there to find a routine. Back in college, in an unnaturally still town in the mountains, I had owned a little machine that approximated the whirring of a fan. I needed it to sleep. I wanted a drill: waking up at five in the morning, going to the gym, eating breakfast, sleeping every afternoon, playing squash in the evening, and kissing the hills goodnight from my bedroom window.

I also wanted to write. Having tried my hand, and failed, several times earlier – in the in-between-work spaces, evenings, weekends and days off – and hating what I produced, I was convinced that the only way to write well was to keep one's mind uncluttered. Like everyone else, I suppose, I imagined that cold showers, mountains, and babbling brooks would somehow transform me into a writer.

When I finally arrived in Dehradun to start work, I was jet-lagged and exhausted. The week before, I had spent one day each in Corfu, Brindisi, Rome, Paris, and Delhi, wearily shifting a heavy backpack on and off ships, trains, buses, and planes. It was the end of a decent holiday I couldn't really afford. At the school, I was allotted a set of rooms on the third floor of a dormitory called Triveni. Students surrounded me on all sides. My flat was dark and damp, and had running water for only two hours a day. Dehradun in August is a hot, humid town. My first night was spent shifting sweatily on a plastic mattress (I had no sheets). The electricity frequently went off, cricket balls periodically assaulted my door, and Snoop Dogg's thumping growl relentlessly blasted on endless repeat somewhere very near.

• • •

I didn't have an alarm clock at first, and relied on the muezzin's call from the colony next door to wake me up. It came every day, loud and clear, which was very convenient for me. The previous squash coach, Mr Baghel, was in the process of moving to the American school in Mussoorie. He asked if there was anything I needed. Yes, I said, I would love to look around. We went out for dinner, and it was the first time I saw the town. He took me for a long drive on his motorcycle. Dehradun central was trapped inside a grim, grey cloud. The streets were a mass of desperate motion, like the last gasps of a wilting town. Electricity was intermittent; the buildings were flecked with soot; people looked tired and surly – and the effect was something like science fiction. Soon, it began to rain, and Mr Baghel drove into a large complex of shops and subsequently introduced me to every single shopkeeper therein. Then he drove me to his parents' house. By this time it was midnight, it was still raining, and we were thoroughly soaked. I'd have liked to be bathed, dry and asleep, but he was determined to be hospitable. His elderly parents – bless them – showed no surprise at being woken up in the middle of the night to confront a completely wet stranger.

My squash duties quickly resolved themselves, and I found myself pulled into all kinds of other jobs, the first of which was teaching economics. I found it difficult to write in the day, and what with squash taking up only my mornings and early evenings, I was glad for small distractions to see me through.

Mr Roy took me through the finer points of classroom instruction. I was to help him teach. 'I like the chairs neatly placed along the lines on the floor, ten inches away from the desk, and everything at exact right angles,' he said, looking at me intently. Expecting an economics drill and instead getting a lesson on symmetrical interior planning, I was caught unawares. But Mr Roy was a man of decidedly fixed ideas. He had previously worked in the management of India's largest heavy engineering company, and was a graduate of the Indian Institute of Technology and the University of Tokyo. In college, he represented the West Bengal cricket team in the Ranji Trophy tournament. Teachers of his calibre were rare, and the principal, appreciating that, gave him some privileges: a desirable flat in the new block, immediate housemaster-ship (teachers usually moved up to it) and control of the much-used Internet centre. Mr Roy shouldered this last responsibility diligently. He spent his evenings hunting for pornography, browsing through every single website that students had visited each day, updating the blocked list. Expectedly, he was thwarted by the burgeoning population of pornographic sites, far too many for even someone with his zeal to control.

Thus he was, among other things, an unlikely encyclopaedia of Internet porn. He relished uncovering the devious truth behind innocuous banners. 'Did you know,' he would say triumphantly, when we met at breakfast, 'that whitehouse.com is a nasty site? Imagine that.' We were friendly, though there were some differences in how we approached our common profession. Mr Roy had been blacklisted by students after slapping a senior – a thug of a boy from whom experienced teachers kept a healthy distance – for saying 'fuck' in the dining hall. His fury and his complete ignorance of how many millions of times it was being said in the dormitories were things I couldn't understand. I put it down, at first, to his age. Later, I realized it was a stronger moral sense, not one that I could relate to, but admired anyway. Mr Roy would go away at the end of that year to a management consultancy job in Tokyo.

• • •

It didn't take long for me to develop a reputation, and I suppose it was my fault. I was closer in age to the senior students than the teachers. My attitude towards the students, and my feelings about their general self-development, mirrored their favourite word: whatever. And in that way, they recognized me as one of their own. Various kids started falling into my orbit: young and old, shy and forward, but especially the misfits.

The mullah gang, as it was affectionately known, consisted of Osama, Ijlal and Aslam. They were virtually the only Muslim students on a campus of some five hundred people. Osama was Kashmiri, his family still lived there and even back then, in 1999, he was sick of the joke '... bin Laden?'. Ijlal came from a wealthy family in Moradabad, and had a brother in a madrassa. He grew his beard in a manner that would have warmed an orthodox heart. Aslam was from Aligarh, his mother was no more, and his father worked as a journalist in Kenya. 'My dad smokes pot,' he said once, laughing nervously, 'and keeps telling me that he won't mind if I do.' Aslam was trying to better his acquaintance with Islam, and in the process causing some strain within his freewheeling family. They were all, in different ways, popular students. Osama and Aslam were involved in relationships with non-Muslim girls from the school next door. Though 'relationship' meant little more than exchanging notes every week, and meeting in a chaperoned space once a month, they took these things quite seriously. And I only realized how much I wasn't aware of when one day, in the middle of an unrelated conversation, Osama looked at me evenly – perhaps sensing, in my disconnectedness, a kindred spirit – and said, 'Muslims should stick together.'

In November, I discovered that I was the drama coach as well. It was time to stage a play. My acting experience was limited to playing one half of the donkey that carried the Virgin Mary around at my convent school's nativity celebrations. But I quickly realized that I could bring my 'contemporary world view' to bear on the opportunity. A famous actor from Bombay had just helped stage *Androcles and the Lion* at the other boys' school next door. The play was replete with good boys speaking good English. A geriatric resident of the Doon Valley – about the only kind there is – wistfully remembered the time he directed the same play at the same school. That was forty years ago. He remarked, with stunning simplicity, that time seemed to be standing still.

I chose Mahesh Dattani's *Final Solutions*, a reaction to the Hindu–Muslim riots that had rocked Bombay in the early 1990s. The play was blunt, simplistic and therefore perfect, replete with good Muslims, bad Muslims, misunderstood Muslims and reformed Hindu bigots. I directed the play with a colleague from the junior school. We had five main characters and several foot soldiers to cast. Two of the main characters were Young Muslim Men at Crossroads. Bharat, chosen to play the Muslim who walks the razor's edge without falling off, exploded with anger when he found out what his costume entailed. 'Do you know who I am?' he said mockingly. 'My family is Rajput. My uncle is a *king*. See this earring? I'm not going to wear that dirty cap.' We chose Bharat because he seemed interested in having a part, and I had no idea that he would object, or express his objections to me so plainly.

I could have got angry. It would have been the sensible thing to do. As much as I ignored the variously vicious feelings that passed between students of different kinds, there was no denying that they existed. I let the incident pass. I was going to stage a play. I was being paid for it. I would do it within the vague boundaries of my conscience, and decided that I couldn't care less about how and whether it affected anyone else. I was more upset that the two young boys playing women's roles – Angad and Harpreet, plucked against their will from the junior school on the strength of their unbroken voices and long hair (they were both Sikh) – were already being harassed. This, I was casually told, was the bane of all-boys' schools.

I let the play take over. There was little else I could do.

In the months we rehearsed, things began to happen. Muslim prayer caps gradually became a fashion statement among the Hindu kids. Bharat started spending more and more time with the mullah gang – from which, Aslam was playing the role of the Hindu patriarch in the play. The multipurpose mobsters, once they had been restrained from setting fire to each other's hair for fun with their flaming paraffin torches, switched between Hindu slogans (*Har Har Mahadev*) and Muslim ones (*Allahu Akbar*) with a slightly unnerving ease. Rubina, my co-director, looked happier with every passing day. As we progressed further into rehearsals, and as the final performance drew closer, it became apparent that something good might come of it. The day we staged it for the public, Bharat came running up to me, bristling with anger, to say that one of the onlookers, a local supporter of the RSS, had caught hold of him and asked, 'But why are we trying to be so nice to these Muslims anyway?' That night, I'm fairly sure, I heard the sports captain speak to Angad politely.

But the play sparked off something that I would not know about until it was too late. Arjun was another of my favourite students. I considered him a friend, in part because he was a key student representative for the dining hall (and therefore, the one-point contact for coveted extra helpings as I ate all my meals with the students). Arjun played one of the mobsters. It was at the rehearsals – held late at night to avoid disturbing a packed day schedule – where Arjun met the young student he would later molest. They marched together in the mob, and walked home in the night, which was when, no doubt, the trouble started.

Arjun took him into a room, locked it, and demanded a blow job. The boy apparently refused, at which point he was beaten up, and after which he ran all the way to the principal's house to complain. He was a plucky little fellow, and survived the experience rather well. Arjun, on the other hand, became a shadow of his former self. The principal asked me to talk to him.

Counselling Arjun was an onerous task. He was a golden boy – captain of the hockey team, highest scorer in the school's cricketing history, fastest runner in town. He walked with a cocky swagger: girls swooned, the boys hanging around him got their ears boxed and cows flinched with pain as he hit them with stones for fun. That was then. One week of denial later, he grudgingly admitted he might have done a few 'bad things'. I tried to talk him through what those bad things were. In the long-established tradition of all-male boarding schools, the prospect of homosexuality didn't faze him in the least, because lusting after little boys was hardly considered deviant. This sexual nonchalance was balanced by his complete inability to understand why beating someone up for sex wasn't the right thing to do. The more I tried to understand him, the deeper I found myself slipping into the murky morass of boarding-school values. In the strange, crazy – and very real – world that he lived in, everything he had done actually made sense. It made no sense to me at all: I was from south India and I had never been to boarding school ever. Finally, I had to stop meeting him, just in order to clear my head. I don't think I affected him in the least bit.

He did, however, tell me about himself. Home was Sitamarhi, near Muzaffarpur in Bihar. He remembered that evening when his mother broke the news of his sister's death. She was fifteen, and he could picture her lying on a bed, hand outstretched, saliva spilling out of her mouth – his mother told him that she died from 'too much love', but nothing more. He was excited when Muzaffarpur got its first Internet service provider. His father couldn't afford to buy a jeep. (He let me in on a big secret. It wasn't his parents who were paying his fees but a rich uncle.) He was being groomed for the Indian hockey team, but that meant he would have to drop college and join the railways. He wondered if it was worth it.

One night, I was woken up at two o'clock. It was Arjun, gruffly bearing gifts, two orange-yellow bed sheets he had secretly tie-dyed in the school arts room. I used them as curtains, their bright psychedelics every bit as mystifying and compelling as their maker.

• • •

One afternoon, I noticed Bharat suspiciously obsessed with his handkerchief. I was in the library, reading the day's papers. I attempted conversation, but it was clear that Bharat was elsewhere. He was languorously sprawled out in the afternoon sun, and in his element: dazed and somehow, still devious. 'Want a sniff?' he asked pleasantly. I hesitantly approached the proffered kerchief. It smelt faintly alcoholic and very sharp.

'Erazex,' Bharat said, grinning.

Erazex, it turned out, was the narcotic of choice on campus. Everyone who could was doing it. Otherwise known as typewriter correction fluid, a typical package contains two bottles, a whitener, and a diluter. It is the diluter that is particularly popular. Portable, innocuous and cheap, when sniffed, it provides an instant low-grade hallucinogenic escape. Kores India manufactures the stuff in a factory at Nagpur. Inscribed on the packaging is this feeble admonition: 'Contains Toluene. Do not drink or inhale.'

All over India, children whose home is the street inhale Erazex incessantly: it is the easiest drug they can get their hands on. In that world, it's called 'sollution'. Activists who work with them curse the thing, worrying about the long-term effects of toluene use, of which little is known. It's clear that it is harmful, and as clear that its manufacturers know exactly how it is being consumed. Bharat, happily ignorant of the implications of its wider use, was unstinting in his praise. 'One sniff,' he said, 'and you get all dizzy and see colours. It's fantastic. I do it every day in class.'

Undoubtedly, it was a convenient way to get through a particularly tedious maths lesson. And it was an arresting picture: rich Bihari boys and poor street kids from Bangalore simultaneously getting high on the same substance. I, however, was transfixed by the idea of any narcotic that had the ambition to call itself Erazex. (Why is it that the majority of drugs have names that are either clinical or demonic?) Here was a lovely prospect: Control-Alt-Delete for the mind.

School broke up in the winter. As I was getting ready to leave, Ugarnath, a perky ten-year-old from Darbhanga, walked into my room clutching a soggy, brown paper packet. It was food, now badly decomposed, that he had saved from his tuck shop allowance a week ago – a goodbye gift. 'I can't behave badly with you,' Ugarnath had once said to me pensively. 'You are too mod.'

• • •

In what was one of the unexpected turns of my Dehradun life, I found myself befriending students much more than my fellow teachers. One of the exceptions was Jagmohan, a portly, bearded man of minor royal descent who taught geography and favoured a racy brand of sunglasses. With a habit of walking about in determined little steps, he encouraged the impression of being the sort of person who might have to leave any minute to fearlessly lead a dangerous jungle expedition. Jags – he liked being called that – threw a party in the winter. One of his guests, a man known mainly for his uninvited passion for the junior school matron, brought out a gun and shot the glass dining table. No one seemed to mind that it came crashing down. Jags's home befitted such eccentricity. He employed a harassed khansama who did his every bidding. He had overstuffed antique couches, old copies of *Marg* magazine strewn about the coffee table and crockery stamped with the family insignia. The walls were crowded with sepia photographs of his ancestors' hunting parties, rows and rows of overdressed brown people – and their inevitable white guests – staring balefully at heaps of dead birds.

Jags's friend, the one with the gun, asked me how I managed without a weapon. With genuine concern, he suggested that the offices of his father – a notoriously insane Haryana politician – could be put to use to secure a licence for me. In shock, I mumbled back something about not being interested in shooting ducks or dogs or whatever it was people shot. Jags admonished me later for passing up this opportunity. Guns, it seems, weren't offered to just anyone.

Once, after a rambunctious barbecue evening on the lawns of his home, Jags stood up and said, 'I'm sick of all of you. Bugger off everyone. I'm going to bed.' Then he noisily tripped over a row of plants, regally extricated himself from the debris, and went to bed.

• • •

March was time for the annual school trek. This was a long-standing tradition, borrowed from the mightiest boarding school of all, the other boys' school in Dehradun, whose name people still whispered with unnecessary reverence. The senior students were going away to Auli to ski. Normally, they tried their best to avoid taking teachers with them. Being seniors, they were allowed the privilege of an unescorted holiday. My inability to discipline being notorious, I was asked along. Sandeep, a rotund boy from Aligarh, caught hold of me one afternoon and hesitantly asked if he could come too. Of course, I said, and gave him some forms to fill out. Later, his housemaster accosted me. Apparently, Sandeep had a diagnosed heart problem. I forgot about the incident for a while, until the housemaster came up to me again, waving a faxed letter of permission from the boy's parents. 'They say he's fine,' he said, 'so if he still wants to go you can take him.'

Starting out at the crack of dawn, Sandeep was the last to arrive. Each of the three hired cars was full. He ran around in the bleak morning chill, between cars, being teased and pushed out as he tried to get in. I brought him to the car I was travelling in, forcing everyone to squeeze in tighter. I had made another friend by then. George was British, and employed by the school for his gap year – that was what they called a year off – while calmly recovering from a series of traumas he had encountered along the way: a strictly regimented public school education, little boys with lots of money and the death of friends by drug overdose.

George was easy-going and friendly, strummed a mean guitar and lived his evenings in a happy herbal haze, which is to say that we got along very well. The climb up was slow and precarious, but eventually we made it to Joshimath where a cable car awaited our ascent. Joshimath to Auli: one minute, we were standing on firm ground, in a place which was cold, but bearable, and the next, we were high up in the clouds, with snow all around us. The cable car gave way to a ski lift, whose handles barely fastened. It was a frightening ride: I worried about not getting off in time and being knocked senseless by a thundering mass of solid steel. But Auli was beautiful: Nanda Devi, among other significant Himalayan peaks, lay waiting in view. The Garhwal Mandal Vikas Nigam (GMVN) set-up was pretty basic, like its prices – possibly the cheapest skiing anywhere in the world. The students had a large dormitory, and we 'escorts' got cottages. Meals were served in a restaurant that lay steeply above us, the ascent to which was by a set of steps so smoothly frozen over, it was like walking up a dangerously tall playground slide.

I was constantly referred to as the 'escort' through that trip.

George, being English, was merely a useless foreigner, and thus it was I who would be shouted at with 'Escort! Your boys are misbehaving,' or, when my patent lack of authority showed, darkly asked, 'Are you really an escort or just a student?' I wasn't sure what to say; I had no authority anyway. The students saw my presence as a favour they had enabled – since they could have done this alone – and had made it quite clear that they expected to be left alone.

In the morning, piping-hot bathing water was delivered to our doorsteps. The breakfast trek was difficulty negotiated with clumpy ski boots on our feet and heavy skis on our shoulders. I had skied before, as had George. For everyone else, snow was a brand-new experience, thrilling and strange. The first night we got in I tried to phone the school, but I couldn't. The telephone lines were dead. They had been, for about a month. The closest communication point was the Indo-Tibetan Border Police (ITBP) outpost, half an hour away on skis. I let it be.

Nights were surreal. It snowed constantly, our translucent night sky scarred by wet little white streaks. Apparently, given the time of year, the amount of snow was unusual. On our first night in Auli, we discovered a tiny little hut where a Tibetan couple offered momos and tea. There, in crackling, sulphurous gaslight, under a thick tarpaulin, we huddled on damp benches, discussing the day's adventures and recovering complainingly from the cold. By the third day, just as we were getting into the groove of things, Sandeep went down with a headache and mild fever. I had brought along a medical kit, so I gave him some Crocin. I asked around for a doctor. The phone lines being dead, there was no one available immediately. The director of GMVN said he would make sure we got a doctor in the morning.

By morning, Sandeep was unconscious. He had altitude sickness. Why no one there could anticipate this the night before, we would never know. Now, as he lay in his bed, gasping for air, soaking in his own urine, everyone seemed to have the answers.

'You have to take him down.'

'Take him to Joshimath ...'
'But Chamba has a better hospital?'
'The only heart and lung machine is in Dehradun.'
'This is bad. Didn't you read the notice on altitude sickness in the walls of the office?'

Communication with the world at large didn't exist, so even at three in the morning, after we went from door to door, waking officials from deep slumber, there was no transport available. The vital thing was to get him down, to lower elevation, where he could breathe again. Sandeep had advanced high-altitude pulmonary oedema. It starts out with a persistent headache and mild fever. In the nights (when it is at its worst), breathing gets increasingly difficult, and the afflicted person eventually passes out. At that point, the lungs have accumulated so much fluid that it is impossible to breathe properly. The simplest rescue is rapid descent.

Someone went to the ITBP unit to call Joshimath for a taxi. In the hours it took to come, Sandeep got worse. We sped down the icy, winding hill path that had been closed off these last three days, owing to the heavy snowfall. Sandeep lay with his head on my lap, straining to breathe like a fish on dry land. His eyes opened once in a while, and he looked at me with gentle confusion. I held him close, manually assisting his breathing while flushing out the bits of yellow fluid that leaked from his mouth and nose. I stroked his face and kissed him uncontrollably. At Joshimath, the only hospital – two rooms actually – was of no help. A small bribe, however, secured the services of a male nurse and an oxygen cylinder, with which we hoped to keep Sandeep going until Chamba.

Chamba was a bigger town, and had a real hospital. It seemed like everyone, from Auli to Joshimath, only wanted to get rid of us, to pass us on to the next person. Sandeep was in rough shape, and no one wants trouble on one's hands. It took all our powers of persuasion, at each point, just to have him admitted and examined. The taxi driver wanted more than the usual fare to take us down.

When we finally got Sandeep into the Chamba hospital, I rushed over to the district magistrate's house.

I walked past the neatly gravelled path, past the whitewashed walls of the veranda and stood by the door. I was stinking of sweat and urine and my thick woollen clothes were flecked with phlegm. Through the doorway I could see cane chairs, potted palms and white curtains: I became oddly conscious of my appearance. Sandeep was slipping, and I was suddenly concerned that I didn't look respectable.

DM saheb was lunching. I was asked to wait. A minute later – a long, frustrating minute later – the DM sauntered out. He had been alerted of the situation already, the principal of the school having reined in all bureaucratic contacts to help. Was there a helicopter that could take Sandeep to Dehradun, or just anywhere lower? No. Was there anything he could do? No.

When I got back to the hospital, Sandeep's body was jumping several inches into the air with the combined force of manual thumping and electric shocks. A few minutes later the thumping ceased, the masks came undone, and that was how we knew Sandeep was dead. 'I'm sorry,' said the doctor, putting his arm around me. I shook him off, stumbled out of the hospital into an ordinary afternoon on a quiet hill road, and cried.

It took nine hours, between six in the evening and three in the morning, to reach Dehradun. Sandeep needed to be covered up. The hospital couldn't spare the sheets he had died on (rules were rules). I went to the market and bought two cotton sheets. Transport had to be organized. No driver was willing to cart a dead body anywhere. 'Police trouble,' they said, begging off. Finally, someone agreed to take us for roughly five times the normal price. Sandeep's body wouldn't fit sideways or lengthwise. We placed him diagonally on the floor of the jeep, his head protruding from under my seat. With my hands, I shielded his head from banging against the steel supports of the jeep as we drove. 'Laash,' I explained at police checkpoints. 'Here is the death certificate. We have all the papers.'

Osama came back with me. His sombre presence was comforting. 'They teach us all sorts of things here,' he said, staring out into the night as we swept through the silent Garhwal hills, 'but not how to be gentle.' I suppose we were both thinking the same thing: what it must have felt like to be fat, short and the editor of the school's Hindi magazine, read by exactly no one. What it must have been like to be constantly teased for being slow, studious and Sikh. And what a life it must have been to want to throw it away by skiing with the boys.

There is an arresting line in Daphne du Maurier's operatic shocker, *Don't Look Now*: 'What a bloody silly way to die,' a man blurts out in panic, moments before his own unbelievable death. I touched Sandeep's face through that thin cloth that protected him. What if he wasn't really dead?

• • •

The mullah gang camped in my rooms for a couple of days after that. They moved in without asking and I was grateful. It was frustrating, explaining things to people on the outside, and complicated conversations were impossible on expensive long distance. The other teachers had their own lives – their families, their mutual alcoholism – in which I had no part. I only had a month left at the school anyway. I had been offered an editor's job at one of the innumerable media outfits that were cropping up at the time, and was headed to Bombay and London. After a year of insufferable telephone connections, which assured that I could read no more than about one email message a week, I was among the least qualified people alive to join the Internet publishing industry. But stranger things had happened.

In fact, I had been mulling over the offer for a few months. It was Sandeep's death that decided it. Dehadrun was supposed to have been my getaway, but now the thought of getting away to another place, to a new profession, was suddenly liberating. I thought of it as my own personal Erazex.

In the present, however, there was a dangerously lurking

melancholia to be considered. George tackled the despair by coming up with an idea so attractive, it instantly became a plan. Stiffing the system seemed like an urgent necessity. It was a simple idea: we would dress up in burkhas and infiltrate the girls' school next door.

Being the oldest, I was saddled with the organization. Salim from the paan shop down the road helped with the burkhas, borrowing them from his amused wife and her mystified friends. The junior school matron gamely donated her old brassieres with strict instructions that I didn't disclose whom they had come from. Anant, a senior student whose natural voice was a high-pitched squeal, was selected to do the talking. Expectedly, the task of conversing in drag with the girls' school headmistress (a formidable woman whose name, quaintly, had become a local synonym for female underarm hair) was not one he looked forward to. It was only after we appealed directly to his greed, with a full butter chicken, that he agreed.

As soon as we walked through the gates, I noticed that the hair on Varun's leg was showing. That George was wearing distinctly masculine hiking sandals. And that Bisharath had hitched his gown so high, his school pants were clearly visible. But it was too late to turn back. We walked in, to be faced by about two thousand young schoolgirls, all looking at us intently. A middle-aged man winked at me, jocularly patted my bottom and said, 'Good disguise boys.'

So much for subterfuge.

Nevertheless, we were in. Now, something had to be done, and said, in order for us to get out again. I pushed Anant towards the unsmiling headmistress, who stood with arms locked in combat mode.

'Excuse me,' he began, while the rest of us fidgeted behind him, 'we are from Dubai. We would like to get our daughters admitted to the school. We want to spend some time in the dormitories to see if they are okay.' This was his brief, and this was how we thought we might invade the school's sanctum sanctorum.

'I see,' said Mrs D, without flinching.

'My sisters,' Anant continued nervously, turning around and pointing at us.

'Why don't you come with me and I will take you where you need to go,' she said, catching hold of Anant's arm with unexpected ferocity.

'Can I call my sisters too?' Anant bleated wildly, trying to wriggle out of her grasp.

'But they're leaving,' she said.

And so we were. Realizing the direction this conversation was taking, we were backing away from him, closer to the side gate. Anant turned around, saw us leaving, wrenched himself free of the headmistress and fled. There was nothing left for us to do but run. We reached the side gate and tried to work our way through a horde of small girls coming in from the opposite direction. We could barely see through our veils. Bisharath tripped and fell. 'Damn,' he said in a gruff voice, and the little ladies were audibly startled. They moved away immediately, and we got to the gate. A burly guard swooped to catch us as we left, but there were too many of us, and he only managed to rip the veil off Varun's face.

'Catch him!' I heard a shrill, schoolteacher-like voice cry with unbridled excitement, 'It's a *boy!*' We didn't stop running until we got to a construction site, where we hid ourselves for a while. Then, throwing off the burkhas, we emerged in our usual clothes and innocently walked home. It had been a while since I felt such achievement. Happily, from what I heard immediately after the affair, the blame seemed to be directed at the other boys' school. It was the perceived sophistication of the crime. We were strictly a UP–Bihar school, while they were famously Delhi–Bombay.

At the principal's house for dinner, some weeks later, he and his wife (an extremely warm couple, and equally shrewd) asked me, much too casually, if I knew anything about this 'burkha incident'. The principal opened up an avenue of reply by suggesting that our school often got blamed for things the other school did. I concurred vigorously.

• • •

I left in April. Arjun came to visit me that summer, and he wasn't the only one. Bharat came in from Scotland, where he had been on a student-exchange fellowship. His boarding school sanctioned beer and wine: Bharat, of course, was caught drinking whisky and narrowly missed being expelled. On his last night in the land of lochs, he went to a nightclub, bought a few tabs of Ecstasy (more cost-effective than alcohol) and saved cab fare by walking home, a full hour's journey. On the way back to India he expended these scrupulously saved finances on an enormously expensive present for me.

The last time I visited Dehradun was in August that same year. Lakshmi, a single mother whose son I used to coach, gave me a book to mark our parting. The journey from Dehradun to Delhi was five hours long. I didn't want to think of the school on my way out, so I got straight to *The Glass Palace*. In fact, I had never read Amitav Ghosh before. I had always suspected his typical reader of being someone else – some stern, ambitious Indian graduate student in Chicago or Manhattan, his life a joyless blur of vexing deviations from stern, ambitious social theories.

And then, towards the end of the journey and the end of the book, overcome by its sentimentality, I gave in. It was just the moment for a good cry. For, I knew that I could reconstruct the shattered fragments of Ghosh's world by simply turning his pages back. The people, the places, the palaces – they were mine and they would wait. But Dehradun was slipping away. We were already transforming. Some of us would grow up, others would change their minds, combinations would rearrange, and that extraordinary moment I had experienced was never going to exist again.

I thought of Sandeep. I thought of Aligarh. When I eventually got there after that fateful ski trip, Sandeep's parents were frozen in a state of inconsolable shock. A fellow teacher accompanied me on the journey, and he took a tour of their palatial home. 'He was their only hope,' he said to me on our way out. 'Look at all this wealth. That is why they are so upset. He has another brother, but –

you saw him – he is mentally retarded, not all right. They have a big vegetable oil factory. Who will continue that?'

At the time, it had seemed like one long delirium. Months later, now, it still did.

The woman sitting across the aisle from me – expensively dressed, perfectly made up and smelling of something strong – looked over to see what I was reading. 'Oh Amitav *Ghosh*,' she said, elegantly wringing her hands, 'I just *love* his books. How is this one?'

I thought about that question for a bit, and wiped my face with the free mineral water that had been handed out earlier. 'I was silly to have thought I wouldn't like it,' I said, 'because it turned out that I did. A lot.' But she wasn't listening any more. The journey was over. Our train was pulling in to New Delhi station and she was speaking into a cellular phone, instructing her driver to jump on to the compartment and get her bags.

THE REMEMBERED VILLAGE
U.R. Ananthamurthy

Swadesho bhuvanathrayam – your own place is all of the three worlds. I had everything I needed to grow up right there in my little village, Kerekoppa. I must explain the word 'village' here. It was a one-home village, and a half-kilometre walk through the forest paths was another one-home village. We were, in reality, living in a jungle.

We lived with tigers. They were the unseen presence in our lives, their roars reverberating through the walls of our village home. The cows tethered in the adjacent shed seemed to know that a tiger was in the vicinity much before we did. The little bells slung around their necks would begin to tremble. It was a peculiar sound, and a signal for us to shut all doors and windows. We would huddle around my mother in a corner, as my grandfather recited slokas in the hope that the chant would keep the tiger away. We invoked the several names of Arjuna – Phalguna, Partha Kireeti, Shwethavahana ...

The forest enveloped our home and the arable lands around. It was the dominant influence on our everyday life. Each morning my grandfather, sickle in hand, would chop away at the undergrowth to keep our clearing free from the relentless march of the forest.

My father was a shanbaug, a tax collector who also doubled up as a legal counsellor for the villagers. Once a year, the collector, in a top hat, would visit the village – reminding us of the omniscience of the Empire. But copies of Gandhiji's *Harijan* had already made inroads and fierce nationalism was a badge we all wore on our sleeves. A few kilometres away was Thirthahalli, the taluka town with a school in which I studied – it was the same school that one of my literary icons, Kuvempu, had attended. A ten-kilometre radius (beyond which I never travelled) constituted my entire universe for sixteen years. This was the world that grew within me.

Agriculture was a cyclical profession, and people had a lot of leisure time in which to cultivate the mind. The stories we told each other, and the dramas that were enacted for us, became a world of ideas that have seeped into my consciousness.

People tracked the rains by looking at the movement of clouds and watching for the appearance of particular insects. Medicinal herbs (along with quinine, if a post office was nearby) were used to combat malaria, which, like the forest, was a constant factor in our lives. Folklore dominated both our workday world and the world of our imagination. My mother and almost every other woman seemed to know songs that lasted for hours. Yakshagana troupes would travel to the village, as would groups of acrobats from a local community called the Dombarus, who performed during the jathre (village fair) every December. The sight of sinuous girls balancing on impossibly high sticks was my first glimpse of the beauty of the human form.

Time here was not linear, rather it moved in a cyclical pattern where both the modern and the ancient coexisted. My father, a Sanskrit scholar, taught himself English and cleared the London Matriculation Exams. But my first sounds of spoken English were heard in the clipped British accent of Srinivas Jois, who brought a little bit of England into my Brahmin agrahara. Jois – who anglicized his name to Sinha – listened to BBC broadcasts on a radio (powered by a dynamo) in the house of Achuth Rao, a sophisticated and well-read elder citizen in Thirthahalli. Defying tradition, Rao, a Konkani Brahmin, had married a widow. And in his well-stocked library – where Jois always lounged – I read my first books in English, particularly those that someone called

Reynolds wrote, romantic tales of dukes and duchesses printed on double-sided yellowing pages. My elders watched adaptations of Shakespeare's plays performed in Kannada, as also Kalidasa's *Shakuntala*. The great names in theatre then were Varadachar and Gubbi Veeranna. We boys loved romances like *Sadarame*.

The Agumbe mountains, a few miles away from our village, was where we went to watch the sun sink into the horizon.

There was a small library in the Sri Rama Temple within our village which stocked Kannada books, on mythology, and of the literary greats, Shivarama Karanth and Kuvempu. The forests of Malnad are a recurring feature in contemporary Kannada literature. There is an apocryphal tale of Kuvempu himself reading a translation of Homer's *Iliad*, surrounded by the dense stillness of the forests in his family home in Thirthahalli. A scene he has recreated in his novel *Kannuru Heggadthi*, where the protagonist reads Matthew Arnold, perched on a rooftop eyrie in a traditional Malnad home, even as below in the forecourt of the house a bleating goat is being readied for a ritual sacrifice.

In the Malnad that I grew up in, times ranging from the medieval to the modern could overlap in the blink of an eye. One didn't have to watch a movie or go to a library to learn about ancient India, it was all a part of one's consciousness, and the experiences of centuries past lived on in people's memories. The contrast with linear movement of time in the Western tradition came alive to me once I moved to England for my doctoral studies in the early 1960s. Watching Ingmar Bergman's *Seven Seas* in the company of my guide Malcolm Bradbury, I realized that the 'past' a Western mind was searching for already existed in the mind of many Indians.

Being raised in an intellectually rich tradition like the one which Thirthahalli offered allowed my mind to roam free. The veteran socialist leader Gopala Gowda often travelled to our taluka, speaking to large crowds of the dream of a new India, an India less superstitious and more tolerant, with space for both our ancient learning and modern thought. My father was a nationalist and open to new ideas; his attitude, in turn, have had a great impact on me.

We never lacked for entertainment, despite living without electricity. It was not just travelling troupes of Yakshagana artistes who fired our imagination, theatre came alive in the forecourt of our own home as well. Tala-Maddale, the narrative component of the Yakshagana minus the costumed dancers, was a familiar winter pastime. And oftentimes, travelling Vedic scholars would hold discourses in the Madhva Matha in nearby Bhimanakatte, challenging scholars from Sringeri's Advaitha Matha to a debate on dualism. It was a world of ideas and thought that seamlessly flowed. Growing up in an extended family housed within the Brahmin agrahara, I was privy to traditions that devolved from both the front yard of the house, where the men dominated, and the backyard, where I learnt of the mysterious lives of the women of the household. As the errand boy who fetched their medicines from Dr Charles, the village doctor, on my way back from school, it was also my task to smuggle in the snuff that they dared not ask their husbands for.

The Melige Jatre, an annual festival, brought the world into our homes. A ride on a richly decorated bullock cart, seated behind the lovely animals who paraded with gejje (ghunghroos) tied to their horns, was the highpoint of our lives. Every community participated in the fair: a Muslim (whom we called byari) was just a person from another jaathi (community) with his own customs. The concept of religion did not exist, people just belonged to different communities. When we adolescent boys thronged the fair to catch a glimpse of images, objects and pictures from lands faraway, the slide show would flip from a picture of a prostitute in Bombay to an image of Tirupathi's Thimappa lest we be incorrigibly corrupted. The jathre was also the place where women from all communities came by. And for a Brahmin boy raised to believe he was first among equals, this brought with it the realization that the woman he could never marry was also the most beautiful one he had ever seen. I might have learnt logic from the Brahmins but my aesthetic education came from all communities.

The start of the Second World War saw the advent of steam

buses in our hilly region. These ancient machines would puff uphill and then stall, only to be hand-pumped again to restart their engines. This was also about the time that bicycles came to Thirthahalli. And by then, discontent with the British was rampant. Local artisans – like the metal workers in nearby Kavaledurga – could turn out the most sturdy ploughs, knives and sickles from iron ore mined there. But the British disallowed it, instead importing steel from Birmingham. The industrial age had begun to intrude into my agrarian idyll, much as it did in D.H. Lawrence's *Eastwood*, even as the winds of socialism and self-determination were blowing ever stronger across Malnad. I moved to Mysore for a college education and then on to England. But the green hills and misty valleys of Malnad are fused in my consciousness for all time.

THE ARCHIVIST

Ananya Vajpeyi

Pandurang Vitthal Sukthankar woke with an unfamiliar taste in his mouth. 'What's this?' he wondered, as he lay on his narrow bed, running his tongue along the roof of his mouth and in between his remaining teeth, where his gums were shrivelled. He tried to recall what he had eaten for dinner the previous night – nothing out of the ordinary, as far as he could tell. But in a second the answer came to him from the morning stillness of his little room: 'It's Death. It's here.' He sat bolt upright, feeling with both wrinkled hands for his heart under his dirty white singlet. It was beating all right. Perhaps it would cooperate with him for the time it would take to finish his work for this life.

He made himself some tea, did his business, bathed, prayed, ate, dressed. He did not pick up his frayed cloth jhola from the chair near the door. He would have liked to confirm his appointment with Nira, but he had no telephone at home. He put on his worn out sandals. As he turned to bolt the door, he glanced up at his dead wife's photograph on the wall at the end of the small corridor. 'Goodbye Panduranga,' she said, in a faded sepia voice. He locked the house behind him as he set out. He slipped the key into his pocket. From his tiny place in Sadashiv Peth, off Tilak Road near the Jnana Prabodhini School, by foot to the Oriental Institute would take him a good forty-five minutes, maybe an hour. At his age, through such bad traffic, one had to walk slowly. The good thing was that by the time he got there the Institute would be open at last, and Nira waiting for him. She was always punctual.

The traffic was terrible; people were driving to work. He got to the bridge with great difficulty. When he was halfway across it, he stopped to regard the filth below that passed for one of Poona's twin rivers, the Mutha. He fingered the key in his pocket, wishing he could throw it down. But there was no flowing water to take it away, to other rivers, to the Arabian Sea. He looked to Sambhaji's statue on the far side of the bridge, thinking how the great warrior must be choked by the vehicular fumes and deafened by the noise, parked as he was on the city's busiest traffic island, with a hundred billboards for company. This was no place to dally, contemplating the final destination of a castaway key. He let the key drop back into his pocket, and went on towards Deccan.

Here was his favourite bookstore on the corner. Pandurang considered stopping by, saying hello to his good friend the owner. But could he really afford to begin something new? Who knows what a conversation might lead to? His heart had given him a final deadline, he had to respect it. He slunk past the entrance, never looking inside, lest the prospect of undiscovered books on the disorganized shelves and stands tempt him in even after he had dismissed the thought of talking to the owner. He turned into a little alleyway, cut across a small vegetable market (sluggish at this hour, thriving at night), and came to the road that circled around the Gymkhana. Suddenly the roar of the traffic became muffled and the shrill messages of advertising text receded from his consciousness. A group of boys played cricket in the Gymkhana grounds. He could be back in the colonial Poona of anglicized Brahmins. It used to be called the Oxford of the East back then, while Calcutta was the Paris of the East and Benares the Athens, in a mirror-image world where the West saw itself when it looked at its colonies.

Pandurang wound his way through the lanes of the Deccan Gymkhana neighbourhood, sandwiched between Karve Road and Prabhat Road. Some old stone houses still stood undisturbed by the construction boom, modernity literally at their gates in the form of trenches hastily and untidily dug to lay fibre-optic cable.

But many of these houses, behind the thinnest residue of transplanted English charm from a century ago, were shabby to the point of being uninhabitable. Pandurang dimly recalled happier times. 'It's Death,' he called to one period house and the invisible people within, over a cable pit, through its rusty iron gate, across its sad compound, 'it's here.' And he kept moving, feeling the sun beat down on his head. Had he been of another caste, he would have gladly worn the white Congress cap that so many of Poona's men used, if not to signal their politics any longer, at least to guard against the city's short sharp noontime heat.

Pandurang felt an increasing urgency to get to the Institute. It wasn't just mortality – they would close for their first coffee break of the day if he didn't get there soon, and then his meeting with Nira would be in jeopardy. Their working hours were a joke. And today was his last chance to be there. One might be devoted to a place for forty years, but when Death comes knocking (filling one's mouth with its own ineffable flavour), one still craves whatever extra snatches of time can be had to spend there. Off Bhandarkar Road to his left was a street he passed with a pang. There used to be the home of a renowned professor, long dead, one of India's greatest. He had been a mathematician and an archaeologist, a Marxist long before the days when it became fashionable for Indian intellectuals to be Marxists – and, somewhat unexpectedly, the builder of a beautiful house, with a red-tiled roof, a verandah running around its sides, and a courtyard at its centre. The house had been sold off to builders now, and Pandurang didn't want to contemplate its present form.

How often did scholars, penurious or careless, live in beauty? The architectural style chosen by the famous man was reminiscent of coastal homes on the other side of the Western Ghats. The front room was preserved as his study, his desk in a corner, his things scattered about, as though he had just got up and left his chair momentarily. Only a very large photograph of him that hung on the wall suggested that he wouldn't be coming back in from another part of the house. Pandurang realized he ought to be able to remember what his presence had felt like, but memory was becoming more and more unreliable as a friend. And right now all he could think of was getting to the Institute. What exactly did he expect would happen with Nira? He didn't know. He didn't care. Reaching there before it was too late, that was his only goal.

Ah, finally. Pandurang's homing beacon flashed furiously at him. There, over a particularly perilous stretch of Law College Road, diagonally across from a fast-food place where youngsters sat sipping juice, was the Oriental Institute. Roadworks, related or not to the fibre-optic revolution, had swallowed its perimeter wall. The frail trees on the inside seemed like feeble protection for the old buildings against further encroachment from all of the city's aggressive impulses to reinvent itself in an ugly avatar. Pandurang dodged speeding two-wheelers, stepped over piles of rubble and mud, heaps of broken-up tar, and barbed wire that intermittently snaked around what used to be the Institute's boundary wall. At last, he was there.

He slipped through the passageway leading to the yard behind, successfully avoiding the man currently holding the post that used to be his. He went quickly to the library in the back, a relatively modern-looking structure, lacking the decrepit loveliness of the manuscript archive and the offices in the front. Fortunately, today none of his friends or acquaintances sat on the table near the card catalogue. He could disappear into the stacks without being seen. Most of the Institute's permanent members and fellows occupied their customary places – at creaking tables next to spider-webbed windows, in cramped rooms they had been allotted decades ago – poring over researches begun in the middle of the twentieth century. Only Death would stop their scholarly quests. One was almost blind, another deaf, a third amnesiac, but they carried on working, often dressed in suits that would have connoted impeccable breeding thirty or forty years ago. Pandurang glided past them like a ghost.

The ancients – they were older even than Pandurang by almost a generation – would not have known that he was there anyway, unless he had gone up to greet them. But had any of the staff seen him, precious time would have been wasted talking of this and that. Or worse, if the current librarian were to come upon him, there would be acrimonious vibes exchanged. Pandurang would be made to feel uninvited, and in turn he would be unable to resist insinuating that the man didn't know how to do his job. Luckily, Pandurang penetrated deeper and deeper into the stacks undetected by a single soul.

He breathed deeply the dampness of a library full of Sanskrit books. He was taking his last gulps of this peculiar air, laden as much with learning as with spores of mould and particles of dust and drops of moisture. He could feel his heart, so sluggish that morning, pounding in his chest. 'Soon,' he said to the bird of life within him, whose call was his heartbeat, 'soon you will fly this cage.' The musty air of the library that used to be his charge was a cocktail for him, it went to his head, made him giddy. He closed his eyes, leaning against a wooden shelf of texts on grammar dating from before the Christian Era. When he opened them again, Nira stood in front of him, asking, in her gentle way that conveyed concern without seeming intrusive: 'What's wrong, Sukthankarji?'

Pandurang came to. So she had kept her word. Nira was a doctoral researcher he liked, unlike most of the other academic specimens who came to Poona from all over India and the world in a continuous untiring tiresome stream. She seemed dedicated to her study without being too earnest, she had a nose for elusive pieces of knowledge that she pursued without the irritating doggedness of many of her colleagues. He had run into her on several occasions at the Institute while she tracked down a disintegrating manuscript or puzzled over some impossibly old phrase that needed deciphering. Other times, they had been invited to the same social gatherings.

These were tea parties for Poona Indologists, where in addition to transient populations of American and European research students came the same small group of Indians who had taught generations of foreigners Sanskrit, Pali, Marathi, Hindi, Bengali for a steadily increasing price. And peppering this mix would be librarians like Pandurang, who provided both communities with texts for them to respectively be taught and teach. Pandurang didn't care much for most of the invitees, but he went along anyway. Sometimes (rarely) excessively polite Japanese or Korean scholars would turn up, the women most often in Indian clothing. They always combined their own traditional bow with the namaskaar, so that the overall effect of their greeting was of extreme humility, almost supplication. There were a large number of East Asians in Poona to study Buddhism, but they tended to be shy, discouraged perhaps by the general use of English at these sorts of social occasions.

In addition to the core of students, teachers and bibliographers, others came too. They were mostly uninvited, but then they didn't need invitations. For her part Nira was wary of them. They were the locals – unsuccessful artists who introduced themselves as 'artistes', wily yoga practitioners and lascivious tabla players looking for gullible trainees, seedy Hindu fundamentalists with a variety of untenable linguistic theories, vaguely right-wing Brahmins retired from government bank jobs, landlords who serially rented to Sanskritists from out of town at preposterous rates. Some were fixtures at these parties – a plump young divorcee who for some reason always volunteered to sing German drinking songs from before the War, an aging and reputedly wealthy man with hair dyed jet-black and kohl-rimmed eyes who claimed to be a 'lover' of Krishna, the bookstore owner from the Deccan corner, discreetly asking the American guests if they'd like to catch a beer later on (and maybe a spin at the disco). Then there were the white people – kirtan groupies, sitar junkies, India hands, potheads, religion chasers, Dutch anthropologists of Vedic ritual, Indian-American undergraduates discovering their roots ... Pandurang went, because more than mixed company he feared loneliness. But he had noticed that Nira had not come to the last few teas.

'Hello!' he said. 'I'm fine, thank you. Just getting old, you know. Where have you been? I didn't see you at our little gathering in the Fergusson College auditorium annexe the other evening.'

Nira smiled apologetically. 'I couldn't make it,' she said. 'Before you contacted me last week, I was away from Poona for three months.' She didn't mention that she was to leave again the next day, this time indefinitely. Nor did she say that the institution of the Indology tea party was too absurd for her to keep returning to it once the novelty – the surprise that such a confluence of eccentric and unhappy individuals could exist at all, leave aside repeat itself at regular intervals – had worn off. There was no community of people like herself, there couldn't be. It seemed to her at this moment that Pandurang looked quite unwell. 'Are you headed somewhere from here?' she asked. 'May I give you a ride?'

Pandurang was silent for a few seconds. He had been so intent on getting to the Institute, he hadn't considered going any further. But he still had his key in his pocket, awaiting disposal. And he had needed more time with Nira, to really get to the point. 'Where can you take me?' he asked, partially afraid that her answer might disappoint him.

'I was going to the Dakshina Academy,' Nira said. 'I needed to return a few books there.' She always spent her last day in Poona returning books at the various libraries she had used during her stay.

He couldn't have hoped for a more appropriate destination. It was far away, he and Nira would have plenty of opportunity to talk. No matter which route she took, the river and he would once again cross paths, and this time he would take his chances. After that he could always use one last trip to the Academy Library, as well known and almost as beloved to him as the Institute's own. 'Let us go, then,' Pandurang replied, ushering her out of the stacks. Now that he had decided to go, he was reminded again of how little time was available to him.

Nira hadn't intended to leave immediately. She might have enjoyed having coffee with the Institute staff in the tiny cups they used to drink their oversweet mid-morning beverage. Who knew when she would have her next chance? But something appeared amiss with the old man. It wasn't clear to her why he had asked to meet, but she wanted to do what she could. He had helped her so many times in her research, and unlike Poona's many professional teachers, he never sold his priceless knowledge for a paltry fee. He simply loved to share whatever he knew. And he already knew everything that she might ever need to find out. She had often wondered how an archivist could become so knowledgeable. If you move books around on shelves long enough, if you arrange and rearrange and label and number and bind them, do you begin to absorb, by some magical osmosis, all that's in them? Before his retirement, for all of his life he had been the guardian of the Institute's massive holdings, their nurturer, their caretaker. He had tended each page, each tome, like a child, like a plant.

She walked him to her car, a large uncomfortable third-hand diesel-run vehicle that she loved because to her it signified driving about by herself in a place that, strictly speaking, was not her home, a place whose cartography she had no native knowledge of. Unlike her, the truck-like monstrosity lived permanently in Poona. Thanks to this car, too worthless to sell off, each time she came to town she had the luxury of traversing the city with her body even as her mind wandered over the spaces that her study opened up for her. Sometimes serendipitously she came to a turn in the road where the inner and outer landscapes overlapped, and she felt overcome by an acute sense of the meaningfulness of the world into which she had stumbled.

She unlocked the passenger side door for Pandurang. The car had a high chassis, he had trouble climbing into it. But there was nothing she could do to help him in, not being able to touch him. She held the door open, made encouraging noises. When he was properly ensconced, she shut the door firmly but politely. Whenever her passengers were old or small or wore saris, Nira was prone to feeling embarrassed about the lumbering size and inconvenient height of her car. She ran to jump into the driver's seat, starting up the engine quickly so she could turn the air conditioning on for Pandurang. The entire contraption shivered, making enough of a racket to threaten the precarious integrity of the buildings. As she reversed out of the Institute property, he said, inevitably, 'This is a very big car for a lady to handle. You are very courageous.' Nira had heard versions of this statement so often from all the people she knew in Poona, either as teasing or as admiration, that she almost didn't flinch. At least he hadn't called her a 'girl'.

On the way, Pandurang was unusually quiet. He seemed to look carefully at everything visible from the windscreen and windows. Nira had met a historian that morning, a more eminent one of the city's innumerable historians, and she went over the interview in her head. What was it with history in Poona? It marked the streets, it moved the people. Its professional practitioners tok-tokked away at its thick trunk, like diligent woodpeckers. Everywhere stories of what had happened were written and recited, everywhere statues of heroes and leaders exhorted passers-by to advance in this direction or that. The past filled out the present till, like colour, it became a more saturated version of itself, luminescent to bursting. Pandurang blinked in the light, Nira squinted to keep her eyes focused on the road ahead.

Up and down the hilly Senapati Bapat Road they went, past the Chatushringi temple with its spectacular hilltop view and its aniconic gods and goddesses that looked like aliens from outer space, then out onto Ganesh Khind Road. But instead of turning towards the university, they went into the Kirkee Cantonment, whose – Scottish? Irish? – name had been indigenized beyond recognition. At first trees lined the road, and fruit vendors stood beneath them with carts piled high, their wares glowing like jewels in the dense shade. Poona always had impressive quantities of fruit that changed with the season. Nira liked that – the fruit marked time for her as weeks of research changed to months, which were now becoming years.

Then the greenery dropped away and the aspect of the road changed to extreme dryness. They were on the Deccan Plateau after all, in the rain shadow of the wet monsoon winds, and stark semi-arid scrubland stretched away to the south and east. Here in

'Khirki' the houses and gardens meant for military personnel and their families wore a parched look, neat but water-starved. Nira nearly forgot that she was not alone in the car. She felt the strangeness of the familiarity of Poona, a familiarity that had developed over the very short time that she had known the city, and that never seemed to wane, no matter how frequently she left, or for how long.

They went under railway tracks, across the old Bombay–Poona highway, past a British war cemetery where flowers spilled over picturesque gravestones, past fenced farmland, around a bend where there stood the gates to an enormous ammunition factory. The road narrowed. They were almost upon the Holkar Bridge, which would take them over the Mutha's twin, the River Mula. Pandurang held his breath. His hand was in his pocket, clutching his key. A uniformed sentry, armed with a gun, looked out from an old watchtower that stood where the road, the bridge and the riverbank met. He seemed entirely unthreatening – and unnecessary – in the broad daylight.

Nira slowed down. She loved this bridge. The way the river below wound away from the city into a green distance, it always made her think of an etching from the Raj. Each time she crossed she wished she could stop the car and figure out the anachronistic tranquillity of the vista by leaning over the railing. The most she had ever managed, with traffic behind her and oncoming, was to roll down her window to feel the riverine breeze. That was a mistake! A stench rose to fill the car, from the water slowed almost to stagnation by the hyacinth that covered its surface. The army had a special unit to fight the weed – they kept on removing it, it kept on coming back. She had come over the bridge rolling up her window.

That day Pandurang suddenly cried, 'Stop! Please!' Nira was startled by his request. He looked at her beseechingly. 'I need a moment,' he said, beginning to open the car door. Nira braked and put on her parking lights. 'I'm not sure this is safe,' she said, 'perhaps we should be quick.' He was out already, he was taking something out of his pocket, he flung it over the railing into the hyacinth-choked water. Before she could see what it had been, he was back in his seat. 'What was that, Sukthankarji?' she asked, unable to resist. 'Oh nothing,' he said, 'something I needed to get rid of.' She said nothing more. The old have their reasons.

They were across the bridge, going towards the Bombay Sappers. In her mind's eye Nira still saw the sandy banks of the river, the low hills, the trees, the fields, all arranged in painterly perspective, the way they looked from Holkar Bridge and nowhere else in the city. She tried to restore perfection to the vision, erasing Pandurang's taut figure and his raised hand from her memory of the scene, weeding out his strange unexplained gesture, like a clump of hyacinth. But the smell of the water, rushing in from his open door, still clung to her nostrils.

They rode on in silence once again. Young soldiers wearing camouflage fatigues crossed the road in orderly files, but grinned and nudged one another as they caught sight of Nira behind the wheel, driving her truck. After a bit a wide road turned away on their left, leading first to Alandi, where the visionary poet Jnaneshwar had lived in the thirteenth century, but past that too, to the other holy places of Maharashtra. It went to Jejuri, the abode of Khandoba, god of the shepherds, and thence to Pandharpur, home of Vithoba, the god after whom Pandurang was named. Thousands of believers walked this road each year. Nira had yearned to take it, but doubted each time, with reason, whether she had enough fuel of faith to carry her through the journey. Pandurang had been down that way several times, but he wondered if those pilgrimages had prepared him for the path he now had to follow.

They went on a little further, to the gates of the Dakshina Academy. On the right was the Archaeology Department. They turned left, to go to the library. The grounds were arid and unkempt. There was a small museum of – what else? – Maratha history to one side, dirty and ill-maintained, like the student hostels. Resident students, many of them young Buddhist monks in mustard yellow Burmese robes or cranberry-coloured Tibetan habits, wandered about looking unbathed and depressed. Their meagre washing was hung out to dry, empty buckets stood here and there conspicuously. There was a perpetual water shortage in this part of town. Yet the main buildings were magnificent survivals from the early nineteenth century. They were neglected and underused, but inviolate in their original grace.

Nira stopped at a discreet distance from the Library. Her car may have been so rickety as to be nearly unusable, but sometimes it raised eyebrows in academic circles. PhD students, more so women, were not expected to have personalized modes of transport, at least nothing larger than a two-wheeler, preferably gearless. It was lunchtime. 'Where will you eat, Sukthankarji?' she asked, as he began to get out of the car. There was no food to be had anywhere nearby, just concoctions that were putatively tea and coffee, and unidentifiable snacks, available from a disgusting little shack off to one corner of the campus. 'At my age you don't need to eat more than twice a day,' Pandurang said. He turned to climb out, then seemed to change his mind, and turned back to her. He shut his door. Nira was still, attentive. The car was cool from the air conditioning that had been on for the whole ride. It was not unpleasant to just stay put for a few minutes. She felt no fear of the old archivist, just curiosity at what he might be about to say.

It caught her by surprise then, when he reached out and took her hand in his. She began a thought about the inappropriateness of this move, about how a passing student from the hostel might see them and balk. She remembered the sick check-out clerk in the Dakshina Library whom women readers always avoided, lest he try to paw them in the stacks under the pretext of accompanying them to help find a misplaced book. But something in Pandurang's face stopped her mid-thought. His gaze bored into her eyes, his hand that held hers trembled. With what seemed like a great effort, he turned her hand over so her palm lay open. Then he closed her fingers over her palm with his other hand, as though giving her something for safekeeping. He pressed her fist tightly between his two hands. He closed his eyes. His pupils darted furiously to the left and to the right behind his lids. Then he opened them, and dropped her hand, in the same instant.

Nira waited, her hand curled into a ball. She saw the man crumpled up on her passenger seat, his head hung, his arms limp. He had never seemed so old, nor so tired. She realized that he ought to have looked like this most times, given his age. It was his usual energy that should have amazed her, not his present exhaustion. 'I must go now,' he said, raising his head as though coming out of a long inadvertent sleep. 'God bless.' She nodded again and again to indicate that she understood, but it was as if invisible lids had dropped over his open eyes. He let himself out of the car, and disappeared into one of the main buildings. He must be going to the bathroom before he got into the labyrinth of the library, Nira thought. She sat by herself for a bit, clenching and unclenching her fingers over her empty palm, and then headed indoors.

• • •

She was at the airport the following afternoon. Someone from the university had called her in the morning to tell her that the ex-librarian of the Oriental Institute had passed away the previous day, and that the funeral would be at 4 p.m. They had had quite a time trying to get the body back into the owner's house to prepare it for the last rites, since the key was nowhere to be found. She said that it was too early for her to have bought a newspaper, and that there was no TV around, so she hadn't caught the announcement in the local news. When pressed further she took shelter behind the north Indian preference – an injunction, really – that womenfolk not attend cremations. She had a confirmed ticket, she was leaving. After she put the receiver down she didn't call anyone to say goodbye, lest they too insist that she join in the mourning. By noon, it was a relief to be at the airport, which always felt to her to be outside of Poona, not a part of it, even though it was not much further out from the centre of town than the Dakshina Academy.

The place Nira lived in most of the time made little sense to her. She would never have chosen it. It had no river, clean or otherwise,

The Archivist

and it wasn't close to the sea. Its people were oblivious to their past. But she had to be there, so she switched into a different mode of being in order to cope with it. In this mode, she never sought meaning, she never found it. Perhaps it was because she never sought it that she never found it. Or perhaps it was the other way around. She had given up trying to solve that conundrum. All she knew was, when she left Poona, her precious oversized and underpowered car parked at a friend's garage, geography ceased to matter. It was like rolling up and putting away maps. Everywhere else was Elsewhere. Yet she felt relieved to be on her way. What she had found from journeying back and forth so often was that the only thing more painful than leaving a beloved city is returning to it.

After checking in her baggage – rather heavy for being stuffed with the research materials she had collected – she wandered about disconsolately for a few minutes, trying to find something to distract her in the small airport. She couldn't bear to dwell on Pandurang's passing. Had Death come upon him suddenly in the stacks of the Academy Library, creeping out of the leaves of some old book, where it had lain pressed like a dried flower? She had not succeeded in editing him out from her mental photograph taken at the Holkar Bridge. Perhaps his soul had leapt out of his body at that moment, and somersaulted into the porous carpet of hyacinth, thrashing its way to the water below like a fish escaped from its net. But he had returned to the car, still animate, still clutching something to be passed on to her. What was it he had thrown away? What was it he had saved especially to give to her a few minutes later?

Then she spotted it, her favourite thing – in fact, the only thing she liked about departure from Poona. This was the mural on the wall above the doors to the restrooms. She settled herself on a chair to study it. It was a linear scene, in nouveau but proportionate and tasteful bas-relief, depicting many of Maharashtra's medieval personages all at once, negligent of their actual order in time. There was Ramdas, the militant mendicant, irate and almost naked as one might expect. There was the portly poet Tukaram, recognizable mostly because he bore an uncanny resemblance to the film actor who played him in an unforgettable musical from the 1930s. And there a whole row of saints and holy men – perhaps the precocious Jnaneshwar, the peripatetic Namdev, or whomsoever else fancy might fit to the figures depicted. But best of all, there, astride a horse and sheltered by an umbrella; bearded, turbaned and bejewelled; almond-eyed and hook-nosed; surrounded by generals, bards and standard-bearers, was the great Shivaji himself, most beloved to the people of this state. Floating somewhere in the spaceless, timeless stretch of the mural was Shivaji's royal seal.

And below the oblong tableau were etched the words of Ramdas (who was not a bad poet, for all his militancy), describing this hero of heroes in what must have been a booming voice, a commanding tone:

> Unwavering, like a mighty mountain
> Rock for teeming multitudes
> Dispenser of their ultimate fate –
> *Effulgent Sage!*
>
> Endowed with Fame
> With Glory
> With Power
> Generous
> Pious
> Just –
> *Knowing King!*

Nira went over these Marathi verses, faux copper-tinted, formed in a particularly well-balanced Devanagari font, over and over again. She read them out to herself, under her breath but loud enough for others around her to give her startled or amused looks as they came out of the bathrooms or brought back cups of coffee from the eats counter.

Shriman Yogi, Nira repeated like an incantation, the Effulgent Sage. But Shivaji was also Jaanata Raja, the Knowing King. What was this effulgence in him, this sagacity, this knowledge that shone through the centuries and dazzled her? His was the light that bounced off the mirror of Poona, and lit up the imagination of those who lived in another time. She recognized that Bombay was a different kind of mirror. It reflected shining Shivaji so fiercely that it burned holes in the hearts of the people in that city and they forgot how to love their fellow human beings, it burned holes in their eyes and they were blinded to the pain of others. The brilliance that belonged to the golden king could be illuminating, but it could just as easily be searing. Nira understood only that it would take her a long time to understand.

The announcer asked passengers to proceed for their security check through the only gate there was. Nira rose from her seat in the lounge with the greatest reluctance, keeping her eyes fixed on the mural till the last possible minute. She stepped up in the queue, her head still turned to the words on the wall. As she went in past the guard towards the metal detectors, she had her purse slung over her shoulder, her boarding pass in the one hand, and in the other, held fast, the nameless legacy of the late Pandurang Vitthal Sukthankar.

EXIT THE GULF

Shougat Dasgupta

My parents moved to Kuwait from Bombay when I was six weeks old. We left Kuwait in 1990, a few months before I turned thirteen. To say we left is not accurate; it implies agency, that we had a choice. Our leaving was not part of the pattern of migration that had brought us to Kuwait. We did not leave Kuwait, like so many other Bengali families we knew, for the greener pastures of Canada or the greenest pasture of them all – the United States; we were removed from Kuwait. Removed by a murderously whimsical dictator who, on a murderous whim, invaded a country because he could. Early on the morning of 2 August 1990, the Iraqi army – hundreds of thousands of soldiers hardened by a ruinous, nearly decade-long war with Iran – annexed Kuwait. They met with little resistance. Iraq is twenty-five times larger than Kuwait and has a population of thirty million compared to Kuwait's two million, half of whom are expatriates. It would have been like grass resisting a rhinoceros.

I slept through the invasion, waking to the sound of my shortwave radio which I realized with annoyance – and possessiveness, scything through the fug of sleep – that my father had commandeered. This radio – an industrial, slate-grey Grundig Satellit 650, stolid, weighty and unglamorous, ('Just like German girls' my Calcutta-born, German-educated father would say, ungallantly) – was a major presence in my life. The hours I spent with my ear soldered to it, listening to the BBC World Service, were the cause of what my mother called 'Britification'. My Anglophilia had long made me the object of family scorn. Hobson-Jobson, or Suited-Booted, my dad would call me when he was feeling affectionate; Ingrej when less so. Football was where my devotion to all things English was most manifest. I lived then for Saturday evenings, discarding my homework (Saturday being Kuwait's Monday) to coax from the radio's bleeps and crackles the classified football results. These were the scores of an entire afternoon's football played across England and Scotland, read, incongruously enough, by an Australian, Len Martin, whose voice bobbed like a buoy against lapping waves, up for a home win, down for a home defeat, so you would know before he had read the score how your team had done.

Martin, I believed, revelled like I did in the poetry of the classified football results, in the sound of those long lists of British provincial centres and market towns. For all the evocative power of England's various Wanderers, Rovers and Rangers, for all its Tottenham Hotspurs, Sheffield Wednesdays and Accrington Stanleys, it was the Scottish teams that were unmatched for euphony. Cowdenbeath, Stenhousemuir, Arbroath, Partick Thistle, Hibernian, Hamilton Academical, Queen of the South and, most stirring of all, Heart of Midlothian. Only the Scottish league could have produced (though it never actually did) a scoreline such as East Fife 5 Forfar 4.

My experience of football was more vivid because it was untainted by saturation television coverage. We got weekly highlights of the games and one live broadcast a year, the FA Cup final. Radio commentary and hagiographic magazine profiles of the players were our regular fare. In lieu of the thing itself, what mattered were the stories, the lore, the private pleasures of the imagination rather than the community solidarity of following one's local football club.

'Listen,' my father said, retaining, in the midst of crisis, the paternal imperative to needle his son, 'it's your prime minister.'

Margaret Thatcher was denouncing the Iraqi invasion as

'absolutely unacceptable', her peremptory tone typical of the more fearsome teachers in my English colonial school. It was a tone I was familiar with, being the sort of feckless pupil teachers feel compelled to hector. My father thought the whole thing would blow over. 'Bush and Thatcher won't allow it. Saddam will pull out within a week,' my parents told their children, their friends, our relatives in Bombay, London and Manila, and each other. After all, the previous day's *Arab Times*, the bigger of Kuwait's two English-language dailies, had announced on its front page that the problem 'between brothers' had been settled.

Then the Iraqis cut the phone lines. My parents, all the while making nervous jokes about their caution, withdrew as much money as they could from ATM machines. We drove to the Sultan Center, the neighbourhood American-style hypermarket, combing the vertiginous shelves – filled with cereal boxes, oversized fruit, bottles of perfume and tennis racquets – for frozen meals, cartons of long-life milk, mineral water, and food in tins and cans – the classic items on a survivalist shopping list. Through the large windows, I saw an Iraqi soldier turn a hose on his pals. Others poured bottles of water over their head for respite from the white heat of mid-morning. My mother hissed at me not to look, 'Go help your sister find bread.' My sister, a year younger than I, was employing a singular definition of bread. She had stocked our cart with boxes of Japanese confectionary inscribed in swirling font with such legends as 'Kabaya Can Baby – pop flavours!' and 'Kasugai Lemon Gummy'. Taking my cue, I grabbed as many bottles as I could of the British elixirs Lucozade and Vimto. Even in Britain, Lucozade, traffic-light amber in colour and served in British hospitals, and Vimto, a cordial the blue-purple of a night sky, were probably not much competition for Coke or Pepsi. But I was steadfast; my willingness to accede to all things English extended even to packages of frozen steak and kidney pie.

In 1990, globalization was an idea gaining currency in academic circles. As twelve-year-old cosmopolitans, defined not so much by where we came from as what we read, watched, heard and thought, you could say my friends and I anticipated the zeitgeist. So in Kuwait in 1990, in this tiny, undistinguished country in the Arabian Gulf, I drank Lucozade and ate Hardee's roast beef sandwiches whenever my mum could be persuaded not to feed us daal bhat; I loved *The Real Genius,* starring Val Kilmer, and sneered at Bollywood; I supported Liverpool Football Club; I listened to New Order and The Smiths and Gang of Four and Orange Juice. On my bookshelf at home I had Sherlock Holmes, Walter Scott, P.G. Wodehouse, Richmal Compton's William, Enid Blyton, Tintin, Asterix, Amar Chitra Katha, the Phantom, Tinkle and – because I had been taking piano lessons for years and I was a show-off – biographies of Bach and Chopin and Scriabin and Rimsky-Korsakov.

Such scattershot particulars, such quirks of personality, I understood. 'Indian' and 'Bengali', I did not. My migrant parents still sought succour in a collective identity, in forming organizations like the Bengali Cultural Society, in putting on plays and evenings of Rabindrasangeet, in the films of Satyajit Ray, in maacher jhol and adda, in creating a facsimile of the world they had left behind. Every weekend, my sister and I, and dozens of children just like us, would play, bicker, eat pizza and fall asleep in each others' bedrooms, while our parents would gossip late into the night about this servant or that relative, about how impossible it was to move back to India and how much they missed the rain.

When my father joked that Margaret Thatcher was my prime minister, he had stumbled upon a truth about me, a truth about so many of us who had grown up in the Gulf. Margaret Thatcher, prime minister of a country to which I had no ties (none that an immigration officer would recognize anyway) might as well have been my prime minister, just as George Bush père might as well have been my president, or Sheikh Jaber al-Ahmed al-Jaber al-Sabah my king; I did not know what it meant to have such allegiances. We had not immigrated to Kuwait. We would, however long we lived there, never be Kuwaiti citizens. Kuwaiti society, with its tribal and Bedouin roots, is a closed shop even though Kuwait is near the sea and Kuwaitis, before oil, were traders. The Gulf Arabs, even the Saudis, have long been considered provincials by other Arabs. Only Iraq was different: older, cosmopolitan and sophisticated. In Kuwait, expatriates were guest workers, there to make money, with no investment in the country as a home beyond mere familiarity. Such a circumscribed life as the one we lived in Kuwait, privileged and comfortable – in the way suburban American lives are privileged and comfortable and materially rich – forced on me an elaborate inner life.

And I was profoundly self-absorbed and self-contained. I lived in my head even more than children ordinarily do. The idea of home was ectoplasmic, chimerical. Identity, I knew from an early age, was nebulous; its edges unruly as an ink stain. Britain, England particularly, filled my imagination. English, after all, was the language I thought in, the language I read, the language I spoke at school and even, for the most part, the language I spoke at home. My curriculum was the standard colonial one, an Anglo-Saxon version of European history. India offered me my external identity, Britain my interior one, and Kuwait was the metaphorical suburban bedroom in which I played out my fantasies. Not that different, I suppose, from the boy in Armpit, Alabama who stares at a David Bowie record sleeve and imagines he is Ziggy Stardust.

The Iraqi invasion barely made a scratch on the resilient carapace of my fantasies. I felt no fear, no swell of sympathy for my few Kuwaiti friends (mostly teammates on the school soccer team), all of whom were still on their summer holidays in luxury hotels and yachts across Europe. I thrilled instead to the novelty of the invasion and the promise, thanks to Saddam's rush of blood to the head, that our school term might not begin as scheduled. The early days of the invasion passed slowly. For news, we were reliant on the elusive shortwave signal of the BBC World Service. The only Kuwaitis we spoke to were my mother's business partner, whose English wife and son were in England, and Asrar Al-Qabandi, a young woman my mother knew, who had been educated in the United States and whose short hair, glasses, baggy trousers and strong opinions had made her unpopular with her family and who was a frequent visitor to our home. Asrar used to complain to my mother about Kuwait – the country's conservatism, the easy money that had made its people lazy, their lack of interest in education, even the country's 'insipid' men. Until the invasion, I had never heard her express any affection for Kuwait. Kuwait was a scab on her knee, irritating and unsightly but comforting to pick at.

Our encounters with the occupying soldiers were infrequent and farcical. Indians were relatively safe in occupied Kuwait. We were of no interest to Iraqi soldiers, unlike westerners who made valuable hostages and, for obvious reasons, Kuwaitis, small bands of whom – Asrar among them – were organizing and mounting a sporadic, flickering resistance. On one occasion, my mother found three soldiers hiding in the lift; they had rung our doorbell and then had second thoughts when they heard our Alsatian bark. They were armed with sticks and asked very politely if we could spare them a bottle of water. The stories told about Iraqi soldiers among Indians were not of the rapes and torture I read about when we finally left Kuwait, but stories of buffoonery, stories imbued with condescension for soldiers who stole computer monitors thinking they were TV sets, for soldiers who were not Iraqi at all but bewildered Bangladeshi gardeners or Filipino drivers forced into the army as casualties in the war with Iran mounted.

When my father told the story of walking into his office to see one Iraqi soldier wheeling out my father's leather chair and another helping himself to the coffee mugs, he did it with a seen-it-all shrug. Yes, he and the other men would say, lighting another Marlboro, offices were being looted and cars stolen, but what did one expect, and besides they weren't Iraqi soldiers but Palestinian kids. The unflappable, phlegmatic Bengali male couldn't be put off his stride by such trifles as invading armies. Wasn't Mr Majumdar stopped on his way to work by an Iraqi patrol on that first morning and ordered to go home, only for him to try another route and then a third and a fourth before bowing to the inevitable? Only the visit to Iraq of I.K. Gujral, the then Indian external affairs minister, jolted our fathers out of their implicit faith in our safety. On television, everyone saw Gujral greet Saddam with a hug. I remember looking at my father's face, seeing the initial embarrassed cringe transform into incredulous rage by the time Saddam and Gujral disengaged. I remember thinking how he must wish now that Margaret Thatcher was his prime minister too. Soon, the story doing the rounds was that Kuwaiti resistance fighters had murdered an Indian man in revenge. Apparently (in a gesture so ghoulish that the story must have been apocryphal) they propped his head on the spikes of the Indian School's iron gates.

We stopped going out or answering the doorbell. A large Gujarati family of diamond merchants, old family friends of my mother's from Bombay, moved in with us. When Gujral left, he had select women and children flown out on a military plane, the so-called 'millionaire's flight' much derided in the Indian press. The women and children of the family that moved in with us left on that plane. My mother refused to take us because she did not want to leave my father behind and because of her distaste for Gujral; a decision my father protested as wilful, melodramatic and, above all, irresponsible. We decided to join several Bengali families who had coalesced in two adjoining apartments, seeking safety and comfort in numbers.

These communal living arrangements lasted till nearly the end of September. It was an idyllic time. The days assumed a rhythm. We played football all morning in the building's empty parking lot and in the evenings raided one particular uncle's extensive VHS collection. One movie I distinctly remember watching is the pulpy 1978 thriller, *The Medusa Touch*, in which Richard Burton plays a crepuscular misanthrope whose bleak Weltanschauung is unfortunately coupled with a gift for telekinesis. A gift he uses to murder his parents, his nanny, and later, his adulterous wife, before sending a Boeing 747 straight into a skyscraper. Every night we ate mutton or chicken or egg curry, mopped up with khubus and rice. Newspapers were spread over the carpet and we sat cross-legged on the floor. Everyone talked at once and talked throughout, as if to stay silent was a dereliction of some essential duty.

Our parents heard of a close friend, a man with a pendulous belly and spry wit, who had been arrested in Iraq for carrying counterfeit dollars. He had been sold those dollars in Iraq. Our parents panicked about their own dollars, bought at five times the usual rate, and the only currency Iraqis would accept in exchange for a plane ticket to Jordan – the only country that had kept its border with Iraq open. Our parents panicked about our schooling. There was a half-hearted attempt by one mother to teach us to read and write Hindi, a language that might come in handy back home. What good, they asked each other, had come of enrolling us in expensive British schools? Of turning us into deracinated half-and-halfs they couldn't even understand any more? It was preposterous to her that I learned French at school and read the Italian *Gazzetta dello Sport,* but struggled to hold a conversation with anyone in the city of my birth who didn't speak English. And how would we, turned soft by foreign schooling, cope with the notoriously rigorous mathematics classes and winner-take-all final exams of Indian schools?

These were not subjects that interested my friends, my sister or me. We sought desperately to tune the radio to the BBC World Service for scraps of information – not about the occupation or whether the United Nations, led by the United States, would enforce Security Council Resolution 660 demanding the withdrawal of Iraqi forces from Kuwait – but about Liverpool's form, about injuries to star players, about the team's chances (very good, as it happened) of winning the league and extending the most sustained run of success in the history of English football. Not once did we discuss Iraq's invasion or what it would mean to leave the country we had lived in all our lives. As children who lived in one country, came from another, and took our cues from another still, our minds were elsewhere.

We left Kuwait in the last week of September. My father and some of the men staying with us had arranged for a bus and a driver to take us to the southern Iraqi city of Basra, and further on to Baghdad. As we crossed the desert at night, we were held up by

Iraqi soldiers. They stole a computer monitor. At dawn, we arrived in the Iraqi capital, where we stayed at a hotel for a week before we were able to board a flight to Amman. Bengalis are, of course, India's doughtiest tourists, our motto: 'Have monkey cap, will travel.' For that one week in Baghdad, my family reverted to type, eating fish and chips on the banks of the Tigris, riding the creaky rollercoaster in the empty but functioning amusement park, visiting the National Museum, taking in the sights of the world's oldest civilization. Back at the hotel, we boys discovered that the bread rolls, hard and heavy as bricks, could cause significant pain. Reality – the reality of us being refugees fleeing from Kuwait, a country occupied by Iraq, an international pariah, in which we were now vacationing – only occasionally intruded, usually in the form of empty supermarket shelves or a tour guide who begged us for chocolate milk for her baby because the powdered variety was all that was available. And there was a parting reminder of the invasion. On our flight to Amman, I noticed Kuwait Airways cutlery and upholstery in what was ostensibly an Iraqi Airways plane. A hasty paint job to create the illusion that this Kuwait Airways plane was Iraqi property summed up Saddam's shoddy invasion: an event more bathetic and comic than sinister. Or so it seemed from my sheltered vantage.

In Amman we slept at the airport for a night before we were able to board one of the many free flights Air India had laid on to transport Indian refugees to Bombay and safety. Two months after Iraq began its invasion of Kuwait, we were on a plane to India. I didn't know then, still arguing with my friends about the relative merits of Liverpool and Manchester United or AC/DC and Iron Maiden, how lucky we had been, how smooth our passage was. Because our parents had presciently queued at ATM machines for hours in the first couple of days of the invasion, we were cash rich. We had dollars and we packed lightly. Others had no money, or had saddled themselves with the material possessions they had worked to accumulate – big-screen TVs, Bang & Olufsen stereos. They had gathered in tens of thousands in refugee camps on the Jordanian border. It took until the third week of October to repatriate refugees bound for the subcontinent, by which time, in the will-sapping heat and wind of the desert, in conditions that were unsanitary, with little by way of rations, hundreds died.

Smothered by relatives in Bombay, in my grandmother's apartment bursting with books, art, furniture, and the detritus of an entire life, indeed the lives of entire generations, I began to realize how evanescent my experience in Kuwait was, how thin my connection to that place, this place, or any place outside my own head. To see my mother so at ease in her home, to see her speak Gujarati to her sisters and Marathi to the servants, to see her act younger, accept the affectionate admonishments of her brother in the same mock-restive fashion I accepted her less serious complaints, was unsettling. My mother loved Bombay as one loves one's home – unheedingly, complacently and without effort.

I was fascinated by Bombay as only a foreigner could be; fascinated by its mephitic drains, its rusting, red double-decker buses, and the clamorous panoply of its streets. For me, even the acrid tang of Thums Up and a furtively gobbled mutton frankie was wondrous. Those long months in Bombay, while I waited to go to school in January, have now been reduced in my memory to a scant slide show. Slow afternoons spent playing carrom, eating softies at Snowman's ice cream parlour in Breach Candy, and riding forlorn ponies down Chowpatty beach. I remember our mint-green Ambassador. And I remember grime, paint peeling from walls like skin, the fur coating our apartment building on Nepean Sea Road like verdigris, the building rotting like the city around it. From our balcony, I watched girls dressed in green-and-white checks walk to Walsingham School; I threw water balloons at them, missing every time, but enjoying their surprise, their terrified screams and the way they looked around for the culprit.

My parents may have belonged to Bombay in a way I never could, but it didn't stop them returning to Kuwait a few months after it was liberated, even as the sky was still obscured by the soot from oil fires the Iraqis had lit before running away. Everyone they knew did the same. They had found homes, not in Kuwait – which had the wherewithal to quickly resume looking like an unimaginative American suburb – but in each other, in the idea that it was people who mattered, not place. I had acquired something else entirely in Kuwait – the armour of solipsism. I read so much, I sometimes think, not from any literary leaning but only so as to always have something to hold in front of my face.

Shortly before the Allies began Operation Desert Storm on 17 January 1991, I began my first semester at a boarding school in the Palani Hills. In the library at my new school, I discovered in *Time* that my mother's old friend Asrar had been arrested by the Iraqis. She had been shot by the Iraqis, I read, in one account, seven times in each breast and seven times in the vagina. In another, I read that she had been shot four times in the head, once between the eyes and that the right side of her face had been cut open with an axe. She was hailed in death by her family as she never had been in life, held up as a martyr for the cause of a country she could not regard as her own until it was taken away.

That January, I also saw the famous *Time* cover of Saddam Hussein patting a nervous British child on the head. It was the picture that some say turned public opinion, in Britain at least, decisively in favour of the war. The child in that picture was Stuart Lockwood; his mother worked at my mother's school. My sister and I used to think he was insufferable. And when the kids at my new school asked about the Iraqi invasion, I didn't tell them about Stuart. I didn't tell them about Asrar. I didn't tell them that when I boarded the Air India flight out of Amman and a sympathetic stewardess handed me an extra bar of Amul chocolate, all I could think was, what's the big deal?

SKELETONS

Naresh Fernandes

The bass notes of *The Tennessee Waltz* ricocheted across St Andrew's Road. Wedding celebrations were on at the Bandra Gymkhana, and the windows of my parents' flat grumbled like a herd of autorickshaws. Still groggy with the jetlag of five years in New York, I bristled with an American sense of violation. I dialled the club's office and assumed an icy tone.

'Your music is so loud, it's making my windows rattle.'
'Where you're calling from, men?' a woman's voice inquired.
'Park View building,' I snapped.
'Which floor?'

I sputtered at the irrelevance of the query. Struggling to make myself heard over wails of nocturnal betrayal in bluegrass country, I yelled, 'Second.' A chuckle of delight greeted me. 'Ah, you must be Ernest's son,' the woman cooed. 'Your daddy told me you were coming back. When you returned from the States, baba?'

My belligerence evaporated. The band played on.

Days later, an article in *The Indian Express* caught my eye:

Skeleton of man, dog surface in Bandra bungalow

– Express News Service, 1 May

They never parted company, neither in life nor death and even beyond. But the grim reality of their solitary world was bared on Saturday, when the Bandra police chanced upon two skeletons in a bungalow that shares a compound with Rebello House. The human skeleton is presumed to be that of 63-year-old Dr. Rebello and the other, that of his faithful dog, who seemed to be gazing at his master even in death.

The article went on to say that the doctor hadn't been seen for almost a year, which led his nephew – who lived a mere fifty metres away – to finally summon the police. 'When the police stepped into the doctor's house, they seemed to have walked into a time warp,' the newspaper stated. 'Amid scattered medical books and magazines and on a floor that was covered with a thick layer of dust, Dr. Rebello's skeleton lay sprawled, face down. It was completely bereft of flesh, hair and nails. Next to it lay the remains of his dog, which appears to have died after his master passed away.'

I was perplexed. Peter Rebello had lived in the heart of Bandra, the tight-knit Bombay neighbourhood in which my mother's family has lived for hundreds of years. Peter descended from a prominent family of doctors, so prominent that several streets – including the one I live on – bore the names of his relatives. If my futile battle against noise pollution had shown that I could never be anonymous, Peter was even less likely to be able to walk down the streets without being recognized by at least a dozen pair of eyes. Besides, his sister and her family lived almost next door. Surely they checked up on him. How had the skeins of community frayed so completely as to come to this?

• • •

Bombay lore maintains that if you climb to the top of Mount Mary – the highest point in Bandra – and throw a stone, it will hit a pig, a priest or a Pereira. The porcine reference is to the peculiarities of Catholic cuisine; not many other religions would deign to let such delights as vindaloo or roast piglet pass their followers' lips. The name 'Pereira' of course, refers to Bandra's Portuguese past. The European power acquired the neighbourhood in 1534, though most of its residents – my ancestors among them – converted (or were made to convert) to Catholicism only seven decades later. In 1661, England's Charles II was offered the largest dowry in history in an effort to coax him to marry the Portuguese princess Catherine of Braganza, a woman whose legendary ugliness had deterred other prospective husbands. Her trousseau included five hundred thousand pounds in cash, the city of Tangiers, and the seven islands of Bombay. But Bandra, across the creek, remained in Portuguese control for another hundred-odd years. It was during this period that the neighbourhood acquired its Indo-Catholic flair, setting itself apart from the rest of the city.

My ancestors were farmers who lived in Pali Village, which would later find itself at the foot of a ritzy sprawl of Bollywood bungalows. My forebears were a geographic incongruity: though they lived on the western coast, they called themselves East Indians. The odd nomenclature was a manifestation of their eagerness to stay on the good side of Bombay's second European rulers – the British. In 1887, in celebration of the Golden Jubilee of Queen Victoria's coronation, Bombay's native Roman Catholic residents sent the sovereign a charter praising her stewardship. The Catholics proclaimed that they would thereafter name their community after the British East India Company, both in acknowledgement of the economic benefits they believed colonialism had brought, and because they hoped that this new allegiance would afford them priority in being granted the minor clerical jobs that were, then, a sure path to prosperity. In no time, many East Indians were speaking English at home; some even anglicized their Portuguese surnames.

Notwithstanding any of this, until the early decades of the twentieth century, my family – as I learnt from the reminiscences of my grandfather Ammon Rodrigues – was still battling deprivation. Grandpa spoke of hungry days when drought withered the paddy crops, and of terrified nights huddled in the fields as great plagues swept across Bandra. (To sleep in a crowded village was to risk catching the infection from your sick neighbours.) The epidemic resulted in a profusion of streetside Plague Crosses, built by the faithful, to seek divine protection from disease or in gratitude for survival from it. Grandpa was the first member of his family to get an education; he took the train into town to be instructed by stern Jesuits at St Xavier's School. After he graduated, in 1916, he sought employment in a Greek trading firm. Summoned for an interview, he realized that he didn't own any long trousers, and borrowed a pair from an affluent cousin. He got the position and rose to become the firm's chief accountant, a job that required him to wear a suit to work, and came with a paid holiday to Europe every six years.

Grandpa soon became a pillar of the community. He was an enthusiastic member of the Men's Sodality at St Peter's Church and volunteered to keep the books for various Catholic charities. In 1965, in recognition of his role in helping organize an international Catholic conference in Bombay, Pope Pius XII made Grandpa a Knight Commander in the Order of St Gregory. After that, people began to address him as 'Chevalier'. He attended weddings and other formal occasions dressed in an impressive close-necked jacket with silver buttons and a set of matching black pants. My cousins and I referred to this costume as his pyjamas; it was, after all, his knight suit.

In 1984, when I was in my final year in school, Grandpa lay in a hospital bed weak with cancer. Often, when walking down the street, strangers would come up to me to inquire about his health. To be fair, these people weren't strangers at all. I may not have recognized them, but they all knew me: I was (I realized with some horror) a member of a long-standing Bandra family. The bonds of community weren't always so comforting. Every time I tried to sneak off to the Bandstand to watch the sun set with my latest object of affection, some relative or acquaintance would invariably happen to be taking their evening stroll. In fact, until I heard the circumstances of Peter's death, I didn't think it was possible to avoid Bandra's sticky embrace.

I never actually met Peter. However, there were people around me who remembered him well. My father had known him as a boy, and Peter had gone to boarding school in Darjeeling with Darryl D'Monte, the man who gave me my first job at *The Times of India*. Peter was also close friends with a set of distant relatives on my father's side. Piecing together his story wasn't difficult.

Though Peter's school record was uneventful, his family's tradition in medicine, two generations long, could not be ignored. He went to Kasturba Medical College in Mangalore, despite a lack of enthusiasm for the subject. He struggled through his exams. Along the way, he developed a circle of devoted friends, many of whom remained loyal to him until he died. 'He was a loner,' one of his college friends said, as we sat in his spare clinic. 'But once you got to know him, he was a friend for life. Peter was the kind of friend who would do anything in the world for you.' Apparently, he was a voracious reader and brilliant conversationalist. 'Peter could talk about anything under the sun: astrophysics, geography, even something as trivial as why bubbles are formed when you wash your hands with soap,' this friend recalled. He asked me to avoid mentioning him by name; he did not want to risk offending the Rebello family.

Peter's idiosyncrasies were evident to everyone who knew him. Dr Ashok Kothari had been to college with Peter and was allotted the room next to his in hostel; he remembered his friend's peculiar habit of 'collecting things' – as he charitably put it. Peter would buy his supplies in bulk and stash them around his room. Old newspapers and bottles never seemed to find their way to the dustbin. Another doctor friend said that Peter was a nervous sort of chap. 'No,' he corrected himself; 'He wasn't nervous. He was hyper-nervous. If someone pointed out a minor mistake, he'd stop eating and sleeping for days.'

Though Peter eventually graduated from medical school, he never got around to completing the internship that would certify him to set up his own practice. The urgings of friends went unheeded. Dr Angelina D'Souza (who asked me to give her a pseudonym because, like others I spoke to, she was friends with

Peter's family) believed that Peter, who was older than the other interns, was embarrassed at having to work with his juniors. D'Souza married Peter's boyhood friend Loy, and her husband once managed to persuade Peter to join the internship programme at the prestigious King Edward Memorial Hospital. But he kicked it up just three months before he was due to finish. 'He was an extremely intelligent man, but he couldn't seem to finish anything.'

Peter could afford to be nonchalant about his career: his father's flourishing dermatology practice had left the Rebellos with a healthy portfolio of shares and property. After medical college, Peter began to display a penchant for elaborate practical jokes. He also began to disappear for long periods of time. Occasionally, he would land up at the homes of friends, especially if they were ill or needed help, and take care of them for weeks on end. Then, he would revert to type, taking offence at the slightest thing, and cut himself off for months.

'He wasn't the easiest person in the world to love,' a friend concluded tartly.

• • •

In the mid-1970s, Bombay's real estate boom began to infect Bandra. As the city sprouted up around it, Grandpa Ammon's vegetable patch had come to be a relatively large plot. The government promptly took it over to build a public hospital. Other Bandra families sold out quickly – and often, cheaply – to avoid surrendering their land to the government. Developers swooped in and the vegetable fields and cottages began to give way to apartment blocks. There was, however, another compulsion for the building boom: single-family cottages were becoming too small to house growing families. Inevitably, bungalows made way for tall buildings in which each member of the family could have their own flat.

With more housing available, Bandra's residents became a truer

Skeletons | 119

reflection of Bombay's cosmopolitan ménage – and stones thrown from the top of Mount Mary were now as likely to hit Punjabis zipping around in their Porches as pork-loving Pereiras. Many of Bandra's Catholics were overwhelmed by the change. Some were bedazzled by slick developers and sold out for much less than their plots were worth. Others, blinded by fortune, attempted to trick their relatives out of their fair share of the sale proceeds. The crumbling of this semi-rural community proved disorienting for many people, as it may have for Peter Rebello.

As Bandra was changing, India was changing too. Reality began to catch up with Bandra's Catholics. Jobs in the service industry – as secretaries, at the airlines and at hotels – previously assured to them on the basis of their English-language skills, could no longer be taken for granted. The trickle of young Bandra residents to Western shores swelled to a gush. Of Grandpa Ammon's eleven grandchildren, I am now the only one who still lives in India.

Today, large-scale migration has turned Catholic Bandra into a geriatric ward. Dinner conversations at family gatherings revolve around the latest visa legislation in Canada or New Zealand, and how these new measures will affect the chances of cousins attempting to gain permanent residence in these countries. There have been some unexpected consequences too. Migration means homecoming as well, and this has swelled the fortunes of my friend Clement's home-repair business. Every year, around October, he is besieged with contracts to renovate bathrooms. The orders come from elderly Bandra residents whose children have acquired white spouses. Clement explained, 'They're afraid that if their bathrooms aren't modern enough, their new sons- or daughters-in-law will get constipated when they come to visit during the Christmas holidays.'

• • •

By the late 1980s, Peter Rebello's idiosyncrasies had become impossible to ignore. 'One would see him wandering aimlessly around Bandra, looking fairly unkempt,' recalled Darryl D'Monte. 'He took to wearing a big beard, like the Jesuits of yore. He was dishevelled and his clothes were crumpled. You could see that no one was taking care of him – and that he wasn't taking care of himself.' With some embarrassment, D'Monte added, 'If I saw him in the street, I'd try to avoid him. After all, he wasn't the sort of person one wants to be seen with.'

Peter had become a recluse, and pushed the meaning of the word to its very extreme even as he continued living on Bandra's busiest street. His neighbour, Farida Merchant, a recent arrival in Bandra, told me that she had not once set eyes on Peter in the eight years that she lived downstairs from him. She had only heard his feet on the wooden floorboards late at night, and occasionally, the bark of his dog. Peter, she said, lived 'in his own sweet world'.

It was generally concluded that Peter's quirks became more pronounced after the death of his mother, Mary. 'He was always his mother's baby,' one of his friends told me. 'She smothered him. That's probably why he didn't get married.' Mary Rebello had been housebound for many years, crippled by diabetes, hypertension, ulcers and obesity. Peter lavished attention upon her and was left shaken upon her passing. His mother's death also marked the beginning of his financial descent. Apparently, many of the shares and bank accounts that Peter relied on for income were in his mother's name, and he couldn't find the nerve to do the paperwork required to transfer them. His family began squabbling over property and gave Peter a raw deal.

One day, Peter had an argument with a neighbour that made him upset enough to turn his life upside down to avoid running into the man. Peter would sleep all day, venturing out only at night or very early in the morning.

Letters, bills and dividend cheques piled up on his doorstep. Peter's main source of income was the rent he received from a spare flat. But a dispute with the building's management – 'They saw his weakness and bullied him,' claimed a friend – dried that stream up. With no money to pay the bills, his electricity and water was cut off. No one is sure where he bathed or even where he went to the toilet. He would occasionally be spotted on the street, late in the evening, carrying jerry cans, as he ventured out in search of water. One of his college friends took to calling him the Scented Man. 'Between the booze, the bidis and the economy with bathing, he got quite fragrant.' Sometimes, Peter would land up at D'Souza's home, with a bucket of clothes in need of washing. Often, he appeared to have been drinking – though she did add that he was never inebriated. They would converse warmly, she said, only for him to vanish inexplicably again.

Peter took to eating his meals at Cafe Delight, a grimy restaurant down Hill Road. The menu at Delight was basic – ground beef, greasy biryani, milky ginger tea and dal fry. The cafe was patronized by taxi drivers, petty tradesmen and labourers on daily wage. Despite a signboard that firmly stated, 'Please don't sit longer', the cafe's owner, Abdul Rauf, indulged Peter. He was allowed to stay as long as he wanted to, puffing up a cloud of bidis and working his way through the English newspapers Rauf laid on for his clients. He was even allowed to solve the crossword. When Peter abruptly stopped visiting, Rauf and the waiters made inquiries. They were told that he had probably gone to Nashik to check up on the family vineyards.

For a time, it seemed like Peter had managed to achieve the impossible: he had got Bandra to stop recognizing him. Or was it that Bandra had changed so much, none of its new residents recognized Peter Rebello?

• • •

The circumstances of Peter's death caused considerable consternation among old-timers. People huddled in churchyards after Sunday mass to discuss the tragedy; they wrote agonized letters to *The Examiner*, the weekly magazine of the archdiocese. 'We, as Catholics are a cohesive community, keeping in touch with other members through church organizations, through social functions and through relationships,' one correspondent declared. 'We care for each other, but clearly not enough is being done ... In these days of migratory trends, many from the older generation are left back alone to fend for themselves. They are at an age when any amount of monetary assistance cannot satisfy their thirst for love and drive away their acute sense of loneliness ... Forgetting that the success stories of the younger generation were scripted by the hard toil of these seniors, they are easily weeded out from the family and consigned to a lonely existence!'

However, one Bandra resident, a counsellor who knew Peter slightly, didn't subscribe to the theory that his death resulted from the lack of community. Rather, she thought it was too much of it that did him in. She believed that the fear of having their family name ruined drove Peter's family to downplay his illness as eccentricity. 'Family name, family pride, family reputation ... were put above the need to attend to his pain.'

One May morning, a neighbour told Peter's sister, Helen Saldanha, that the back door of his flat was open and flapping in the wind. Saldanha had noticed her brother's absence, but it was hardly the first time he had disappeared. 'A series of precedents caused him not to be missed for several months,' D'Souza told me later. The family didn't know what to do. 'Suppose we said, "Let's break down the door," and it turned out he was only at a friend's house – after all, he often went away for months – he'd have got very upset.' Eventually, the unlocked door seemed unusual enough to warrant the invasion of Peter's sanctuary.

With typical disregard for science, the Bombay police told journalists that the absence of odour in the flat was because Peter had not eaten for days before his death. 'Moreover,' a report in *The Indian Express* claimed, 'he always kept dogs and pigeons in the house and never cleared out the mess. Hence, any odour that the body may have emitted blended with the stench in the house.'

Peter's skeleton was sent to a hospital to be examined. The doctors established that the bones were of a man in his sixties, about five feet ten inches tall. The police ruled out foul play. They told journalists that he had probably collapsed after a massive stroke. They concluded that the dog, used to being fed from Peter's own plate in his lifetime, had starved to death.

There was no memorial service for Peter; it appeared that his family was not keen on having one. As for his bones, no one knows what happened to them. When I last spoke to her, Angelina D'Souza could not bring herself to refer to Peter in the past tense. 'I keep thinking that this is one of his pranks,' she said, a full year on from the discovery of his death. 'I think that if we held a service, Peter would suddenly walk down the aisle to the skeleton and laugh at us all.'

BUILDING BRIDGES
Manu Herbstein

One Sunday in 1941, Sir Benegal Rama Rau came to lunch at our home in Muizenberg, just over the road from the old wooden footbridge across the Vlei. He and my father sat chatting on the green wicker chairs on the front stoep. My mother flitted in and out, from stoep to kitchen to dining room. I looked on in awe. I was five.

It was not often that a non-European sat on our front stoep, let alone joined us at the dining table for a family lunch. The non-Europeans I knew worked for us in the kitchen and the garden and lived in quarters at the back of the house.

Sir Benegal was fifty-two, eight years older than my father. He had been India's deputy high commissioner in London before arriving in South Africa in May 1938 as agent-general. After the war he was to serve as his country's first ambassador in Tokyo and later in Washington DC. He wound up his career as governor of the Reserve Bank of India.

I can no longer tap my late parents' memories and none of my siblings recalls details of this visit. In June 2008, I phoned Sir Benegal's younger daughter, Santha (b. 1923). She lived in New York and could look back on a long career as a writer. She confirmed that her father would have been alone. At the outbreak of World War II Lady Rama Rau had taken Santha and her older sister back to India. The Summer/Fall 2009 Bulletin of the Authors Guild reported Santha's death on April 21 2009.

As I grew up, literary fantasies embellished my mental picture of Sir Benegal. In my imagination he wore a richly embroidered silk sherwani and a striped turban secured with a huge pink diamond.

• • •

Muizenberg High School didn't have its own sports ground, so every Wednesday afternoon we took the train to Steurhof and walked to the False Bay fields for rugby practice. Afterwards we would call at the Indian shop opposite the station. On the counter there were heavy glass jars with sweets in them: nigger balls and bullseyes, black liquorice twists and ropes and marshmallow fish, jelly beans and lifesavers, barley sugar and hard-boiled sweets, Turkish delight and home-made fudge. The shop was full of unfamiliar spicy smells. I have only the vaguest recollection of the shopkeeper and his family. We bought our toffee apples, dripping with treacle, and hurried off, anxious not to miss the next train.

• • •

In 1957–58 I worked for consulting engineers in Victoria Street, London.

I had to go back to Cape Town to finish my degree. I flew to Nairobi, which was as far as my finances would permit. There were two YMCAs there, one in a township, for blacks, one in the city, for whites. The city YMCA, where I stayed, had admitted its first two non-white guests. One was an Indian, Hari Sharan Chhabra, who was doing research for a PhD. He was to establish African Publications (India) at 9M Bhagat Singh Market, New Delhi, publishing *Africa Diary*, a weekly record of events in Africa for many years. In 1964, we would meet again in New Delhi and share a meal. When he wrote and published *South Africa: One year after Mandela's release* in 1991, Nelson Mandela wrote the foreword.

• • •

As soon as I had my degree I headed back to London, staying for a while at the Yusuf Meher Ali Afro-Asian Socialist Students' Hostel, named after a Muslim leader of India's Congress party in Bombay whom the British had interned during the Quit India movement in 1942.

I spent 1959-60 at Imperial College in London. In a class of forty engineers, all men, nine were from India or Pakistan: one of them, Sudhu Prabhu would spend his whole career with Pell, Frischman and Partners in London, rising to become its chief executive.

When I was in Bombay in 1963, Sudhu returned to get married. I visited him at his home in Dadar. He told me there was a problem. The family astrologer did not like the date they had chosen for the wedding.

'But Sudhu,' I troubled him with a customary lack of tact, 'I know that you have a brilliant, rational, scientific mind. Do you really believe in this stuff?'

He just shook his head. It is possible to live in two different worlds at one and the same time.

• • •

In 1960–61 I was working for a firm called Gammon in Nigeria. A new managing director had good contacts in Ghana. He negotiated a road survey and design consulting contract. I was the only qualified engineer in the firm. Jack Thompson sent me to set up an office in Cape Coast and run the project. I was twenty-five.

A Ghanaian asked me, 'Where do you come from?'

'South Africa,' I said

'Oh,' was the reply, 'Have you met your countrymen?'

My countrymen, teachers at the Anglican Adisadel College, perched on a nearby hill, were Manilal Moodley and Roeps Ramdas.

Mani hailed from Durban. His forebears were from south India and he was very dark, darker than any African. He sported a handlebar moustache and an upper-class British accent. He had completed his law studies in London but hadn't been called to the Bar. He was teaching English. In spite of his colour, Ghanaians insisted on addressing him as Kwesi Oburoni, Sunday-born white man. That amused him. He had a relaxed sense of humour.

Mani took charge of me. Within a week I had a large circle of friends, Ghanaians, West Indians and South Africans. Cape Coast was good to me and it was Mani who made that happen.

• • •

Gammon India, our parent company, sent two professionals to assist me with my work. I announced the impending arrival of the first, engineer Jayaram Nanjangud, to my new-found friends. Hard of hearing, they promptly named him Mister No-Damn-Good. He hailed from Mysore, from the small temple town which shares his surname. I met him at Accra airport. He told me that he'd left his new wife behind because the job description required a bachelor.

'What led you to apply for a job in West Africa?' I asked him.

'I want to learn something about Western culture,' was his reply. I raised my eyebrows. Then I smiled.

That Saturday night, a nightclub called Weekend in Havana was hosting the Cape Coast heat of the national Star Highlife Competition. I took Nanjangud along with me. Out of his hearing, I asked an attractive girl at our table to invite him to dance. He declined politely but she refused to take no for an answer. He had never danced before, not highlife, not Bharatanatyam, not Kathakali, not anything. He did his best but was clearly relieved to return to his seat. The next Saturday night there was a dance at the Monte Carlo. I invited him to join me, but he wouldn't come.

The other expatriate member of our team was a surveyor of Sri Lankan Dutch Burgher origin. The Burghers were the descendants of eighteenth-century Dutch settlers who had stayed on when the British captured the island in 1796, the abandoned flotsam and jetsam of a now-vanished empire. Burgher worked hard during the week but at weekends he was bored: there wasn't much by way of entertainment in Cape Coast. Then he discovered a cinema which showed three-hour Hindi films on Saturday nights. He had never watched a Hindi film before. Now he became an addict. He even watched the repeats.

The third South African Indian in Cape Coast was Hari Sewpershad, who taught Latin at the Aggrey Zion Memorial School. He had a car with the number plate CR999. As he drove around the town, calls would follow him from the pavements, 'Nine-nine, nine-nine', most of them from pretty young girls. When he came to the end of his contract, he put a 'For Sale' notice in his rear window. The calls changed to 'For-sale, for-sale'.

Sewp suffered from athlete's foot. His doctor advised him to give his toes plenty of air. He might have bought himself a pair of sandals. Instead he applied a scissors to the front ends of a pair of running shoes. He would raise his toes repeatedly, ventilating the oxygen-hating fungus which plagued them.

'Ag. Sewp.'

We would shake our heads. The man was incorrigible.

The Queen of England paid a state visit to Ghana. There was to be a ball in her honour at the Town Hall, though, sadly, she was too busy to attend. All our friends received invitations. Only Sewp and I had been left off the list. We sat on the stools at the counter of the California Bar, morose, drowning our sorrows, listening to the band at the Town Hall just down the road.

After a few beers, Sewp flapped his running shoes and told me, 'Come on, let's go.'

'Go where?'

'To the Queen's ball, of course.'

Having imbibed less beer than he had, I was reluctant. Even if we got through the door without tickets, we would surely be thrown out. I was concerned for my reputation. Sewp accused me of cowardice and I caved in. We did get in. And we were thrown out.

• • •

There were two distinct classes of Indians in Ghana. The first were traders of long standing, who ran stores like Chellarams and Kewalrams. The second were professionals on contract – doctors, engineers and academics. Many of them were Bengalis. One of them, Debu Chaudhuri, whom I had met in London, had joined Gammon after returning to India. We renewed our friendship when he turned up in Nigeria on a business trip and then again in Ghana. We were to meet and work together yet again in Bombay.

• • •

In 1919 the young English civil engineer John C. Gammon gave up a secure career in the Indian Civil Service to strike out on his own as a contractor. His first big contract was to construct the Gateway of India. It was a long-term project. The foundation stone was laid in 1911, marking the visit of the King-Emperor, George V. It wasn't until 1924 that the monument was completed.

By the time I arrived in Bombay, Gammon India Ltd had grown to become the second largest contractor in the country.

In January 1964 J.C. Gammon visited Bombay for the annual general meeting of the company, of which he was still the chairman. I met the great man at a cocktail party. The managing director was James Bates, but he was soon to depart, to be replaced by the first Indian managing director, leaving me as the only non-Indian at head office, just down the road from the Gateway of India.

There were two Englishmen in the Calcutta office. I described one of them in a letter as 'another of the type who have to explain away their superfluity here by a display of arrogance towards the natives and also, by hearsay, since he's never been to Africa, to Africans.'

Gammon's chief engineer was T.N. Subba Rao, who was to become managing director some years later. When last I heard from him he was still at work in Bombay (now Mumbai), running his own consulting engineering firm. During my two years with

Gammon he was responsible for the design and construction of several kilometres of prestressed concrete bridges as well as other major civil engineering structures. He was a charismatic leader and an outstanding and innovative engineer. I recall him with affection and respect. I would hazard a guess that if you could put all the bridges he had a hand in, end to end, they would stretch to something approaching a hundred kilometres.

I had come to Gammon India via Gammon Nigeria and Gammon Ghana. Both the latter subsequently shut shop but Gammon India has evidently gone from strength to strength. J.C. Gammon died in 1973, T.N. Subba Rao, at the age of 80, in 2008.

• • •

I arrive in Bombay early in June 1963. Gammon India's personnel officer checks me in at the Grand Hotel, a short walk from the company's office. I'll stay here until I can find a flat to rent and a car to buy.

The hotel dining room is lit by a skylight and lined with potted palms. On a small stage at one end two elderly Anglo-Indian men stroke violins and a tiny grey-haired European lady does pizzicato on a cello. They play popular music from the time of my parents. (My mother's favourite: *If I should plant a tiny seed of love, in the garden of your heart* ...)

The head waiter asks me whether I would mind sharing a table with another bachelor guest. We introduce ourselves. He is Jaroch Losuvalna, an oil engineer from Thailand, in Bombay for specialist training. We become friends.

Jaroch is going to a concert and invites me to join him. I agree. My supply of reading matter is running low.

The hall of the Bharatiya Music and Arts Society is enormous: rows upon rows of seats seem to stretch to distant horizons.

Three musicians sit cross-legged on a low carpeted dais. The first is fiddling with an unfamiliar stringed instrument. A sound box shaped like a cutaway calabash rests on the carpet next to his right knee. The wooden neck extends way above his left shoulder. It seems to have many strings, perhaps twenty, but they are too far away for me to count. The sounds are strange to my ear. Every so often the player pauses and adjusts the pegs. It seems that he is still tuning his instrument. Perhaps I'll get a better feel of what is going on when the real performance starts.

'That's a sitar,' Jaroch whispers to me.

I nod wisely.

Next to the sitar player, his companion's busy fingers and thumbs create a complex rhythm on two little drums, one hand serving each.

'Tablas,' Jaroch advises. 'One male, one female. And that instrument at the back is the tamboura, the drone.'

I nod again.

The sitar player ups the tempo. The drummer responds. They seem to be conducting an improvised dialogue. Like in jazz, but these are not jazz sounds. The guy in front of me slides his head out onto his left shoulder and then back over to the right shoulder. He does it again. I get the message: he is overcome by an ecstatic auditory orgasm. Now his wife does it too. Discreetly, I try to emulate them. My neck is too stiff: I might as well try my hand at the sitar.

I close my eyes and try to focus my attention on the music. My concentration is soon interrupted. Small children are playing tag in the aisle. At the end of our row, two guys seem to be negotiating a business deal. I'm tempted to direct a rude shush at them, but decide against. When in Rome ... or rather, when in Bombay ... Finally they get up and take a stroll. My bladder advises me to follow them. The doorman hands me an outpass. Without it he won't let me in again.

The programme continues. The audience is fired up by the performers. There are calls for encores. The performers are fired up by the audience. It is already past midnight.

A late train takes us back to Churchgate Station. Carefully skirting the pavement sleepers, we walk back to the hotel. It is early the next morning before we get to bed.

I learn the names of the star performers, Pandit Ravi Shankar and Ustad Alla Rakha, Mani Iyer, Ali Akbar Khan. I begin to grasp the difference between a morning raga and an evening raga, or think I do. I can't say that I become any sort of expert, or that I learn to roll my head from shoulder to shoulder, but I do learn just to relax and enjoy. And in the course of time I include Indian classical dance in my repertoire.

My taste is catholic. I listen to the Trio de Bolzano playing Beethoven, Mozart and Schumann at the Taj Crystal Room. When Ravi Shankar reaches out to the same audience, the members of the Bombay Madrigal Singers Association, the programme includes a two-page introduction to Indian classical music, directed to Western listeners unfamiliar with the tradition.

A year later Acker Bilk and his Paramount Jazz Band perform to a full house at the Bhulabhai Desai Auditorium.

It wasn't until 1965 that George Harrison took sitar lessons from Ravi Shankar. I never did get to hear the Beatles live.

• • •

In 1959, while studying at Imperial College in London, I was invited to join the Goats' Club, where the rule was, one country, one member.

In 2007 I learn from the Internet that, 'The purpose of the club was to foster a deeper understanding of Britain through the appearance of influential guests (politicians, authors, actors, academics, etc.), each giving a talk about the particular aspect of British life in which he/she played a part.'

That was their agenda; mine was to meet girls. Amongst them was a striking Indian medical student, Durreshwar Dhanrajgirji.

Princess Margaret was our next guest. A musical play was staged in her honour. Durr played the lead, a seductive witch girl. She was no mean performer. She stole my heart.

• • •

June 1963. Durr has qualified and is back home in Bombay, soon to embark on a short-lived first marriage. I have arrived in Bombay to work for Gammon India Ltd. I track her down. She invites me to her parents' home for a meal. They live in a large apartment in a solid old building called Dhanraj Mahal, not far from the Gateway of India.

Dhanraj Mahal. The implications escape me.

Durr answers the doorbell and welcomes me.

(Did we shake hands or exchange namastes? Only Latins embraced and kissed on both cheeks in those days. I don't recall: this is after all forty years ago. But I do recall her grace, her ever stunning looks and the warmth with which I was received and made to feel at home.)

She will soon introduce me to her parents, of whom I have no prior knowledge.

Durr's father is Raja Narsingir Dhanrajgir Gyan Bahadur. He is a man of manifold gifts, a widely-read collector of books, an accomplished cook and a master raconteur.

Durr's mother is Zubeida Begum Dhanrajgir. She was born in 1911.

Begum Zubeida's father, Major HH Mubariz ud-Daula, Muzaffar ul-Mulk, Nawab Sidi Ibrahim Muhammad Yakut Khan III Bahadur Nusrat Jang, was the last Nawab of the princely state of Sachin, with, like the Dhanrajgirjis, a family history running back hundreds of years.

Zubeida's mother, Durr's grandmother, Fatima Begum, was a remarkable woman in a remarkable family. In the 1920s and 1930s she was not only one of India's leading movie actresses but also the country's first woman film director. And this at a time when acting was hardly considered a suitable career for a girl from a good family.

Encouraged by her mother, Zubeida started her own acting career at the age of twelve, with a part in the silent movie *Kohinoor*. Her two sisters, Sultana and Shehzadi, were also actresses. After honing her skills and building her reputation in a number of silent films in the 1920s, Zubeida hit the big time with her starring role in India's first talkie, the great hit, *Alam Ara*, released in March 1931.

Famous throughout the subcontinent for her beauty and acting skills, Zubeida was also a talented singer and dancer. She made her last film in 1949.

Of all this I know nothing.

Durr's mother, the very same Begum Zubeida, appears and greets me warmly. She is in her early fifties. It is from her, I see at once, that Durr has inherited her fine features. She asks me about myself, where Durr and I met, what has brought me to Bombay.

After lunch, Durr takes me to meet her father. He is drinking whisky in his den with two friends. He offers me a glass. Politely, I decline. A card table has been set up nearby. Durr tells me later that they will play poker until the early hours. Her father seldom rises before noon.

I am subjected to another gentle grilling. He gets me talking about South Africa and raises his eyebrows at my optimistic prediction of the early collapse of apartheid. Then he begins to tell me something about himself. He is a Hindu, by birth, if not by religious conviction. His status in Hyderabad imposes upon him the obligation to perform certain religious rites. His subjects' respect for him borders on worship. He does what is required of him, concealing his lack of fervour.

He believes in the unity of all mankind. We all see the first light of day in the gap between a woman's legs. (I am surprised at the words he chooses. I think Durr is too.) We all share the unavoidable expectation of death. There is no essential difference between us.

Durr listens with evident astonishment but says nothing. She tells me later that her father's declaration of belief has been a revelation to her.

Many years later, Durr's daughter Rhea will write, 'Living in big, grand homes with an overdose of luxury, I saw intimacy and emotional bonding taking a back seat to materialistic satisfaction.'

Forty years have passed. Researching this memoir I wonder what has happened to Durr. A web search leads me to an interesting blog in which the writer, Altaf Abid, describes a meeting with Durr's brother, Humayun Dhanrajgir, a leading player in the Indian pharmaceutical industry. Altaf gives me Humayun's phone number; Humayun gives me Durr's. She lives in California. I call her and we chat. Her voice, at least, hasn't aged.

• • •

I found a wonderful, inexpensive house to rent, in leafy Silver Oak Estate, off Warden Road, now Bulabhai Desai Marg. It belonged to a German company and the only condition the landlord set was that if they needed it themselves I should not make a fuss about being asked to vacate it at a month's notice. I hired a houseful of furniture from the Bombay Furnishing Co., opp. Central Bank, 30 Bruce St., Fort, Bombay. On 21 June 1963, they delivered: two beds

Manu and friends, Silver Oak Estate, Bombay, 1964

with salva underlays (whatever those are), two cotton mattresses, one bedside table with glass top, one wardrobe – half hanging half shelves, one bookcase, one dining table 3ft x 4ft, six dining chairs – cane seat and cane back, one chair for cook, one sideboard, one large meat safe, one kitchen table, one writing table with two drawers only and two peg tables.

I employed a cook-cum-steward, an elderly Christian Sri Lankan Tamil of Indian origin who had migrated to Bombay years before. Natu was a professional. I never had any complaints about the way he did his job. There was, however, one serious difference between us. He refused to clean the WC, even though that meant nothing more than sprinkling some Harpic and using a brush. He wanted me to pay for a lower-caste man to come in once a day to do that job. I reacted with supreme insensitivity. I invited him to watch while I demonstrated. Then I told him that if he wanted to subcontract the work he would have to pay the subcontractor himself. He did so, without complaint.

• • •

My Thai table-mate Jaroch introduced me to his colleague, Servulo Colaço and Servulo (also known as Bulão) introduced me to his fellow Goans.

My Goan friends loved parties. These weren't just Goan parties – there was always a broad ethnic mix. I was a welcome guest and not only because, as a privileged foreigner in the age of Morarji Desai's prohibition, I was entitled to purchase a weekly ration of hooch. What made the parties distinctively Goan was that round about midnight the record player would be switched off and guitars and violins would materialize; and then we danced to live music.

The object of Bulão's affections failed to attend one of these parties – she might have been ill or studying for an exam. As we dispersed in the early hours of the morning, Bulão gathered the musicians and insisted that they, and I, accompany him. We ended up under Carmen's window listening to Bulão serenading her to his own accompaniment. When Carmen qualified as a doctor, they got married and emigrated to Canada where I lost track of them until May 2009 when we spent a pleasant morning together in Toronto. Neither of them had any recollection of my story of their courtship.

Dr Luis-Felipe de Souza had learned to play the violin as a child. In 1960, at the age of forty, he took it up again. As his children grew up he started to give them lessons, Ralph, the firstborn, at five, Harvey at four. I was often in their home and when Ralph was reluctant to go to bed would tell him concocted African folk tales as bedtime stories.

We remained in touch at least once a year after I left India and so it was that I learned that Yehudi Menuhin had offered Ralph a scholarship to attend the school he had founded in Surrey, England, in 1963. (Harvey, the third-born, six years younger than Ralph, was to follow.)

Years later – it must have been in the early 1980s – I spent a few days in London. At a loose end, I scanned the entertainment columns and saw advertised there a violin recital by one Ralph de Souza at the Queen Elizabeth Hall on the South Bank.

How many violinists called Ralph de Souza could there be? I checked the telephone directory but there were just too many R. de Souzas. I decided to go anyway.

The scene in the concert hall was unusual. Many of those in the audience seemed to know one another. There was a great deal of waving and shaking of hands and conversations in the aisles. Then the violinist came on stage and took his bow. There was no mistaking him: this was the son of Luis-Felipe and Sheila de Souza.

During the interval I struck up a conversation with the man sitting next to me. He was the English master at the Menuhin school. He told me that the year before my friends had visited England for the first time and he had met them at the school.

After the concert I went backstage and joined the queue of those lining up to congratulate Ralph on his performance. When it was my turn to shake his hand, there was a puzzled expression on his face: who was this stranger? I introduced myself and he remembered me at once. That night I wrote a long letter. Luis-Felipe's reply was longer: thirteen pages.

Ralph has been a member of the Endellion String Quartet since 1986 and Harvey has been a member of the Academy of St Martin-in-the-Fields since 1993. In his late eighties Luis-Felipe was still going strong and still teaching children not only the violin but also dancing.

Every December Ralph and Harvey go home to Mumbai (as Bombay is now called) where they organize the Sangat Chamber Music Festival, bringing home the host of talented Indian musicians who live and work abroad.

• • •

On 12 December 1963 the Bombay Branch of the African Students Association of India (Charles Odede was the chairman) organized a dinner-dance to celebrate Kenya's independence, and Zanzibar's.

As I sat out a round I noticed the unusual haircut of a man dancing with his back to me. I had only once before seen such a distinctive style and that was in Ghana. It could hardly be the same guy. I could see his partner's pretty face but didn't recognize it. Yet she was wearing a typically Ghanaian kaba. They turned and I was on my feet.

Tony Mensah's surprise was as great as mine. The last time we had met he was the manager of Kingsway Stores in Cape Coast. He introduced me to his wife, Mary. Tony was on secondment to Hindustan Lever. Mary was attending a course of some sort. She was not happy in Bombay, complaining of constant racist abuse whenever she was on her own in a public space. I think she must have been the only African woman in the city.

The African students also had it tough, but being men, were perhaps better able to cope. Their problem (and mine too) was finding girls to date. An Indian girl might ruin her marriage prospects if she were seen out with any foreign man, let alone a black man. Even without foreigners, Indian society was run through with prejudice. In the matrimonial columns of the newspapers typical classified ads might invite correspondence from a 'beautiful, educated bride, preferably fair-complexioned' or a 'college graduate, very fair, accomplished beautiful bride'.

The African students' activities were not confined to their studies and organizing independence dinners. Late in November 1964 the *Times of India* reported: 'Eleven members of the African Students Association in Bombay were arrested by the police in front of the Belgian Consulate ... The students were staging a demonstration against Belgium's 'intervention' in the Congo. They were arrested when they tried to break through a police cordon to reach the consulate.'

Amongst those students at least one is still active in politics. Samson Ongeri is Kenya's minister of education.

Prohibition was in force in the state of Maharashtra and only certified alcoholics and foreigners were entitled to a weekly ration of beer and spirits. I took full advantage of my allocation and consequently had a regular stream of visitors.

One of my most radical occasional guests was Richard Hove. When he got his degree he returned to Zimbabwe and at once joined the struggle against Smith and Co.

In 1992 Ghana Airways was the only airline flying from Accra to Harare and on to Johannesburg. This was my first trip home in thirty-three years. I decided to break my journey in Harare and restore links with old friends. Hove had by that time been minister of defence. When I said I planned to call him my host raised his eyebrows but said nothing.

Hove had no problem remembering me but apologized profusely: he was about to leave for his farm and wouldn't be back until after my departure. He was a key senior member of ZANU-PF and his name appeared on the blacklists of both the USA and the EU. I guess he was proud of that. He died on 22 August 2009.

I don't recall any black South African students in Bombay but there was a South African Students' Association. Within a couple of months of my arrival I attended their Freshers Social followed in November by a 'cultural talk' by Shri V.K. Krishna Menon, distinguished Indian nationalist and erstwhile minister of defence. All the SASA members were South African Indians. They wanted closer ties with the African Students' Association – some of them even favoured a merger – but the East African students would have none of it. They regarded all Indian descendants in Africa as racists. This was hardly an issue for the West African students.

When I threw a party I invited friends from both camps and don't recall that that ever caused a problem.

• • •

Arun Gandhi was born in Durban in 1934, son of Manilal and Sushila and grandson of Mohandas Karamchand 'Mahatma' Gandhi. In 1946 his parents took him to India where he lived with his grandfather until shortly before his death at the hand of an assassin in 1948. Arun returned to South Africa and took his matric. There was a family prejudice against universities so that was the end of his formal education. Back in India in 1956 he joined the *Times of India*. When I arrived in Bombay in 1963 he was in charge of their library.

The Hindu establishment, citing ancient laws and customs, frowned on widows remarrying. Arun married a widow. When Sunanda died in 2007, they had been married for nearly fifty years.

Sunanda suffered from a serious spinal complaint which caused her constant pain and required surgery. During her convalescence her doctors prescribed a special diet. I was assigned the task of delivering a daily flask of bone soup to her in the hospital.

They both delighted in telling me the story of the birth of their son. They were travelling by train from Bombay to Calcutta when Sunanda went into labour earlier than expected. It was on the cards that their child would be born before they arrived at the next station and who knows what emergency medical care would be available there. Sunanda was a nurse. She took charge, acting as her own midwife, giving Arun instructions. Sheets were borrowed and hung up to create a private delivery room and in due course Sunanda gave birth to a son whom they named Tushar.

Sunanda ran a vegetarian home, more for reasons of economy, I suspect, than ideology: the *Times of India* was not the most generous of employers. When they came to visit me, Natu would offer them a choice of veg or non-veg. Tushar had a hunger for meat. His parents did not object and let him eat his fill.

Arun and I decided to set up an Indian Anti-Apartheid Movement. Our resources were extremely limited and we were operating in a society which was deeply divided internally by its own ethnic, caste and colour prejudices. We decided to concentrate our efforts on providing a source of information for opinion leaders. Using material from the International Defence and Aid Fund and other sources we produced a duplicated monthly news digest and circulated it to the media and members of the Lok Sabha.

Cape Town's Bellville Jail was reported to have become a local torture centre. Adolfus Malgas was subjected to electric shocks there. Elijah Loza, a Cape Town trade union leader, had been badly beaten. Jackson Tayo and Simon Xamlashe (arrested 24 June 1963) were in hospital, both with broken jaws. Xamlashe also had head wounds and it was feared that he would die. An affidavit alleging torture was submitted to the court conducting the inquest on the death of Looksmart Solwandle Ngudle. Twenty-three-year-old warder Johannes Bronkhorst was fined £40 or 80 days imprisonment (half suspended for three years) for shooting a prisoner with a blank cartridge as a joke. His unnamed sixteen-year-old colleague, who tried to repeat the joke with live ammunition, was due to be tried for attempted murder. And so on.

In 1964 Dr Yusuf Dadoo and J.B. Marks toured India as guests of the Afro-Asian Solidarity Committee and the All-India Peace Council. Both were leading lights in the South African Congress movement and the South African Communist Party. We went to call on them at their hotel. Dr Dadoo was somewhat under the weather and cool but J.B. Marks received us warmly. It was not until a few years later that Alfred Nzo would establish the first ANC office in New Delhi. By that time I was back in Ghana.

• • •

I met Dr Rustum Gool in Ibadan in 1961. He was teaching anaesthetics at the University Medical School. Both Rusty's mother, Cissie Gool and his grandfather, Dr Abdullah Abdurahman, were legendary figures in Cape Town history. His father, Dr Abdul Hamid Gool, had been briefly involved in the anti-apartheid struggle before World War II but later maintained that his medical practice allowed him no time for politics. In November 1963, at the age of seventy-six, he visited India for the first time. He told the *Times of India*: 'South Africa's 500,000 Indians are well-to-do, but are compelled to live in "group areas".' He is reported to have said that he was lucky to be classified as a Malay and not as an Indian and was therefore entitled to own land. (In 1937, my uncle, the architect Max Policansky, designed a three-storey block of flats for him in Buitencingel Street; it didn't progress beyond the project stage.) Cissie had died shortly before his visit and I recall (no doubt unreasonably) resenting the way he appeared to exploit her reputation: 'an undaunted politician'. Whether through Rusty, or through Arun, I found myself providing him with the use of my car.

Over the years after I left India, I lost touch with Arun. Then the Khadi and Village Industries Commission sent an exhibition of hand-spun and handwoven fabrics to Accra under the leadership of Tara Bhattacharjee, a cousin of his. It was Tara who put us in touch again, sending me at the same time a cherished snapshot of herself and her grandfather.

• • •

In a letter to the editor of the *Times of India* dated 4 December 1963 and headed 'Racialism in Bombay', Dale Harrison reported: 'My wife and I are white. On Sunday ... we invited three Negro Americans (colleagues of ours working in Kerala) to join us in a swim at the Breach Candy Swimming Bath in Bombay.'

They were denied entry.

In his 6 December leader the editor commented: 'Many (of Bombay's citizens) have no doubt heard of apartheid in South Africa, of racial discrimination in the United States, and of the racially exclusive clubs, hotels and restaurants in places such as Salisbury; and many of them no doubt think that it could not happen here.'

The editor demanded a change in the law.

A later edition recorded that they had received only two letters on the subject from readers, both 'so inadequate in their content and composition that they could not be published'.

On 30 December Phillis Taylor reported an interview with the Breach Candy manager. The swimming pool had been built by the European residents of Bombay with funds donated by themselves and now held in trust. It was 'a privileged heritage of the European community'. Europeans only were admitted and compliance was 'judged solely by the skin shade'.

The issue was taken up by R.K. Karanjia, the editor of the muck-raking left-wing tabloid *Blitz*. He chaired a well-attended public meeting at which I shared the platform with Jagjivan Ram ('Babuji'), India's minister of transport and communications and the most influential 'untouchable' in the land; and the powerful trade union leader, George Fernandes, whose hold over the Bombay trade unions was such that when he called for a bandh, the city ground to a halt. My speech, drawing parallels with apartheid, might have had little impact, but Karanjia, Babuji and Fernandes, all charismatic personalities, succeeded in rousing the audience.

African students joined the Breach Candy picket. *Blitz*, 'Free, Frank and Fearless' inscribed on its masthead, devoted its front page to the protest. Sales soared.

I joined the picket line after work. One day while I was standing there, holding a banner, the governor of the state of Maharashtra passed by in her limousine.

Now the governor was no ordinary person. She was Mrs Vijaya Lakshmi Pandit, younger sister of the prime minister, Jawaharlal Nehru, and a distinguished freedom fighter and prison graduate in her own right. She had headed India's delegation to the United Nations in the years which followed independence and had been the first woman to be elected president of the General Assembly. She had, moreover, been an early, consistent and doughty opponent of South Africa's racial policies.

The limousine slowed. She rolled down her window and waved a white handkerchief.

'Well done. Keep it up,' she called.

And that was all. The government failed to take any action. Our protests soon fizzled out.

The Breach Candy Swimming Pool Trust has neither a website nor an email address, but they do have a telephone number. In July 2008 I spoke to the membership secretary. He was evasive. I suspect that they do still operate a de facto colour bar.

• • •

Time magazine reported on 10 January 1964 that a sign at the entrance of the Western India Turf Club read, 'South Africans not admitted', describing this as 'an untypical bit of Bombay intolerance'.

• • •

On Christmas night, 1963, Goan friends invite me to join them at the Catholic Gymkhana. I'm introduced to a woman I haven't met before and ask her to dance.

'Do you know St Thomas Aquinas?' she asks me.

I don't. She remedies my ignorance by delivering a lecture.

All the time, I'm desperately struggling to avoid stepping on her feet. Is the band playing a quickstep or a foxtrot? Not my kind of music.

She asks where I'm from. I tell her.

'Where's that?' she asks.

'Africa,' I reply.

'All Africans are barbarians,' she tells me.

'What? Please say that again.'

'All Africans are barbarians,' she repeats.

'What on earth are you talking about?'

She stops talking and fixes my eye with a beady stare.

'They take nuns behind cars,' she tells me.

I look at her in amazement, tell her thank you for the dance and return to the table alone, leaving her stranded. The atmosphere at the table is strained. Not my best Christmas.

• • •

Soon after I arrived in Bombay I bought a new car. Imports were not allowed and there were only two locally manufactured options. I settled on the Hindustan Ambassador Mark II, which was based on the old British Morris Oxford. The waiting list for new cars was two years or more. There must be some sort of guilt-driven amnesia operating here, because I have no recollection of how I was jumped to the top of the list. My guess is that expatriates were given special treatment. What I do remember is that market conditions were such that I could have sold my new car, now second-hand, at a premium of at least 25 per cent.

Two couples joined me on my first long trip out of Bombay, during Holi in February 1964: Tony and Mary Mensah from Ghana and Luis-Felipe and Sheila de Souza. Luis-Felipe is a Goan; Sheila, Chinese.

We were an unusual multinational party and the object of constant but distant curiosity, particularly since China had recently defeated India in a minor border war in the Himalayas. Only once were we approached directly by anyone other than a beggar seeking alms. A young girl, perhaps eleven or twelve years old, greeted us politely and asked for our names and countries of origin, which she proceeded to record in a notebook. She explained that this was a task her father, who was a schoolteacher, had set her, as part of her education. I sometimes wonder what became of her. There was a rare warmth and directness about her.

Our destination was Aurangabad, from where we visited the caves at Ajanta and Ellora.

• • •

The Ambassador's next trip was to Goa, to attend the wedding of Angela and João Fonseca. I joined the Western India Automobile Association and bought a detailed description of the route. (Sample: 'Road surface good in dry season, but numerous twists & turns: average 20 m.p.h maximum maintained with safety. Astoli – good shikar area: Panthers, Wild Boer (sic) some tigers & inferior deer. It is dangerous to traverse this section at night.')

Luis-Felipe and Sheila were my passengers as was Servulo Colaço, who had first introduced me to Goan circles.

The wedding was held in the Basilica of Bom Jesus which houses the corpse of St Francis Xavier, a Jesuit priest who died in 1552. Roman Catholics believe that his dead body remains undecomposed and has miraculous healing powers. Once every ten years the corpse's left hand is exposed to the view of the faithful. Its right arm, the one the living saint used for blessings and baptisms, was cut off and sent to Rome in 1614.

I don't recall the wedding ceremony. My attention must have been focused on the magnificent gilt altar which dominates the Basilica's nave.

I stayed with Servulo at his family home. In honour of his visit his aunt prepared a baroque dessert, the sixteen-layered Bebinca which, in its effect on the palate, rivals the visual effect of the Basilica's altar. Its principal ingredient is twenty-four egg yolks.

Servulo's father was a professor of English literature. The family were practising Roman Catholics. At the same time they were Brahmins. I asked Servulo whether he would marry a non-Brahmin. (I didn't have to ask whether he would consider marrying a non-Catholic.) He laughed nervously. Then he regained his customary self-assurance. It was quite ridiculous, he told me, not to say un-Christian, for Catholics to be concerned with a concept as irrational as caste. On the other hand, he had to take his parents' feelings into account; and they, sadly, didn't necessarily share his liberal views.

This was really a non-issue: the lovely Carmen Miranda, whom Servulo was courting, was beyond doubt a Catholic and certainly also a Brahmin.

Luis-Felipe had grown up in Goa in a strict Catholic environment. He had suffered such intellectual, if not physical abuse, that he had, as soon as he was able, struck out for freedom and excommunicated himself.

In 1991, twenty-six years after we had last met, he wrote me a twelve-page letter from Bombay, from which I quote this statement of his humanist credo:

> ... man is the product of biological evolution ... he has arrived at a stage of intelligence and consciousness making him different from, and higher than, his inferior kindred creatures ... and nature has created him without purpose (he has to create one for himself) and destroys him without regret ... the world will carry on believing that creation is a whim of God, and man's future is in his hands, irrespective of the fact that thousands of years of religion have not improved man.

And yet in Goa he was back home and clearly relished the return to his childhood haunts.

• • •

My long train journeys have dissolved into the single stereotype, a distant view of flooded paddy fields being ploughed by water buffalo, with small boys sitting on their backs.

A more compelling image is the scene in Satyajit Ray's *Pather Panchali* in which the boy Apu and his sister Durga are transfixed by their first sighting of a distant train of many carriages, drawn by a steam locomotive, thundering its way across the landscape, a powerful symbol of the urban modernity which will draw Apu away from rural India.

But one train journey stays stuck in my memory.

On a trip from Calcutta to Gauhati I alighted at Siliguri and, taking a few days leave, joined the chugging 'Toy Train' on the 2ft-gauge Himalayan Railway, to Darjeeling. Though Siliguri is about 500km from the sea, it is no more than 120m above sea level. The distance from Siliguri to Darjeeling by rail is only 86km, much less as the crow flies. The highest point on the railway, at Ghum, is 2257m above sea level and Darjeeling is only a couple of hundred metres lower. The train winds and jackknifes on a hair-raising five-and-a-quarter-hour journey through forests and tea estates.

A notice at my hotel offered an early morning trip to see Kanchenjunga, at 8586m, the third highest mountain in the world. I didn't read the small print. The sun rose, as promised, but Kanchenjunga refused to emerge from its cloak of clouds.

• • •

For two years from mid-1963 I shared an office cabin with Sankar Lal Chanda. There was barely enough room for our two desks. We sat facing each other, pushing our slide rules or twirling the handle of a mechanical Facit calculator (or, if we could lay hands on one, the latest electrical model.)

Sankar was designing the structure of the 1830m long, thirty-nine-span Thane Creek Bridge which would open up new territories for the expansion of the geographically cramped city of Bombay. Today, with computers, the analysis would not present major problems. In those days, it was tedious.

The three-lane bridge was eventually opened in 1972. Sadly, all concerned had underestimated the destructive power of the extremely aggressive marine environment. The stressed steel cables encased in the concrete members began to corrode and within two years cracks began to appear in the concrete. The bridge has been replaced by the two-lane Thane (or Vashi) Bridge, constructed on a parallel alignment, just 40m to the south. Only two-wheeled vehicles are allowed to use Sankar's bridge. I would like to think that he was not directly at fault but I can imagine that the failure bore heavily upon him.

The news of Sankar's death at quite a young age shocked me. I sent a warm letter of condolence to his wife, Ruby, but never did receive a reply.

• • •

In Cape Coast in 1961, J.C. Gammon's partner, J.B. Murray, asked me how I saw my career developing. 'I'd like to specialize in bridge design,' I told him. He advised me to join Gammon India and promised to persuade them to offer me a job. I held him to his promise. Since I had a South African passport getting a work permit was not easy. I spent three months of accumulated leave wandering around West, Central and East Africa while I waited.

Gammon India really didn't need me: there were many highly qualified and competent Indian engineers queuing up to join them. Apart from the managing director, Jim Bates, soon to make way for an Indian successor, I was the only expatriate on the head office payroll, the only non-Indian design engineer in a team of over twenty.

Our chief engineer, Tippur Narayanarao Subba Rao, soon earned my enormous respect, not only for his brilliant innovative design skills but also for his charismatic leadership. After a short interview on my first day at work he presented me with a challenge I could not refuse, giving me the responsibility for the detailed design of the superstructure of the 400ft-span Barak Bridge. I was twenty-seven. Sudesh Dhawan, about the same age, was already installed as site agent, working on the foundations. It was his responsibility to get the bridge built. Debu Chaudhuri, whom I had met first in London and then again in Nigeria and Ghana, was the head office contracts manager for the job. Once completed, the bridge spanned the Barak River at Silchar in Assam – the first prestressed concrete bridge to be built in India by the free cantilever method. Sudesh later emigrated to the United States where he built more bridges. In May 2009 I spent a day with him and his charming wife Achla in Toronto. They had driven up from New York to meet me. Sudesh presented me with a book of photographs of Barak Bridge which he had published.

Barak Bridge, Silchar, Assam, 2008

• • •

Gammon Pakistan Ltd was set up soon after Partition. In 1964 the West Pakistan Department of Irrigation called for tenders for the construction of a 3220ft-long bridge over the Indus River, based on a design by UK consultants. The bridge was to provide a direct link between the city of Karachi and the rest of the province of Sind.

Gammon Pakistan believed that a more economical solution was possible but lacked the confidence to attempt it. They asked Gammon's London office to pass on a request to Gammon India to prepare an alternative design and tender.

Subba Rao called us into his office. We received the news with great excitement. He instructed us to drop all but the most urgent other work and concentrate on this project, for which he had already devised a conceptual design. The superstructure would be constructed by the same free cantilever method used for Barak Bridge, but with precast concrete units. This would permit work to continue in the casting yard during the months when the mighty Indus was in flood.

He split the work up. Because of my experience with Barak Bridge, I was allocated the design of the cantilevers. We worked flat out, day and night, sometimes falling into an exhausted sleep at the office, going home in the morning for a shower and a shave and then back to work.

After two weeks the job was done. The tender, complete with design drawings, was despatched by air to London, redirected to Karachi and submitted. In due course the contract was awarded to Gammon Pakistan, but on condition that the structural calculations were submitted to independent consultants for checking. One of our engineers would have to go to Karachi to guide our counterparts there through our calculations, line by line. An Indian? Out of the question.

At Karachi airport an immigration official took one look at my South African passport with its Indian arrival and departure stamps and decided to declare me a prohibited immigrant. Fortunately, Gammon Pakistan was there to meet me, in the person, to my great surprise, of an engineer who had been in my postgraduate class at Imperial College in London in 1959–60.

He persuaded the immigration man to let me in, 'in the national interest'. We spent a pleasant week, slowly working our way through the calculations and drawings and the proposed construction programme. We went to look at the bridge site, reminisced about our student days and talked politics and religion.

In due course Gammon Pakistan prepared a fresh set of calculations and, presumably, burned ours. In a paper published after the bridge had been built, they wrote: 'It is worthy of note that this longest prestressed concrete bridge in Pakistan has been entirely designed and constructed by Pakistani Engineers ...' After more than forty years, I can reveal for the first time that that was only partly true.

As the 2010 flood made its way down the Indus towards Sind, I kept a daily watch on the Internet for news of the Thatta-Sujawal Bridge. Checking back on my files, I found that the reported flood volume was marginally less than the West Pakistan Irrigation Department had specified in their design brief. The bridge seems to have survived without damage.

They say that surgeons bury their mistakes. It is not so easy to bury a bridge.

While I was in the office of the Assam Public Works Department, news came in of the collapse of a reinforced concrete bridge which one of their engineers had designed. I joined them on a visit to the site. This is what I saw. One span had collapsed while its twin had survived.

Diagnosis of a structural failure can be difficult: in this case it was easy. The concrete was substandard. Cement was supplied in jute bags. Adulteration by criminals was not unknown. And rumour had it that the contractor was a relation of the minister of works.

• • •

The *Times of India* featured a regular cartoon by Mario Miranda satirizing Bombay life.

At the centre of a street scene of utter confusion, double-decker buses, horse-drawn carriages, scooters and broken-down cars, a traffic policeman directs the chaos while a turbaned palmist reads his fortune.

At the railway station, a jam-packed third-class carriage stands

Building Bridges | 153

Katakhal Bridge, Assam, 1965: the broken span.

Katakhal Bridge, Assam, 1965: the surviving span.

alongside a reserved second-class compartment with just two passengers, a garlanded politician and his wife.

On 30 June 1963 Mario celebrates the arrival of the Monsoon as citizens rush for shelter and try to open rusty umbrellas.

The top prize at the Film Awards Night goes to the best plagiarist of the year.

At the beach, women bathe in their saris, a practitioner of yoga stands on his head, a dhoti-clad swimmer ogles a bikini-clad beauty and a politician harangues a small crowd.

On 1 September 1963 the cover of the *Illustrated Weekly of India* featured eleven of Mario's vignettes.

A politician in dhoti and prison cap harangues an attentive crowd. At the Gateway of India a paunchy American tourist in baseball cap, flowered shirt and short pants, cigar clenched between his teeth, takes a photograph while his stiletto-heeled wife balances a guidebook on her enormous bosom and a ragged street urchin cries for alms. At a pavement café, under an umbrella inscribed 'Society' a man in blazer and tie, pipe in mouth, places his order with a turbaned waiter while his coiffed companion, the height of elegance in black choli, red sari and dark glasses casually flicks the ash from her cigarette. A mustachioed traffic policeman strikes a pose with his folded umbrella. A family has just arrived in town: a porter leads them carrying their suitcases and bundles on his head. At a jam session, a Sikh in tight trousers jives with a pretty girl in a spotted salwar-kameez, to the vibes of an eyes-tight-shut saxophonist.

A red double-decker bus passes a bus stop: in the queue, seen from behind, a man in sola topi, a woman in a Western-style dress and a school boy in shorts and tie; beyond them, running along the centre of the street (to catch the bus perhaps) a barefooted woman in traditional attire balancing a basket of fish on her head.

At the opening of an art exhibition the pseuds discuss the latest abstracts. At a sweet shop the mithaiwalla serves rasagullas to greedy customers. On Dalal Street, traders scan share prices in the *Money Times*. And in the lower right-hand corner of the *IWI* cover, a somewhat inebriated reader has wrapped his bottle in a newspaper whose headline reads: 'Prohibition Enormous Success'.

• • •

What was I reading in Bombay? I still have my copy of my introduction to the great riches of Indian mythology, R.K. Narayan's *Gods, Demons and Others* with its stories of asuras and yakshas and danavas and of a cosmogony measured in yojanas, a yojana being the distance travelled by a horse in one harnessing. My copy was published by Heinemann in the UK in 1965. I bought it from Thacker & Co. Ltd, Bombay.

I remember reading Narayan's *The Man-eater of Malgudi*, published in 1961 and Raja Rao's *The Serpent and the Rope*, 1960, but both seem to have disappeared from my library. Narayan lived to eighty four, Rao to eighty seven.

Mulk Raj Anand's novel, *Untouchable*, appeared in 1935. He was approaching ninety-nine when he died in 2004. Ageing writers, take heart.

In 1965 Penguin published my countryman Ronald Segal's *The Crisis of India*. My recollection is that it was banned. Certainly my copy, ordered from the UK, was in great demand and I am rather surprised that I still have it, albeit sans the first twenty-four pages. It is a remarkable book, thoroughly researched and written with great style. Reading it after I'd lived in the country for nearly two years, I felt that I'd barely scratched the surface whereas Segal had managed to plumb the depths.

Here's a sample. Perhaps, if the book was indeed banned, this is the reason Indians could not be allowed to read it:

> Nehru never wished to be a tyrant, but he became one – not a great one but a petty one, and not through will but through vacillation. He reigned but did not rule, he commanded but did not conduct, he arbitrated where he should have resolved. His Cabinet consisted in the main of courtiers, chosen for

their personal loyalty or influence or political past, for everything but their policies. And because, inevitably, they did not promote his own ideas, he governed by intervention, not control. His was the tyranny of confusion and caprice. He failed – not because he antagonized too much, but because he was afraid to antagonize enough. He never realized that his worst enemies were his own party, undermining his policies, debasing the coinage of his thought. He was not resolute, only obstinate. He retained Ministers whom he should have dismissed for corruption or incompetence or flagrant disloyalty, because he regarded criticism of them as a reflection on himself, and he dismissed Ministers whom he should have retained for their allegiance to his own beliefs, because his support of them did not in itself still the carefully mounted campaigns of criticism. He said and did more than any Indian in modern history to secularize his people, yet he allowed his spokesmen to inflame religious feelings by threatening calamitous consequences for the Muslim minority if Kashmir were surrendered to Pakistan. He fought the power of caste, yet permitted his party to deploy it in electoral tactics. He reverenced the rule of law, yet detained political opponents without trial. He despised corruption and recognized its dangers, but he sat by, silent, while political colleagues, and even relatives, openly engaged in it. He was brilliant, but he was not wise, for the wise have the ability not just to perceive, but also to adopt and pursue the best means for accomplishing an end. He was embarrassed by a richness of ends and a poverty of means. He was not disciplined, he was a romantic repressed. He was impatient with detail – he pursued policy in swoops – and the intricacies of administration merely irritated him. He was lustrously original, but originality must be based in the present if it is to achieve any change. Nehru was wrapped in visions of the future so tightly that he lost sight of the disorder and dismay everywhere around him. Above all, he was not ruthless and he was vain – as none knew better than the parasites who surrounded and threatened to consume him.

Ronald Segal died in Britain in 2008. His obituary in the *Guardian* was written by my cousin Denis Herbstein, a distinguished *Financial Times* journalist who has spent several extended vacations in India since he retired.

• • •

Living in London in the late 1950s, I discovered the first film in Satyajit Ray's Apu trilogy, *Pather Panchali* (1955). It remains to this day at the top of my list of the world's best movies.

My aunt Lilithy, one-time history teacher at Wynberg Girls High School in Cape Town, was visiting London. I took her to see *Pather Panchali* at the Academy Cinema in Oxford Street. On a second viewing I was as entranced and absorbed as at the first. Aunty Lilithy fidgetted and squirmed in the seat beside me. She was utterly bored. Halfway through I had no choice but to give up. We sat in a restaurant with little to say to one another. I had been her favourite nephew. Now she saw me, I think, as a lost soul.

There was only one cinema in Bombay which showed Bengali films. Since it catered for a Bengali-speaking audience, there were no subtitles. I would invite a Bengali friend, often Suhas Mookerjee, to join me and whisper a commentary. There is an episode in *Jalsaghar* where Biswambhar the old zamindar (played by Chhabi Biswas) sits dozing while a small boy searches the hair on his head.

'Do you know what he's doing?' Suhas whispers.

'Picking lice?' I venture.

There is a look of barely concealed contempt on Suhas's face as he turns to me.

'Pulling out grey hairs,' he tells me.

• • •

In Bombay I discovered and quickly joined Anandam, a 600-strong film society which had been formed in the early 1960s by a group of broad-minded scientists from the Atomic Energy Establishment.

At Anandam I saw classics of the French, Italian, Japanese, Swedish, Polish, Bulgarian, Hungarian, British and American cinemas including de Sica's *Bicycle Thieves*, Buñuel's *Nazarin*, Wajda's *Kanal* and *Ashes and Diamonds*, Polanski's *Knife in the Water*, Bergman's *Wild Strawberries*, Eisenstein's *Ivan the Terrible Part 1*, Kubrick's *Paths of Glory*, David Lean's *Great Expectations*, Luchino Visconti's *Rocco and his Brothers*, Truffaut's *Le Quatre Cent Coups* and *Jules et Jim*, Alain Resnais's *Hiroshima Mon Amour* and Jacques Tati's *Monsieur Hulot's Holiday*.

Then there was the Bombay Film Week with shows at six cinemas, where I saw Antonioni's *L'Avventura* and Demy's *Les Parapluies de Cherbourg* and movies from Hong Kong and Turkey.

In February 1964 Anandam ran a festival of mainly silent film classics, Wiene's *The Cabinet of Dr. Caligari* (1919–20), Murnau's *The Last Laugh*, Fritz Lang's *Metropolis*, Eisenstein's *Battleship Potemkin*, Rene Clair's *The Italian Straw Hat* and *Le Million*, Dreyer's *Passion of Joan of Arc*, Sternberg's *Blue Angel*.

In July 1966 Anandam published a special issue of its journal *Montage* devoted solely to the work of Ray. It is a treasure trove of reviews, critical essays and interviews and includes the complete script of *Nayak* and two revealing essays by Ray himself, *Some Aspects of My Craft* and *Why I Make Films*.

• • •

There was, of course, another Indian cinema, or, rather, other Indian cinemas. I kept cuttings of the issues of the *Times of India* which announced the assassination of US President Kennedy and the arrest of Lee Harvey Oswald. On the rear side were the current movie advertisements: B.R. Chopra's *Dhool Ka Phool*, showing at the Maratha Mandir and *Mujhe Jeene Do*, 'regaling thousands daily' at the Opera House, were amongst the ten Hindi films on offer.

Raj Kapoor was pulling the audiences in to see *Dil Hi To Hai* 'for the 7th Delightful Week'. (The term Bollywood, the origin of which is contested, didn't exist until the mid-1970s.) I tried just one Hindi film and that was enough for me.

Elsewhere, at cinemas with names like Strand, Metro, Rex and New Empire one could see Elvis Presley in *King Creole*, Jack Lemmon in *The Notorious Landlady*, Marilyn Monroe in *Niagara*, Marlon Brando in *One-Eyed Jacks* and also Melina Mercouri and Anthony Perkins in Jules Dassin's *Phaedra*. ('As long as you live, you'll not forget the ghastly sins Phaedra committed in the name of LOVE.') And then there was Arne Sucksdorff's documentary *The Flute and the Arrow* at the Excelsior, recording in the Bastar jungles of central India an ancient lifestyle which by now must surely have been consumed by creeping modernity.

One might perhaps say the same about the work of Satyajit Ray except that his work not only reaches back into the past but also forward into almost any imaginable future.

• • •

The English-language theatre scene in Bombay was less lively than the movie scene, but one play was of particular interest.

In July 1963, Zul Vellani's *Africa-Jawan Pareshan* was performed at the Jai Hind College Hall. The guest of honour was R.K. Karanjia, editor of *Blitz*. The five actors were all Indian. Shaukat Faifi played the lead, a Kikuyu woman. The scene was the servants' quarters belonging to a Kikuyu family. A barbed wire in the background marked the boundary of a European-owned farm, a few miles out of Nairobi.

The playwright cited his reasons for writing the play: 'Kenya, the land of my birth is important to me. Violence has a way of changing personal relationships even among those with a common cause. The brutality which now rampages in Angola and South Africa makes this play of urgent interest.'

• • •

My paternal grandfather, Moritz Isaac Herbstein, died six months before I was born. Following Jewish custom, I was given his name. When I was small and learning to talk, adults asked me, as adults will, 'Little boy what is your name?' My name was a mouthful and I answered, as best I could, 'Manu.' It stuck. That's what I've been called ever since.

In Ghana, Manu is a common surname, meaning, literally, the second-born. It is sometimes written Mainoo, for that is how it is pronounced. It makes a good conversation piece. I tell Ghanaians that I didn't acquire the name after my arrival, I brought it with me.

And then there is the famous musician, Manu Dibango from Cameroon, Manu with the emphasis on the first syllable.

The origin of the Hindu Laws of Manu is lost in a period when history was emerging from myth. One reference dates them as early as 1500 BCE, another between 200 BCE and 200 CE.

Some authorities maintain that the influence of the Laws of Manu is still manifest in some sectors of Indian society today, particularly as regards the comportment of women. It is Manu who advises them to dress modestly, to wear no make-up and to keep their heads covered as a sign of respect.

As an indication of friendship I would sometimes find myself addressed as Manubhai.

• • •

Bombay, 18 August 1963.
I'm slowly meeting people – it's much more difficult than in Ghana, perhaps because I feel myself a foreigner here, but also because of the nature of big-city life and the way Indian society works.

Things are looking up though. On Monday night I'll be having my first date, taking a twenty-year-old Goan Catholic history lecturer to a sitar recital. We met at a South African students' dance and she insists, for reasons of common propriety, that we have another couple come along.

2005.
My good friend Yao Graham is in London. He has to change his flight plan and goes to see his travel agent, an Indian woman who operates from a third-floor office in Regent Street. The agent has had to go out on an errand and a friend of hers is holding the fort. There are no other customers waiting. She assures Yao that the agent will be back soon, asks him to wait and offers him a cup of coffee. They chat.

'Where do you come from?' Yao asks.

'I grew up in Bombay,' she replies. 'And you?' 'Ghana,' he says.

'Ghana? Strange, I've never met a Ghanaian before. But years ago, when I was young and pretty, I had a friend in Bombay, a South African guy who used to date me. He'd come to India from Ghana and when he left he said he was going back there.'

Yao asks for her friend's name; and hers. Just then the agent returns and Yao never gets round to asking Biba for her contact information.

Biba Matharu was a Sikh. She worked for BOAC as an air hostess. I was starved for female company and I was grateful to her for allowing me to date her. She had no hang-ups about being seen in public with a foreign man. We could dine in a restaurant and go to the cinema or theatre or a concert. We could spend time on the beach and she would wear a swimsuit.

She was a stylish dresser, whether in sari, salwar-kameez, slacks or a skirt and was pretty enough to turn men's heads. She was relaxed and intelligent company but our relationship went no further than that. She was in charge.

In April 1964 she was due to fly to Israel for the first time and to have two days off there before the return flight. I asked my elder brother who was living in Tel Aviv at the time to show her the town, but with the admonition, 'Keep your hands off, repeat, off.' On 3 May, I wrote to say thank you to both my father and my brother for looking after her so well: 'She didn't stop talking about Israel for three days after she got back.'

• • •

I met Zia at an afternoon party for late teens and early twenties. At twenty-eight I might have been the oldest present. The sexes were evenly balanced and the girls were all pretty. They came from a range of backgrounds. Zia was a Parsee but there were Christian Goans, Anglo-Indians and Sikhs; perhaps a few Hindus and Muslims.

What the girls had in common was that they were all escaping, at least temporarily, from parents who would have strongly disapproved of their behaviour, dancing cheek to cheek with young men, (and young men of different religions at that, perhaps even of different castes), perhaps drinking and smoking cigarettes.

The party was held in the afternoon because it was easier to invent plausible daytime agendas, say studying in the university library or shopping with a girlfriend. There was a scent of danger. There wasn't a chaperone in sight.

Zia wasn't my first choice but I was hers. As I scanned the field, she focused on me. She won. I won't say that I lost, though. We met alone regularly, almost always discreetly, at my home.

Zia had a problem and her problem became mine. The Parsees harbour anxieties about losing their identity through assimilation. ('Marry inside our community, and save our religion,' exhorts a Parsee website.) Zia was of an age at which her parents would have been giving active consideration to arranging a marriage for her within the community.

I could not (and cannot now) read Zia's mind: lovers don't reveal all their innermost thoughts to one another. My guess is that she saw me as a means of escape, firstly from a marriage which might not have been of her choice and secondly, maybe, from the narrow vistas and limited opportunities offered to a woman in a life within the community.

If this was indeed her plan, it was a dangerous one. If it had resulted in marriage to me, it might have led to a break with her family and her network of support within the Parsee community. That would have been more of a problem if we had stayed in India than if she had followed me wherever I chose to go.

A more serious danger, from her point of view, must have been of a rumour concerning our relationship reaching her parents and her prospective husband. Within this conservative community she would almost certainly have been regarded as spoiled goods. Our affair had to remain a secret to all but a few trusted friends. Even her best Parsee friends were not to be trusted. Also, she had to keep her options open. If I failed her, she might end up having to marry her parents' choice. In order to allow for the possibility of that fate, it was essential that she retained her virginity.

Zia had a deep understanding of both male and female sexuality. She catered for my sexual drive in a manner which released it and disarmed it. On the other hand she feared the consequences of being overcome by her own aroused desire. So she imposed strict rules. She couldn't afford to lose control.

I could not see myself spending the rest of my life in India. I hoped to go home to South Africa after the demise of apartheid. I had discovered a good place to sit out the years until that happened: Ghana. I was not confident that after the early passion had worn off, Zia and I could build a life to fit that dream. I decided that it was only fair to her to bring our relationship to an end. I bought her a parting gift, in hindsight, a stupid and insensitive gift: a gold ring. I chose to present it to her at a party at Luis-Felipe and Sheila de Souza's flat. I thought she would understand the logic of my case. I was quite wrong. She was deeply hurt. That ring meant less than nothing to her. It was me she wanted and any ring was a poor substitute. But I had made my decision and I stuck to it.

Memory is so unreliable. After I'd written this, I found among my papers, a poem entitled Z* which I must have written at this time.

> Visit me when I have gone.
> Ring the silent bell at my doorpost.
> (I turned off the mains before I left.)
> Knock at my door, hammer
> As I present my passport to be stamped

At Santa Cruz
And sign the Customs Declaration:
Nothing to declare.
I'm carrying away
No priceless gems, no cherished memories,
Only a tiny irritating bitter seed
In an empty bag (you didn't call.)
Who knows? By the time you telephone my office
In the morning
('He's left, you know: caught the evening plane.')
It will have grown into a pearl.
Visit me when I have gone.
I've left already.
I never was entirely here.

For the life of me, I can't recall the circumstances that inspired it. Memory is so unreliable.

• • •

I had gone to India on a one-year contract and had stayed for two. Mr Subba Rao, I knew, would be happy to offer me another. The time had come to make decisions about my future.

Around that time I made a business call to a man I had not met. He was out. I left my name and telephone number with his secretary. When he returned, his secretary called our switchboard and asked to be put through to Mr Manubhai Harbans Singh. In no time at all everyone in the office was laughing at that story. That night I looked at myself in the mirror. Should I let my hair and beard grow and buy myself a turban? Save up for a large, pink, diamond turban pin?

I flew to New Delhi for an interview for a job in Ghana.

• • •

I was working for the government in Ghana in 1966, when the military, with CIA support, made a coup d'état. The Americans imposed a policy of economic austerity. I was paid every month but it was clear that none of the structures I was designing would be built. Frustrated, I found a job in Zambia. Then I met my future wife, Akua. I took the lead. Akua would follow as soon as I was settled and we would get married in Lusaka.

The Immigration Department headquarters was in Livingstone. I wrote and explained the circumstances. Since there was no Zambian consul in Accra, would they please issue Akua with a visa, to await her at the international point of entry, Ndola Airport? They demanded, quite reasonably, that I pay a deposit to cover the cost of her repatriation should I fail to marry her. I paid the deposit and gave them her flight details. They assured me that the visa would be issued to her on arrival. Murphy's Law. I was not entirely convinced.

Mani Moodley, my South African friend from the days in Cape Coast, had returned to London, qualified as a lawyer and taken a job as a magistrate on the Copperbelt. (He was later to become Zimbabwe's first Ombudsman.) I asked him to meet Akua's plane at Ndola Airport. She arrived. The immigration officer said he knew nothing of a visa. Her plane was flying on to Lusaka. When it returned they would send her back to Dar-es-Salaam, which had been her last stopover. Until then they would detain her at Ndola Airport. She was desperate. What had gone wrong? How would she get from Dar-es-Salaam to Accra?

As she emerged into the arrivals hall in the custody of an immigration officer, Mani recognized the Ghanaian kaba she was wearing and stepped forward to welcome her warmly. She was confused. Who was this stranger? He introduced himself and she was happy to let him deal with her problem.

The immigration officer required payment of a deposit, in cash, before he would issue her with a temporary visa and allow her to proceed to Lusaka, the same amount I had paid to his colleague in Livingstone.

Now the Dar-es-Salaam flight connected to flights from India and its arrival was something of a social occasion for the Indian merchants of Ndola. Mani took a collecting bowl around and raised the cash amount demanded. Akua sighed with relief. She could proceed to Lusaka.

I sent Mani a refund immediately. The Immigration Department took several months to refund the Ndola deposit and several months more, after I had sent them an attested copy of our marriage certificate, to return the Livingstone deposit. Murphy was right.

In 1970, Akua and I returned to Accra, where we still live.

THE MUSE OF FAILURE

Anand Balakrishnan

I vowed to write upon water, I vowed to bear with Sisyphus his speechless rock. I vowed to stay with Sisyphus suffering the fevers and the sparks, and seeking in blind eyes a last plume that writes for autumn and grass the poem of dust. I vowed to live with Sisyphus.

— Adonis, 'To Sisyphus'

The Arabic word for failure is built from the tripartite root of f-sh-l to become fashil, the harshest, most damaging word in the language, at least the way my Arabic teacher pronounced it. The word often twisted his dyspeptic mouth, spattering our lessons like ordnance from a cluster bomb. Everything was fashil. I as a student, he as a teacher, Cairo as a city, Egypt as a state, the Middle East as a region, Asia as a continent, communism as a theory, democracy as an ideal, Islam as it was practised, humanity as a species, and, in the summer when the smog congealed, the sun as a source of light.

'Shams,' I said, when he pointed at the bright yellow ball in our Arabic textbook.

'Fashil!' he exclaimed. 'The sun is a failure in Cairo.'

'Ragol,' I said dutifully, when he pointed at the picture of a cheerful-looking man standing next to a well-fed family.

'Fashil! A man cannot earn enough to support his family. All modern men are failures.'

'Al'iqtisad al'arabi,' I read out loud from the chapter about the victories Arab states had won in the face of foreign neo-liberalism.

'Fashil! There is no Arab economy!'

Thoroughly imprinted by the speech patterns of my teacher, my practice sentences began to read like the polemics of a fed-up dissident (or, perhaps, a smart-ass American – the line is a fine one):

> *Ahmed failed to walk to school. His father failed to pay for gas. The official failed to stamp the passport. The glorious culture of Al'Andalus failed to keep the palm trees alive. The third-world dream of Nasser was an awesome failure. The Arab League failed to do anything about Sudan. The UN fails to do anything ever.*

Luckily for me, my practice was not wasted. It was 2004. Failure was in the air and all over the Arabic headlines. The American invasion of Iraq was fashil. The fruits of the Arab Spring? Fashil, dead on the vine. And the two-state solution was fashil, as always. As I read the newspapers for my Arabic exercises, it became clear that journalists fell into two camps: those who used the word fashil and those who didn't. Of the former, the leading light was Abd al-Halim Qandil, whose weekly denunciations of the Egyptian government's rhetoric and policies introduced me to a dozen synonyms for failure. Arabic is a rich language, book two of my textbook series informed me, rich in nuance and history. A good deal of this nuance and history, it seems, is preoccupied with the meaning of failure.

• • •

At a moulid in Sayyeda Zeinab, a group of people gathered around a one-armed man from Afghanistan. Compared to the other sights to be seen – the fire-eating, the exorcisms, the three-armed man – the Afghan was a minor curiosity. He had light grey eyes, partially occluded by bangs, and carried himself with an unwieldy grace, turning and dipping his armless shoulder to make his way quietly through the crowd. Somehow, word got out that he was Afghan, and, within the whirlpool of the crowd, an eddy formed as men lined up to shake his hand. Several addressed him as Batl, or Hero. One well-dressed sheb passed around his Oakland A's hat to start a collection, and an old woman with a faded blue tattoo on one cheek burst into tears. It seemed as though the madness of the moulid had only intensified the crowd's psychic investment in Afghanistan. The Afghan thanked everyone in exceedingly formal Arabic. 'Allah Khaleek, the Arabs and the Afghans will always remain brothers.' Then he slipped away.

Intrigued and tactless, I followed. It was dusk, and lights were going on in the apartments around us – warm yellow rectangles punched out of concrete walls. I stumbled as I caught up with him, and he turned around to see me trip. 'Your arm,' I blurted out, my attenuated language skills overwhelming my sense of propriety. 'Your arm, why has it failed?' The Afghan, who turned out to be a former Arabic-as-a-second-language student himself, was forgiving of my linguistic butchery.

We walked back to the apartment he shared with two other men, a Malaysian and a Somali. By the time we got there, it was night. The apartment was simple. There were two bedrooms, and the third man slept in the living room. The Afghan offered me tea, and we drank it standing in the kitchen, which was lit by a single bulb hanging on a wire from the ceiling. All three men were seminary students at Al'Azhar; all three were in their mid-forties or so. And all three, strangers in Egypt, clung to each other. The Afghan showed the others the money he'd collected. 'Good,' said the Malay. 'Keep it up, and we'll be able to begin jihad again.' He looked at me. 'Jihad is extremely expensive. If we're lucky, the Egyptians will give us enough money and guns to free our nations.'

'And if we're even luckier, we can get shot and go to school for twenty, thirty years more,' dead-panned the Somali without looking up from his book.

I must have looked confused.

The Afghan explained. 'It was the Arabs that got me,' he laughed, 'not the Soviets.' A visiting Saudi mujahid had mistaken him for a Russian soldier. 'It was noon, though, so I understand.' He didn't harbour a grudge. The Saudi had felt so terrible about shooting him in the arm that he sponsored his education at Al'Azhar. The one-armed man hadn't returned to Afghanistan since beginning his studies twenty years ago. 'We got the Soviets out. We got the Taliban. America got the Taliban out. We got the warlords. That Saudi's bullet probably saved my life.'

The Somali laughed. 'I call it the Failed Jihadi Scholarship Fund. He gets to learn Arabic and understand the secrets of Islam.' He put one long finger against his lips. 'Don't tell anyone – it's a secret.' He picked up his book again. He was reading a faded copy of Sayyid Qutb's *Milestones*.

• • •

Sayyid Qutb came to the United States in 1948 before publishing *Milestones*, a text that some believe inspired a later generation to fly planes into the World Trade Center. Since those attacks, hundreds have travelled East to pursue the story of those men who travelled West. One day I will compile the thousands and thousands of pages produced by these criss-crossing intercontinental passages into an anthology called *A Thousand and One Nights of Al Qaeda: A Tale of Tales of Terror*. It will be filled with Arab characters whose names are now the stuff of myth – Sayyid Qutb, Ayman Zawahiri, Osama bin Laden – and the khawegga who try to understand them – Lawrence Wright, Patrick Fitzgerald, a revolving cast of freelancers and academics.

In *A Thousand Nights and A Night*, fear lends Scheherazade eloquence: a failure to amuse means death. In my version, fear of another terrorist attack will lend a similar urgency to the narration. There will be two differences, however: first, the goal will not be to amuse, but to explain; second, a thousand Scheherazades will die, killed not by an emir but by the knife of another storyteller eager to spin a tale.

Patrick Fitzgerald appears early in the anthology to tell of his prosecution of the 1998 US embassy bombing in Kenya. He speaks in the short, clipped rhythms of a man who knows that time is a privilege he does not have. He will describe the formation of the terrorist plan, outlining with bullet points the backgrounds of the various figures involved, presenting his case to the court.

Next in the book is a series of memos, the interdepartmental chatter of the CIA, to explain what the spooks knew before 9/11. Later still, Lawrence Wright will introduce Sayyid Qutb, the prudish Egyptian whose experiences led him to write *The America I Have Seen* (1951), a sweeping critique of the country, from its racism to its spiritual emptiness to its bad taste in haircuts. From there, I will excerpt from books by historians tracing the roots of Islamic extremism, sociologists tracking the relationship between socio-economic frameworks and the development of terrorist cells, psychologists studying the seductions of terrorism, Internet chatroom transcripts, short stories, and flow charts of terrorist networks and anti-terrorist networks. The anthology will be a cacophonous mess, a contest of clashing cadences and incommensurable registers. Each of its thousand and one narratives will be a failure.

Peter Lance will appear at some point to argue – as he does phlegmatically in *Triple Cross* (2006) – that Patrick Fitzgerald and his team of lawyers failed to recognize key pieces of information that could have stopped later terrorist attacks. Lawrence Wright will describe the institutional dynamics and skewed priorities that undermined CIA efforts to track terrorist threats. A curmudgeonly historian will snipe at Lawrence Wright, dryly suggesting that it takes a writer to attribute such far-reaching impact to *Milestones*, a mere book.

It is possible that the anthology will remain a work in progress. The literature of terror is just beginning to flower. But if the long peace were to come and failure no longer sent writers East in search of stories to tell a hungry audience at home, I would grudgingly end the book with excerpts from Bernard Lewis. Not because Lewis is right or wrong, but because, in doing so, I will ensure that no knife remains unsheathed:

> *In the course of the twentieth century it became abundantly clear in the Middle East and indeed all over the lands of Islam that things had indeed gone badly wrong. Compared with its millennial rival, Christendom, the world of Islam had become poor, weak, and ignorant. In the course of the nineteenth and twentieth centuries, the primacy and therefore the dominance of the West was clear to all to see, invading the Muslim in every aspect of his public and – more painfully – even his private life.*

The failure of his grand narrative of failure will practically guarantee me a sequel.

• • •

According to the political science graduate student who sat next to me on the plane to Cairo, Samuel Huntington's thesis in *The Clash of Civilizations* is wrong. I forget the precise contours of the student's critique, but I do remember the contents of his carry-on bag. We were both subjected to a random search by airport security; I pulled out the second set of clothes that my mom makes everyone in our family pack (in case our luggage goes missing), and a copy of Amitav Ghosh's *In an Antique Land*, which I was inexplicably embarrassed to be caught carrying. The political science student pulled out the latest copy of *Foreign Affairs*, Hannah Arendt's *On Violence*, and his Arabic–English dictionary. He studied the political economy of fear, he told me as I watched the plane's shadow crawl over the skin of the Atlantic. The governments of the Middle East had become anxious institutions, he said, both fearful of the governed and determined to inspire fear in them. 'These are total institutions of loathing,' he said. 'It's really just misleading to say that you can separate the people and the sovereign when one is constitutive of the other.' I didn't fully follow what he was saying, but he spoke with a confidence borne of countless hours of impassioned fighting over methodology, and I myself had nothing at stake. Hours passed; conversation ebbed. The kid in the seat in front of me excitedly pointed at the sinuous curves the wind carved out of the desert. A tiny sandstorm rose up miles below us, giving shape to the air. The kid laughed. 'Imagine the tiny people!'

We were over the pyramids when I could no longer dodge the question of why I was going to Cairo. 'Well,' I hedged, embarrassed, 'there's a book I like, and I have a job for a year.' He pressed me on the book. 'It's more of a short story,' I admitted grudgingly. 'By Abd el-Hakim Qassim,' I said. *Good News from the Afterlife*. I tried to describe it to the political science student. It's a difficult story to describe because it doesn't have much of a plot. A man, an Egyptian peasant, dies. His body decomposes, and his soul is judged by two angels of death – Naker and Nakeer. A small child sits on his grave and falls asleep. The centrepiece of the story is an extended dialogue between the angels and the man's soul about the nature of law and duty, prophecy and authority, knowledge and fear.

I began to wax eloquent. Qassim had managed to blend Islamic theology with a distinctly modernist sensibility, a marriage of deep religious rootedness and existential transcendence. He had spent time in Europe, I explained, but had never left Islam. His challenge was that of our times – to free religion from itself without leaving religion.

My new friend looked at me quizzically. He had read another novel, *The Seven Days of Man*. 'Qassim did a fine job depicting the life of the rural poor,' he said. 'That's important. Literature informs our understanding of politics.'

We lost each other in the snarl of traffic after trading email addresses and making the traveller's promise to see each other soon. Six months passed before we ran into each other again, and, over a beer, it became clear that the Middle East is an especially exciting place for a political scientist. His research was coming along wonderfully, he said, though his focus had changed from terrorism to something more hopeful. It was the first blush of the Arab Spring: Yasser Arafat was dead; Saddam Hussein was in an Iraqi jail; an energized Egyptian Left, with its slogans of *Kifaya*, had impelled Mubarak to announce fundamental electoral reform. A younger generation was emerging, less rooted in the dogmatisms of old – more open-minded, ready to rise to the moment.

The way he described it, a transformative politics supersaturated the air. Its crystallization merely awaited some missing ingredient that would trigger an alchemical reaction in the Arab world. His eyes glowed in the dim lights of the Zamalek bar. This was, I supposed, what a political scientist waits for: a moment when theory is measured against the exigencies of reality, and the social world becomes a living laboratory for the success and failure of ideas.

He asked me how I was doing. I made a noncommittal shrug. He had arrived right on time; I was too late. I had gone seeking Qassim and his Egypt, but the writer was long dead, his body decomposing and his soul judged. I worried that he had been found wanting. His books are perennially out of print.

I ran into the political scientist again another six months later. We were in Tahrir Square and he pulled me into the coffee shop where he sat with his papers. He looked no less excited than before. 'The question I now ask is different,' he said. 'It is a question of why change fails.' Since I'd seen him last, change had, in fact, failed. Mubarak and the NDP stayed in power; Hizbullah rallied for Syria to stay and Lebanon's fragments hung together by the loosest of threads; the death toll in Iraq continued to mount; and the Sunnis continued to feel isolated and marginalized in their newly liberated nation. And the political scientist had traded in Arendt for Foucault. It was now a political economy of failure that he was planning to explore – the way 'the sovereign and the people alike constituted and were constituted by ossified structures that prevented change'. His eyebrows went up with the phrase 'were constituted by'. He used the word aporia a few times, and I nodded gravely as if I understood what it meant. I surreptitiously wrote the word down on a tissue so I could look it up later. He asked me what I was reading, and I told him I was reading a book by Son'allah Ibrahim. He pulled the tissue from my hands to write down the name. Noticing my handwriting, he tucked the tissue into his pocket and, smiling gently, explained what aporia meant.

• • •

Son'allah Ibrahim is Egypt's reigning bard of failure. Ibrahim is sometimes described as the Arab Kafka by dint of his early novella, *Al'Lajna*, or *The Committee*, a deeply paranoid story of bureaucratic decadence and autosarcophagy. But Kafka didn't use footnotes; Ibrahim does. They proliferate obsessively in his work, peeling off from his fictional narrative to tell parallel stories of history and politics. As the narrator of *Amerikanli* describes, in sometimes excruciating detail, his failure to control his sexual urges during his trip across the United States (hiding behind trees to watch the American girls walk by, then masturbating afterwards), footnotes march along in the bottom margin, explaining in small print the cavalcade of failure that is the history of the United States. In *Zaat*, chapters detailing the heroine's struggle through life during the era of Infitah – buying a busted television, masturbating while thinking of Nasser, learning to wear the hijab – alternate with chapters composed of snippets of newspaper articles cobbled together to tell true stories of state corruption, of grand engineering projects left unfinished after their budgets disappeared into the private coffers of Sadat's ministers, of government bread baked with one part wheat and three parts stone – in short, the true story of the failures of the Egyptian state. Ibrahim's stories are comedic without being cheerful, just as the masturbation he inevitably depicts is pleasurable without being fulfilling. The history of failure marches on with every turn of the page; any moment of triumph is necessarily fleeting, a brief respite before the next disappointment.

Ibrahim was part of the 1960s generation of intellectuals, a group whose story is inextricable from the history of political events. There were the secular hopes and promises of Nasser, the 1967 defeat, the crackdown on civil liberties and political dissidents, the dissolution of Arab unity, the rise of Sadat, the peace with Israel, the entrenchment of Mubarak. It's not a hopeful history, and – as my Arabic teacher pointed out – it was Abd el-Hakim Qassim who described it best when he titled another allegory of Egyptian history and politics *Qadar al-Ghoraf Al-Moqbeda,* or *Destiny of Gloomy Rooms.* 'Compared to Qassim,' he said, 'Ibrahim's a failure as a pessimist.'

My Arabic teacher and I were walking through the streets of Ain Shams at night as we talked about Qassim. The uniform apartment complexes, with unfinished upper floors, wore the melancholic, sepia tones of the street lamps. I had told him I had read and liked that story *Good News from the Afterlife.* And my teacher, of course, exclaimed, 'Fashil! The title is mistranslated.' He explained why, though the differences were minor. He was quibbling as a point of pride; he had known Qassim and claimed special knowledge of the man and his work.

Qassim's life was a series of interruptions. Born in a village near Tanta, he studied law at the University of Alexandria but never finished; after working for the postal service, he was arrested and spent several years in prison on suspicion of leftist activity. After a few years working in insurance, he went to Germany to start a dissertation on Egyptian literature, which he later abandoned. After more than a decade in Europe, he returned home, settling in Cairo. He became increasingly religious and began writing for the Islamist newspaper *Al'Shab.* He ran for a parliamentary seat in 1987, but was partially paralysed by a severe stroke during the campaign. He died three years later, dictating his final literary works to his wife.

My teacher knew Qassim during those last years. They would meet once a week and he would take dictation from the paralysed writer, editing and assembling the final product for his *Al'Shab* column. My teacher was younger then, more hopeful, and far more secular. He was ideologically opposed to *Al'Shab* and to the Islamist project in general. The two of them would argue, he said. He still felt terrible about it. Qassim had strong convictions but a faltering voice. My teacher was young enough to substitute volume for logic and was quick to lose his temper, shouting Qassim down when a disagreement arose, calling his choices mistakes, angrily denouncing his decision to turn on his secular friends and join the Islamists. And then, fuming, my teacher would read back Qassim's latest column for Egypt's premier organ of Islamic dissidence and quietly accept corrections.

My teacher's desire to correct language was obsessive. When we watched Al Jazeera, he made a teaching moment out of the commentators' every dropped tanween. He read books and newspapers with a pen, ready to correct copy editors' failures and writers' misuse of classical Arabic. He corrected every written word that crossed his path, without prejudice as to the source: the speeches of doddering Wafdists, the Islamists of *El'Osboua*, the Nasserists of *Al'Arabi*, the jesters of *Al'Dustour*, the liberals of *Misr Al'Yom* and *al'Ghad*; emailed bank statements; flyers from grocery stores; film advertisements; the dropped nuqta of my Arabic textbooks – none was exempt from the judgement of his pen. I once watched, fascinated and a bit horrified, as he compulsively corrected the corrections an elementary schoolteacher had written over his daughter's handwriting. 'Fashil! She is teaching the students to ruin Arabic lettering.' He looked up from the three-inch daad his daughter had written in crayon and stared at me. 'Even you, even you can probably write a daad better than a modern Egyptian schoolteacher.'

Qassim and my teacher were both born to deeply traditional families in small towns outside of Cairo. They were attracted to Cairo through a love of books and an appreciation for the history of a language that represented the fading dreams of Arab nationalism, Islamic glory, and a way out of their sometimes stultifying homes. And, in the decade after Qassim's death, they grew more similar. Six years ago, my teacher stopped going to political meetings. He started to pray, grew a beard that he kept neatly trimmed, and stopped talking to most of his old friends. But he would never join the Islamists, he said. People would call him and ask him to go to Kifaya meetings and protests, but he refused. I asked him several times why he made the choices he did. He didn't give me a straight answer. 'My choices are wrong, of course,' he'd snap at me, before asking why he had been cursed with such a terrible student. 'How can you understand me when you can't even write your sentences properly?' He underlined a sentence in my notebook: *They failed to restore the Caliphate*. 'Yafshilo!' he corrected. 'Present tense.'

THE ADVENTURES OF IDI AMIN DADA

Binyavanga Wainaina

Monday. The hot dry breeze is lazy. It glides languorously collecting odd bits of paper, they tease the ground, threaten to take flight, tease the ground. Every so often there is a gathering of force and a tiny tornado whips the paper into the air and swirls dust around. Dogs lift their ears, tongues lolling, then burrow their faces between their forelegs as the wind collapses, exhausted.

Children are in school, long lines of spittle reaching their desks as they try to keep awake. From the roof of the town, Menengai crater, the flamingoes look like a giant fabric, rising from the lake like a cloth on a hot shimmering line, revealing blue, falling, and turning the lake pink again.

Vishal is at the library. His brother, in school. Mr Shah, at work.

Idi Amin Dada is hunched over Mrs Shah like a question mark, jabbing. She is chewing hard at a bit of blue, gold and red sari, trying to keep from screaming out loud; they have put on a movie at high volume to muffle the sounds.

On the screen, Idi can see a pouting maiden at the edge of a cliff. A man with a giant Afro and big sideburns sings in a shrill voice. The maiden leaps off the cliff and the Afro follows her in a flash. They lie draped elegantly at the bottom of the valley; their fingers touch and they die; then the music escalates in intensity, beyond drama, beyond melodrama, into Bombay Belodrama.

This morning, every weekday morning, Idi drops Mr Shah at Nakuru Grain Millers, the family business; then he drops the petulant maharaja, Rajesh, at school. The Shah Pre-school Academy.

The Maharaja's mother begs him to get into the car. Mr Shah remains silent, fingers tapping the steering wheel. If Vishal was around, he would have something sarcastic to say. You going to cry now, Maharaja? The Maharaja starts crying.

As soon as the car leaves the factory gate in the industrial area, after the yes-sir/afende-sir Amin smilingly sends at Mr Shah, the Maharaja wriggles his way to the passenger seat of the Peugeot 504 Injection, eyes dry and now happy.

Once or twice a week, if they have a few minutes, Idi stops at the kiosk near the General Hospital, where his Ugandan friend Simon sells sweets, and buys some goody-goody toffees for the boy.

Simon punches Idi on the shoulder and announces his fame as the crowds of sick look on, all waiting for some kind of attention at the hospital. As groups of young men wait for somebody to park a car and hire them, for a day of heaving things around, slapping cement, or digging a pit latrine, for ten shillings. It is a good place to have a kiosk. Somebody always needs a loaf of bread or some milk. There are schools nearby too. And a church. And nurses. And the railway. The path across the hospital leads past the cemetery and into town.

'You see this man, you see this man, you know he was the Boxing Champion of Uganda, this man.'

They get back into the car, and the boy is flushed with excitement. Sometimes Idi puts his mouth on the boy's stomach and makes little burping noises. Rajesh laughs and laughs until he starts to cry with joy.

• • •

Piles of freshly ironed clothes sit on a boat-shaped basin next to the bed, clothes Idi has ironed last night. Vishal's bookshelf had been moved to this room since he left for Oxford; the top row is full of Louis L'Amour thrillers and the bottom row has a copy of *Heart of Darkness*, A-level notes scribbled in the margins, biro doodles on the front cover. Next to it is V.S. Naipaul's *A Bend in the River*.

Mrs Shah gives a low gnashing answer that sends a soft cardamom gale into Idi's ear.

He loves ironing. Every afternoon he puts on a Bollywood film and turns the Shahs' washing into a crisp battalion of soldiers. He loves shrugging shirts into broad, identical shoulders, arranging them in wardrobes, watching them stand at attention. The room was once a stable, but is now a servant's quarter. At six p.m. exactly, he will take a shower, then smoke hashish mixed with loose tobacco.

Sometimes he dreams of the embrace of a Luganda prostitute, sucking at his nerve endings like a fish. Once he blew his whole salary on a woman he met at a bus station who told him she was a ssenga.

• • •

The 1960s were full of landslides: as the British administration screeched to a halt, those that were waiting for a trajectory to come and grab a hold of them were left stranded.

Everything changed for Idi. He had considered leaving Kenya and going back to Uganda, but he did not know what to do without a new commander. Sergeant Jones was dead. And Idi had enemies there. Jonas, his junior, was close to Obote at independence – and from the same village. He had hoped to get word of an opening from a friend in the right place. None had come.

By 1970, he was about to give up, was about to hitch-hike to Uganda and sell illegal liquor in Arua like his mother had done, when he had found a frail Gujarati man being beaten by a ten-year-old parking boy outside the wholesale market, with market women cheering the boy on.

He had rescued the man, Mr Shah. And he was given a job. It

wasn't bad. Mr Shah was polite. And Mrs Shah was the same as Sergeant Jones: an insistent fanatic about time and a goddess of routine. Idi had joined the army as soon as age would allow it. It was his way out of aimlessness. His mother sold liquor, was a camp follower, and 'had' several army officers. At the age of thirteen, he beat up a thirty-year-old Acholi private who slapped his mother.

At fifteen, he was six foot four, and when Sergeant Jones saw him walking in Arua, he offered him a place in the army at once. Jones would spend hours with Idi in the boxing ring, teaching him new skills. He loved to punch Idi softly; to wipe sweat off Idi's back; to test out Idi's muscles. Always gruffly.

Idi loved to catch and beat up Mau Maus. One day, after winning a boxing match, he got drunk and came to the barracks with a prostitute. The sentry refused to let him in. Amin left him unconscious on the floor. Jones found him in the barracks the next morning. He slapped Idi twice. Hard.

Idi did not talk to anybody for days. Three days later, after winning the Gilgil Barracks Boxing Crown for a second time, Jones patted him on the back; Idi grinned widely and said, 'Now I am the bull afande.'

'You're a good lad, Idi. A good lad.'

• • •

Mr Shah likes to spend the morning working on his novel, which is titled *Conquerors of the British Empire*.

He is already one thousand words into the preface.

> ... It is the only way to make a National Profit from hundreds of years of British Rule: the more territory we control, the more we can dictate the cost of raw materials. The final profit will be manned by our rupees, our shillings and our guns. Mother India should be Lord of the Commonwealth. Why let the English carry us on their back? Why build afresh when we can inherit what is already there? The Desais will keep the books, the Amins will manage the farms.

We can take the skills the British brought, and add them to the world ...

His firstborn, Vishal, is disdainful of the book. 'V.S. says the Indian industrial revolution is petty and private. We are greedy. V.S. says we are a society that is incapable of assessing itself, which asks no questions because ritual and myth have provided all the answers, that we are a society that has not learned rebellion. Maybe you need to read some real literature before writing this. The Russians ...'

Since his return from England, Vishal treats his parents like they are colourful mantelpiece trinkets.

Last year, at a birthday party, Vishal composed a song that would scandalize everybody (except the Marxist Harbajan Singh, who liked his mettle). He sang it to the tune of a nursery school song about a kookaburra.

Duka-wallah sit by de ole Neem tree
Merry Merry King of da Street is he
Run Dukawallah run
Dukawallah burn
Dukawallah hide your cash and flee

• • •

It started with small things. She would scrub her heel with a stone until it bled. It was better when they had the shop. Now, Ramesh does not come home any more for lunch. He eats fruit instead. Now, she wakes with a surging panic, as her days cannot fill up. The house extensions are finished. At night it seems, sometimes, like the earthworms are coming. They are shifting everything, turning up the earth, dark and whispering. Last month, four families on the street left. Ramesh will not hear of it. Start again where? Then Vishal left. They sit there, on her wall, her certificates. For hockey, for first place in biology and art, Duchess of Gloucester School, Pangani.

When she was twelve, she wrestled her bigger brother to the ground. Her mother found her scratching his face. She was confined to her room for days, and dreamed of becoming Sally, an air hostess. Or Jane, a trauma nurse.

Sitting for tea at the Nakuru Sweet Mart with friends, some days, she pinches herself under the table, harder and harder, and a satisfying tingle runs up her back; she dabs the tears and says they are so strong, these onions, fresh – as they talk about ways to hide gold.

• • •

Between two and four in the afternoon you will find Idi Amin at Nakuru Boxing Club. For years he has been the Nakuru Boxing Champion. Now, he is older and the young bucks are challenging him. Modesty Blaise Wekesa is short. Very short. It is said he once lifted a plough over his head while working as a casual in the wheat fields of Masailand. He is copper to Idi's black. It is his speed – the unbelievable speed of those bowed legs and thighs the size of a grown man's waist.

When Amin first exploded into the Nakuru boxing scene people saw a future world champion, 'Aii Alikuwa kama myama!' – he is like an animal! The discipline of the army added to his natural ferocity to make him unbeatable. He had no wife. Many lovers: mostly market women looking for a man with some skills, who complained that their men were disdainful of frills. These women had heard all the legends about tap-tap and other Ugandan bedroom abilities he never acquired.

He has a son, in Ronda. Twin daughters in Naivasha. In 1957, in Gilgil, a woman once came to the barracks, screaming. She unknotted her baby-kanga and put the baby on the ground. She stood at the gates, tearing her clothes off, and screaming in Gikuyu, as the men laughed. One of the guards tried to stop her, and she slapped him. 'Where is he? Where is he?' Idi was away, at the Police Lines, drinking. The woman walked off, leaving the baby there. She got to the fence of the village, was just about to walk through the ditch that surrounded it – a ditch dug by her and other women – when she turned and ran back. She picked the baby up and walked away, past the village, probably, they speculated, all the way to Nairobi, where the orphans, the rejected, the divorced and the accused go to disappear.

After his sparring session with a nervous young man with even larger limbs than his – a young man so scared he could probably kill in fear – Idi has a soda with an old friend.

Godwin, the only fellow Kakwa in Nakuru. Godwin Pojulu is a tailor for an Indian family, the Khans. Idi speaks his language badly; he speaks Luo and Acholi and Kiswahili better – army languages.

But when he was six or seven his mother took him to Yei town in Sudan – and he fell in love with the mango-lined avenues. Children were generally a nuisance in colonial Arua, but his maternal grandfather's home, just off Maridi Road, five miles from Yei, was heaven. He was free to run and play as far as he wanted. Adults would swell to accommodate him and he would eat in the homes of strangers.

Godwin speaks to him about Sudan. About Inyanya – the war. About old heroic days; about rumour and gossip coming from Yei town. They drink soda and eat mandazi and talk till the people leave their offices, until the surge of workers coming in from factories sets Godwin to work.

• • •

At five thirty, before the last sun, Idi heads to Eunice's for supper. He loves that walk – the railway, with its long straight one-roomed homes, reminds him of his childhood in various labour lines near various railway stations.

One roomed homes – with kei-apple-green doors looking across from each other. He arrives at Eunice's. Clothes flap on the line directly above him.

The buildings are very old, some of the oldest in the country, as old as the railway – the origin and spine of what we now call Kenya. Green fungi on the open pipes; green tears streaming down peeling walls. A toy car leans by a wall streaked with the scribbles of children. Railway children make the best wire cars – crouched and snarling, with steering that makes the wheels turn; with paper mudguards, number plates, and springy aerials thrusting out from the back.

In between the ceilings, under the old corrugated iron roof, young men keep carrier pigeons – the feathers cluster in roof drains.

Eunice is sprawled on the grass, elbow crossed over her eyes, sleeping; her whole body receiving the sun. The smell of cooked fish and boiling, bitter, green vegetables is everywhere. Two women are getting their hair plaited on the sparse patch of grass between the parallel single-room buildings. Both their heads are held at the knee by their hairdressers, legs wide open. There is a pile of discarded pea pods, sukuma-wiki stems and potato peels next to the tap, covered with a large web of slime. Brackish, soapy water glides out into an open drain where ducklings swim. Ducks with mossy muddy bellies wander about. The women are talking and don't stop when they see him standing awkwardly near the tap.

Eunice. She is not young. In her fifties probably. Straight and lean with sharp buttocks and very short grey hair, cut like a boy's.

Her head is a pot gently placed on a long straight neck where it rocks gently from side to side; gold-coloured loop earrings wobble on her ears; her hips and buttocks are a pendulum of tight flesh. Her back is perfectly straight.

She catches Idi's eye, and slips past the open door where four quarters are carefully divided, by old sarongs, into four rooms.

• • •

The only person in the household who threatens Idi's job is Vishal, back from England and full of black-power talk.

That night, Mrs Shah surprises her husband by defending Vishal. She is bent over, head between her thighs, hair over her face, brushing the back of it, metres long, as Ramesh rails on. 'Are we sending him to Oxford to become a black man?'

Idi has been with the family for fifteen years now. Two years ago he cornered some thugs, beat them all up, and received a knife wound in his belly.

He is afraid of only one thing. The market. Those women. Whenever he is shopping for the Shahs, he can see their eyes measuring him, he can hear whispers surging when he turns to leave. One day he hears 'Thief! Thief!' and starts to run. The whole market, until a moment ago a puddle of fast-moving ants, is now an arrow chasing to kill, an arrow surrounded by cheering crowds.

Later, he wonders whether they were chasing somebody else. In any case, he decides to send Godwin to the market on the days Memsahib is too preoccupied to go and buy the vegetables herself.

• • •

It only started recently with Memsahib.

Idi walked in from the kitchen with a big mug of sweet tea and caught her wailing in the living room, a day after Vishal had left for Oxford. He tried to slide backwards, slowly edging his way out, but she leaped up and grabbed him and wept on his shoulder, leaving long trails of snot on his khaki shirt. Then her mood changed abruptly and she attacked him, teeth and nails, her body incoherent.

This change, this new erratic thing to deal with, troubles him. Most times, he does not mind being a houseboy.

MOBIUS

Rimli Sengupta

He always insisted that the liveliest places are the edges.

So he built a glass house around an abandoned camper. The kind of camper you can throw on your truck bed and away you go. That was in the centre, the centre he was trying to flee. So he slept in it, feigning motion. And the edges were kept lively in glass that could shatter at a moment's notice. Except, the moment never came.

Instead, a neat hedge of tulip-like planters showed up along the glass walls, each meticulously carved from old tyres with zigzag slits. On spring nights, rain flirted with the poised rain gauge before getting harvested in ten-gallon drums. And fat-bottomed truffula trees happily settled in for the next hundred years.

And his home sweated the muffled desperation of one centred but not by choice.

NEST

His house had a woman-shaped hole. Or perhaps it was a hole-shaped woman.

If she so desired, hole-woman could primp in front of the oval dressing mirror flanked by exuberant plants in exotic planters while keeping an eye out, chameleon-like, for the hawk soaring above the gorge yonder. Or while taking a pee she could seep through the clear glass walls, slide down the cliff and plunge into the swirling green waters below. Or while dusting the bottle collection that cast a stained glass pattern on the area rug she could caress the leathery braid of dried bull kelp that swung from the rafters yearning for the Tasmanian Sea.

But she didn't do any of these things.

If she had, she might have had to help him clean up the mess after each of the whores he brought home. And stay up with him while he drummed out the wet blood smell with substances being abused. And keep the dogs out of the soft mounds in the morning.

But she didn't. So she didn't have to.

SUGARCANE

Nilanjana Roy

The ghosts who lived in the back garden – behind the mali's small red brick house – left the year we bought the transistor radio. My father always said it was the radio that forced their silent eviction, but that may have been because he disliked the Binaca Geetmala himself, and the tinny distant sounds of bands that wafted across the airwaves all the way from Radio Ceylon. He was a classicist; and on the old wind-up Victrola, he listened to Sibelius and Debussy, Gangubai Hangal and Bismillah Khan.

The silence told us they had gone, and for weeks afterwards I mourned. There had been something friendly, reassuring even, in the soft wails, the discreet thumping and the quiet, almost apologetic crash from the kitchen as a ceramic pickle jar dislodged itself from the shelves. I missed the dog the most, though he was the quietest of all our ghosts; we could only tell he was there from the sound of paws clicking across the wooden floor of the balcony at night, from the swish of a feathery tail felt across the face as I sat out on the long verandah at the back, shelling peas or doing some other kind of make-work intended to keep me occupied and safely out of trouble.

My mother was restless the day after the ghosts left. She paced the back garden, stepping absently on the carrot seedlings she had planted so carefully just the day before, looking for them in the small stand of sugarcane, in the branches of the champa tree, and returning disappointed every time. It was only when a light breeze and the dusty spatter of rain began in the evening that she went in to tell my grandmother, and for a long moment, the two women – one shrivelled into a small, curlicued caricature of herself, the other tall, slender, straight-spined – stood wordlessly in the garden.

Then my mother put out a hand, to steady my grandmother, I thought at first. But really it was to steady herself, and they walked slowly back to the house. The next morning, my grandmother left hibiscuses near the sugarcane field, and the day after that, giant golden sprays of laburnum, and then threaded strands of jasmine, and it was only after my father gently voiced his displeasure against his precious roses being sacrificed that she brought the flower ritual to a halt.

In compensation, she ordered the cook out of the kitchen the next day and made fresh catfish curry for my father. The catfish were replenished from the market on a weekly basis, and lived in a small metal tub where they swam round and round, their numbers steadily diminishing through the week as one after another they were turned into lunch.

• • •

Two months after our ghosts left, Shamala Mashi came to stay. She sliced through the stillness that hung over the house ever since the ghosts had departed with her usual laughing ease. She was famously the first – and for a long time, the only – divorced woman we knew, and her visits usually coincided with the departure from her life of yet another married man who turned out not to be leaving his wife for her after all. My friend Mamta from school would have to stop visiting us while Shamala Mashi was in residence because her mother disapproved of divorced women in principle, and disapproved even more of Shamala Mashi because she seemed to enjoy being divorced in a manner that was scandalous.

I liked Shamala Mashi. She was the only person I knew who didn't have holdalls or trunks, but matching luggage in red leather – a smart suitcase, a smaller vanity case and an exquisite miniature cosmetic case that opened to reveal mysterious unguents in glass-stoppered bottles. This time, she waved me over first, even before she'd greeted my grandmother.

'This, darling,' she said, 'is straight from Paris.' And she handed me a silk bag that I thought was the gift – it was so pretty. She watched me quizzically for a second, then gestured impatiently for me to open it. I did, and my grandmother hobbled in just as I extracted two gossamer wisps, one in black, one in pink.

'Shamala, what on earth are those?' said my grandmother. Her voice quivered with indignation.

'Mashi, there you are!' said Shamala Mashi. 'They're bras, of course. Uma should really have had her first set two months ago, I noticed her molehills popping out at Sati's party, but I've been so busy, I just didn't have the time to get them organized.'

My grandmother said, 'She can't wear these obscene things, Shamala, you have no sense at all,' just as Shamala Mashi turned to my mother and said, 'You can't possibly stuff her into those horrible Liberty bodices, so constricting for the blood vessels, and fatal – fatal, Ruma – for anyone who has the least desire to actually have a figure.'

The fight escalated, but I wasn't listening. The two scraps of lace and gossamer nestled like kittens in my hand, and I stared at them. They were so soft, so silky, so very different from the stiff white cotton contraptions my mother wore, the ones she washed by hand and hung on a discreet line in the bathroom afterwards instead of on the clothes line in the back garden, so that neighbours would not suspect the existence of underwear or the presence of something as undesirable as breasts in our three-woman household. Molehills or not, I knew with a fierce hunger that I wanted to wear these, and I knew that they would unearth something in me that might never emerge into the light otherwise.

I imagined how they would feel against my skin.

'Give them here,' said my grandmother.

I said, the word bursting from me before I could stop myself, 'No.'

Her hand was already extended. I saw the shock on her face rippling across the room to settle on my mother's features. Even Shamala Mashi was stunned. I had always been the most docile of children, but now something drove me. 'It's mine,' I said, making things worse, looking from one adult to another in desperation, 'it was a present. You can't take it away.'

Things might still have turned out all right if only I hadn't started crying. My grandmother's eyes went cold.

'Enough of these histrionics,' she said sharply and held out her hand again. There was no appeal this time. She didn't look at Shamala Mashi, and neither did I, as she led me out of the room, to her own small bedroom, where she deposited the bras at the bottom of the battered black trunk that had accompanied her from Dhaka to Delhi. They looked out of place against the ancient, yellowing newspaper that lined the trunk. It was in Bangla, and its blurred photographs chronicled the excesses of the Bangladesh War; my bras lay across pictures of skeletons and mass graves, and partly obscured the block letters that spoke of massacres and a war long gone. I hated the newspaper lining; it had acquired a dank smell of its own over the years, like unwashed hair. My grandmother made me turn the key in the recalcitrant brass lock, and then she sent me to bed.

I might have cried myself to sleep, but instead I sat by the window and its rickety green shutters for a long time, while something stubborn and unyielding in me solidified into hardness instead of tears. There was a gibbous moon, cold and yellow and distant, hanging over the sugarcane patch. I pretended to be asleep when my mother came in; I lay stiff and unresponsive when, uncharacteristically, she stretched a tentative hand out and lightly touched my forehead. My mother smelled of tiredness and talcum powder. My grandmother smelled of camphor, incense and flaky old skin. Shamala Mashi always smelled of perfume, and underneath that, jasmine soap. I kept my eyes closed but I listened as my mother left the room. One after another, the windows were shuttered, the doors pulled to and closed, each implacable bang reminding me of our missing ghosts. The house was still and close without their friendly bumps and thumps.

The next afternoon, when I was doing my maths homework, my mother knocked lightly at my door. 'This is for you,' she said. I stared dumbly at the two Liberty bodices, which managed to radiate scratchiness and discomfort, even from a safe distance. She hovered for a second, searching for the words. 'I hadn't realized,' she said. 'Until Shamala pointed it out. I'm sorry. Do you need anything else?'

'I won't wear these,' I said. 'They're horrible. I want those bras.'

I saw disbelief and something else, a shrinking, in my mother's face. She pulled the door shut. It was very quiet in my room.

'Listen to me, Uma,' she said. 'Those things are for other women. Not women like us; decent women don't wear things like that.'

'Shamala Mashi does,' I said. My mother's eyes flickered, and she turned to leave again, then she turned back.

'I never said Shamala Mashi was a decent woman,' she said. 'That sort of clothing, it's for whores.'

She spoke coldly, with great precision, the sole English word thrown like a stone into the soft ripples of the sentence she had spoken in Bengali, and then she left.

I didn't hate her then. That came later in the evening, when she, Shamala Mashi, my father and Mr Khanna were playing bridge. Mr Khanna had just smoothed his hair with his hand for the fifth time, leaving a slimy sheen of Brilliantine on his fingers, and was staring at Shamala Mashi's décolletage with open lust.

'That's a very nice outfit you're wearing, Shamala,' he said.

My mother looked at my father, whose eyes lost some of their weariness every time Shamala laughed, or made a clever remark.

'Yes, Shamala,' she said. 'Not all of us women could carry that sort of blouse off without looking, well, cheap – but you have such natural grace ...'

It was when I saw the flicker of pain on Shamala Mashi's face, and when I saw that my father had registered the word 'cheap' and that the tiredness was back in his face, that I began to hate my mother. Shamala Mashi left the next day; she had a friend to visit in Bombay, she said.

I couldn't steal the bras back, not because my grandmother would find out – she seldom opened her trunk more than twice a year, and besides, I knew where she kept the keys – but because I had no hiding places in which to keep them. My mother and I shared a cedarwood almirah, and she meticulously checked every chest of drawers, every cupboard in the house once a week, ticking off the items stored on an old, yellowing list where she recorded everything that was bought or gifted, down to the smallest hand towel. I avoided the Liberty bodices as long as I could, but after the nuns sent me home from school one day with a note for my mother – 'Uma's development will necessitate a change in her innerwear' – I couldn't avoid them any more. They faded to grey after a few washes but retained their essential prickliness. They felt like bandages, like poultices for a permanent injury; there was something of the hospital about them.

If it hadn't been for our quarrel, I might have noticed that my grandmother missed our ghosts as much as I did. I spoke to her as little as possible, ignored her when she called out from her room, pleaded too much homework when she invited me to join her in the evening aarti. Once, waking early, I heard a strange noise in the garden and crept down, shivering in my thin nightgown, to investigate. It was still dark, but there was enough light to see my grandmother outside, leaning against the champak tree, looking towards the sugarcane field where the ghosts used to live. She was shivering, too, but she was lighting diyas with unsteady hands, setting each down on the perimeter of the cane, and there was such grief in her face that I almost went to her side. And then I remembered that we were not speaking, and I left her alone in the grim grey damp of the morning.

A week later, she took a chill and died, and some inexplicable turn in her final moments made her get out of bed, naked, and walk to the kitchen. We found her face down in the metal tub, catfish swimming round her face, brushing her eyebrows and nose with their whiskery snouts. My mother said, 'Don't let anyone into the kitchen until I get back.' I sat there, patting my grandmother's ugly, straggly grey hair, not sure whether I should lift her out of the tub or not, mesmerized by the patterns of the varicose veins snaking up her legs like exotic creepers, like ferns on a crumbling wall, until my mother returned with a sari and a blouse that she wound around my grandmother's body, which leaked water and other fluids onto our hands as we did our inexpert best.

• • •

The day after the cremation, my mother and father argued about what to do with the ashes. They did this quietly, without raising their voices, and that made it much worse. I was hidden behind the heavy velvet drawing room curtains. I had begun to seek out hiding places, little corners where I could be, at least briefly, separate from my world and still be a part of it.

'You promised,' my mother said. 'You told your mother you would take her ashes back to Dhaka.'

'I know I did, Ruma,' my father said, 'but be reasonable. I can't afford it, and what difference does it make if we deposit the ashes in the Yamuna? It's just as sacred.'

'But she wanted her ashes to be scattered in the gardens of the old house in Dhaka,' my mother said, 'you promised.'

My father poured himself a stiff whisky and looked at my mother.

'She's dead now, Ruma,' he said. 'It doesn't matter to her any more.'

My mother straightened her back. 'It matters to me.'

My father downed his whisky in two gulps, and walked out of the room. My mother half rose from her chair, and then her hands tightened over its ornate curlicued arms and her face settled into blankness.

The next morning, my father hired a brand-new black-and-yellow taxi and we watched as he and his mother's ashes jounced off to the Yamuna, the taxi emitting a bumblebee hum all the way down the lane.

My mother waited till he had gone before she allowed herself to cry. She cried all day, soundlessly. She cried as she doled out the stores to the servants, as she dusted the china ornaments in the drawing room, as the gold bangles on her thin wrists rang softly when she wrote out the shraddha cards for the funeral ceremonies in her perfect, calligraphed Bengali script. Her voice remained steady, and her face didn't shift into the rictus of grief; except for the tears that never stopped, nothing else changed.

When I couldn't stand it any longer, I went into the back garden, ducking quietly into the sugarcane stand. In the past, this had been banned to me on account of the ghosts; now that the ghosts had left, it was still off limits, on account of the snakes that were supposed to live in the thickets. But the sugarcane stood high and tall and made the perfect hiding place, and though the leaves were rough and rasped my skin, a telltale line of diyas, faded in the rain and sun, told me that my grandmother had come into their depths not so long ago. I followed the line of diyas as though they were fairy-tale breadcrumbs until they led me to a small clearing in the centre of the patch.

Sugarcane has its own aroma, heavy, dense, sweet but vegetal, almost narcotic, and I found a comfortable spot, hidden by the cane. I must have gone to sleep; it was many hours later that a low moaning woke me up. It's the ghosts, I thought, our ghosts are back, and I stood up, the muscles in my legs aching.

There was a bundle in the middle of the clearing, heaving and moaning. I blinked; the heavy shape separated itself into two figures, the mali and the next-door ayah. I listened for a long while; I heard their skins meeting with a slapping noise and then separating wetly; her skin was dark, her breasts round and heavy. There was a final moan and involuntarily, I gasped. The two shapes separated, there was a whisper, and then the ayah scrambled to her feet and ran, mali behind her.

I could feel the hateful Liberty bodice tight across my skin, and suddenly the thought of keeping it on seemed unbearable. Reaching round, I fumbled with increasing desperation until the clasp gave, and I yanked off the bodice and hurled it as far as it would go into the cane. It soared in the air, like a grey wraith, a dusky lily, a ghostly but oddly beautiful shape.

My mother was standing outside the thicket of sugarcane when I came out. She said nothing, and I said nothing – I had no idea whether she had seen ayah and mali.

In the moonlight, I could see the streaks of silver in her hair, the wrinkles that made her face look harsh and drawn beyond her years. I could also see, for the first time in my life, that she had once been a very beautiful woman.

She was looking down at a dusty black velvet pouch, its gold tassels faded like an expensive but old wig. She held it out to me wordlessly and as I took it, I noticed the delicate skin on the palms of her hands, the first papery softness of approaching age.

My mother gently closed her fingers over mine before I could put my hand inside the bag. It was a warning grip, but it was also very nearly an embrace.

'Ashes,' she said.

'Thakurma's?' I asked.

She nodded. 'I took a little when your father wasn't looking. It's what she did when she left Dhaka, she brought what she could of the family with her. Your father's brothers. He had two. His sister. She was twelve, your Thakurma told me, twelve when she died. They were killed in 1971, in the Bangladesh War. Your Thakurma often said she was lucky to have the ashes, that many families didn't even have that much.'

My missing family, the relatives we never spoke of, the aunt and the uncles I never knew I had, the ghosts who sometimes haunted my father's face, carried here in a faded black velvet bag. What had my grandmother used that bag for before she brought her family back in it? It was probably a jewellery pouch, I thought. Or perhaps it had been an evening bag; perhaps she had used it when going out to parties in silk saris, in a time before the austere white widow's sari defined every single boundary of her life.

My mother tied the tassels of the bag together, enclosing my grandmother within its confines, a handful of fine bone ash mingling with the older ashes of her children.

'Your father will never go back to Dhaka,' she said. 'It was wrong of me to ask him. And I will never go there, I'm too old for these journeys. But I thought some day you might take them back. Back home.'

The bag felt light, almost weightless, in my hands. Such a small container for so much history. I made my mother no promises and she never spoke of it again, but as we walked back to our house that night, emptied of all our ghosts, the familiar and the unknown, there was peace between us. That night, I sank gratefully into the silence of the house and dreamt of golden sugarcane juice, heavy and thick with sweetness, stirred sunlight in a crystal glass. That night, much as I mourned our ghosts, I did not miss them.

RAAGTIME

Benjamin Siegel

I imagine myself at that first New York concert often: the measured steps towards the heavy tanpura, the swish and fall of her dupatta in the silent theatre, hearing the first pulls at taut wire strings. A set of potted poinsettias sits shrouded in curls of incense under the stuccoed ceilings; Ratan Devi's eyes fall downwards past her thin nose towards her pale bare feet, and the first droning raag begins to rise. A set of raags – a simple alap, a ragini bhairavi in praise of Shiva – and Devi disappears from the stage, coming back for an unaccompanied set of hushed Kashmiri folk songs, and later, a climbing second series of raags. The congregation streams out breathless into a cool April afternoon: the next morning, reverential newspaper write-ups interpret the tanpura's drone – 'the eternal, universal reality out of which the individual emerges,' suggests one, 'and into which he recedes.'

The 1916 concert is a forgotten inauguration – the crowds at the Princess Theatre on 39th Street, more used to the regular premieres of Jerome Kern musicals, were the first audience in America to witness an Indian recital. For over a decade, Ratan Devi's intimate performances entranced American and British audiences with Hindustani raags and Kashmiri folk songs, drawing in dazzled listeners who saw in Devi the embodiment of their Indian imagination.

For her fawning American audiences, Devi's 'successful transplantation of Hindu music from its native temples,' as one contemporary account gushed, was the locus of a new American cosmopolitanism. For her tempestuous husband, the celebrated symbolist and art scholar Ananda Coomaraswamy, those audiences were where India's aesthetic potential could reach its fullest bloom – with this ambitious young scholar serving as the lucid facilitator.

Little in Devi's performances, however, belied her beginnings as a Yorkshire mezzo-soprano, whose only journey to India years earlier had seen her sitting at the feet of a Kashmiri jongleur. In spite of her inauspicious origins, the quiet Englishwoman became an unlikely ambassador of Indian classical music, giving feverish American audiences their first Indian forms, collecting glowing accolades from scores of audiences and reviewers, among them Tagore, Yeats, and George Bernard Shaw.

But as America's Indian imagination narrowed and its orientalist fantasies wilted, Devi's star faded as quickly as it had risen, her Indian pantomime cast away in a rising crest of conservatism. And as her moment cruelly ebbed, Devi found herself abandoned not only by an indifferent public, but by the men with whom she had shared her meteoric ascent.

Ratan Devi's disappearance – her absence from the cataloguing of American cultural memory, and the strange erasure of her presence from her lovers' memoirs and files – remains deeply vexing. In the records that recount her rise, the fiercely individual oddity of her journey emerges, in brief and tantalizing flashes.

• • •

In 1910, Alice Richardson fell deeply in love with Ananda Kentish Coomaraswamy. Their courtship was understandably brief. Coomaraswamy boasted watery black eyes, a manicured and thin moustache he would only shave a quarter-century later, and caramel skin gifted by his Ceylonese father and wealthy Kent mother. Richardson was a slight mezzo-soprano from Yorkshire, who first set eyes on her future husband when he attended one of her English folk music recitals that year.

If their coupling ruffled feathers, it was certainly easier for the young couple than it had been for Coomaraswamy's mixed-raced parents. Thirty years before, a tribute recalled, Elizabeth Clay Beeby, 'the belle of the season, entered a London drawing room. There she came upon a student from the East, [the] cynosure of all eyes, the object of all attentions. His exotic beauty, his courtly manner and polished speech – speech in her own language – lifted her off her feet.' Within a year, Mutu Coomaraswamy, England's first Asian barrister, had swept his bride back to Ceylon to give birth to Ananda in 1877.

When Richardson first met the younger Coomaraswamy in London three decades later, the geologist was only months removed from a bitter divorce from Ethel Partridge. Partridge had accompanied him for close to a decade on his early expeditions to Ceylon, first as a precocious doctoral student, and then as the headstrong director of the island's Mineralogical Survey. Coomaraswamy's years of shuffling between London and Colombo had rendered him a vegetarian, a fiery nationalist and an aspiring art scholar, touched by the monomania that his many lovers would find cuttingly romantic. Leaving for Ceylon gripped by the island's uncharted mineral deposits, Coomaraswamy had returned a South Asian art evangelist, lending a lucid and powerful voice to heritages ignored.

Back in London, Coomaraswamy found no little grist for the mill. At a meeting in 1910 at the Royal Society of Arts, the eighty-year-old chairman of the Indian section had lambasted a vitrined Buddha, suggesting that 'a boiled suet pudding would serve equally well as a symbol of passionless purity and serenity of soul.' Ananda, incensed, took his pen to the pages of the *Times*, and shortly thereafter, announced the formation of the Royal India Society. It was through the Society that Coomaraswamy published his earliest pamphlets, and while immersed in its formation and the city's frenzied arts scene that he first met Richardson.

In spite of a generally progressive orientation, Coomaraswamy's early writings were undercut by the disdainful misogyny that would bubble throughout his work. Reeling from his divorce, Coomaraswamy penned a vitriolic apologia, *The Oriental View of Women*, where, in the face of a blossoming suffragist movement, he lamented the sorry state of Western child-rearing. Indian women, he posited, found in intercourse sacrament, while their Western counterparts could, through sex, only vitiate themselves.

None of this seemed to matter to Richardson, who was taken with his charm and quiet intensity. Within months, the two were married, and lecture invitations in hand, Coomaraswamy whisked her off to India.

• • •

The couple arrived on the subcontinent in late 1910, Coomaraswamy having been charged with organizing the Indian art section of the United Provinces Exhibition at Allahabad. The exhibition was to be a triumphant celebration of imperial advance, with modernist Indian painters airing their canvases under the roar of French-manned biplanes.

For some of its attendees, however, the show of the century was tinged with controversy: the celebrated Bengali singer, Gauhar Jan – one of the first singers recorded by India's Gramophone Company a decade earlier – provided evening entertainment, singing the thumris and khayals that had made her a national star. Jan's was an unlikely provenance: she was born Angelina Yeoward to a family of Armenian Jews in Calcutta, and converted to Islam with her mother when the latter remarried a Benares Muslim. Prominent Hindu males condemned Jan's performances, deeming them obscene and debased – but in spite of their threats and outcries, Jan performed to consistently sold-out shows, scalpers hawking tickets for usurious sums. Coomaraswamy and Devi could not but have heard Jan – and for Devi, Jan must have proved an irresistibly compelling idol.

It was shortly after delivering his keynote on Rajput painting that Coomaraswamy headed for Calcutta, meeting with Rabindranath

Tagore for the first time, and collecting the first drawings and sculptures that would, many years later, serve as the seeds of the Indian collection at Boston's Museum of Fine Arts. Returning to Allahabad, Coomaraswamy hatched a plan to conduct a study of Rajput painting from a base in Srinagar.

The roads to Kashmir – from Delhi in the east and Rawalpindi in the west – were traversed in the thawing months by merchants and entertainers who moved towards the mountains, hoping to ply their trade to the trickle of English tourists taking respite from the mounting heat. The apples and mutton to be had alongside Srinagar's Dal Lake could only hint at the English countryside; for more intrepid travellers, Kashmir offered a welcome holiday from the ceaseless illness and dust of their north Indian postings.

Coomaraswamy and Richardson passed at least a few of these travelling musicians on their own meandering journey through Punjab and the Himalayas: first, a sitar player near Rawalpindi, then two 'picturesque and ragged' veena players further north. It was on this voyage that Richardson began to plan a study of Indian music to match her European training in London, though the sarangi player whom they first approached politely turned down their offer for spring employment as a tutor, noting that there was more lucrative work to be had as a musician in residence at one of the many dak bhavans along the road. Coomaraswamy had never shown anything but the most cursory interest in Indian music, and his agreeing to the idea of a spring tutorial for his young wife proved a ready means of occupying her for the season while he obsessively pursued his own writing.

It was Ustad Abdul Rahim, a craggy Kashmiri singer and tanpura player, who would finally accept their offer. Abdul Rahim, whose white swirled turban, high cheekbones and knotted fingers made for a regal contrast to his brown tweed jackets, came from a long line of musicians and mystics – his father, he claimed, had been retained as an entertainer by the princes of Jodhpur. The balladeer was prone to thaumaturgic visions and cryptic predictions: his ancestors had been Kashmiri Brahmins, converted to Islam upon pain of death. Coomaraswamy, while a more talented symbolist than ethnographer, marvelled at Abdul Rahim, seeing many of his cultural traits – most notably, his family's refusal to remarry its widows – as essentially Hindu.

'Slight and delicate,' Coomaraswamy would remember later, 'gentle-mannered and patient, an inveterate smoker of hookah, a first-rate teacher, a great boaster, much too fond of presents and too ready to ask for them, a true artist and often unmistakably inspired, finding his art now less and less appreciated, yet conscious of the dignity of his inherited skill – such are the salient characteristics of a rather pathetic figure, not without nobility, but such as the Board school education of Indian Universities finds little use for.'

Abdul Rahim consented to taking on Richardson as his charge – with the insistence that their lessons be conducted with the gravity and formality befitting a teacher and musician of his stature, however faded. Their relationship began with a series of offerings to Richardson's new teacher, and an invocation to the success of the strange gathering that would ensue.

• • •

The trio made their way north to Srinagar, where the snow had begun to thaw and the expansive houseboats on Dal Lake had begun to buzz with life. Coomaraswamy and Richardson rented one of those houseboats for themselves – and Abdul Rahim began to prepare his lessons, gathering a motley crew of musicians, minstrels, and singers. That spring, Richardson was to trade in her English folk and theatre training for a slow course in the classical and folk forms of Kashmir, purchasing a mother-of-pearl-trimmed tanpura as long as she was tall, its drones tuned to her honeyed soprano.

Each morning, Abdul Rahim would convene a changing assembly of peripatetic musicians who would take turns singing and playing for Richardson, and Coomaraswamy, when he chose to join. The repertoire was a heterodox mix of styles and subjects –

paeans to Sufi pirs and saints and Hindu gods, ballads of romantic yearning and odes to the beauty of Kashmir.

Richardson would listen attentively, the heavy tanpura perched on her lap, jotting down words and notation before singing back short phrases to her company of tutors – among them some of the musicians she and Coomaraswamy had passed on their way to Kashmir. Richardson found in Abdul Rahim an ecumenical but often deeply traditional pedagogue: when the weather grew too cold, he would refuse to sing dipak raags, reserved for the summer months. And while his peers readily traded in their cumbersome and expensive tambouras for cheap and compact harmoniums, Abdul Rahim scoffed at the British substitutes, vowing never to lend his cantillation to such crass instruments.

'Abdul Rahim's faith in Hindu gods,' wrote Coomaraswamy, 'is as strong as his belief in Islam and Moslem saints, and he sings with equal earnestness of Krishna or Allah, exemplifying the complete fusion of Hindu and Moslem tradition characteristic of so many parts of India today.' A century later, it is sometimes difficult to imagine that wholly syncretic Kashmir. The cast of Hindu and Muslim musicians who came to Dal Lake that spring were not reluctantly practising a thin-lipped, self-conscious tolerance, but rather living the mutuality that would miserably implode in the years after Partition.

The couple warmed quickly to their Muslim companions, whom they found gifted with both musical sagacity and deep charm. One minstrel, Abdulla Dar, particularly ingratiated himself to Richardson and Coomaraswamy, strumming devotional songs on a tinny rabab. 'To hear him recite Persian or Kashmiri words, without music,' Coomaraswamy gushed, 'is almost as great a pleasure as to hear him sing. I say advisedly, see him sing, for not only is he a very handsome man with a frequent frank smile and pearly teeth, but his manner of singing is most fascinating, and while during a song he quite forgets himself, at the close he will shyly hide his head behind the instrument in a very coy and boyish way.'

The Coomaraswamys, however, did not particularly care for their Hindu hosts, or at least their music. 'We were told that this pandit was accustomed to singing to sick people,' noted Coomaraswamy, recalling one of many such brought around to perform, 'and even effect cures, but to our thinking, he sang no better than the others – that is, not very well. The so-called various raags sung by the pandits are all very much alike, and musically distinctly uninteresting.'

While Richardson tackled new songs and tweaked and tuned her tanpura, Coomaraswamy brooded on the houseboat with a Kashmiri grammar, his studies aided by a Hindu, Samsara Chand. Chand was charged with transcribing each one of the songs into neat Persian script before giving another stenographer the text to transcribe into Devanagari. Coomaraswamy would then sound out each syllable carefully, his halting efforts met with approving nods and smiles from his tutors.

For Coomaraswamy, however, music was a tertiary pursuit, and while he was quick to peacock his scholarly accomplishments in the slim volume of songs they would publish once in London, it was clear that the spring belonged to Richardson, whose musical acumen made her an enviably quick study.

As his young wife cut her fingers on the tanpura's sharp strings, Coomaraswamy was short in his praise of her, though he did afford reluctant admiration to her tutor. 'At times,' he allowed, 'our Ustad – who could upon occasion shout with the loudest and hoarsest – proved himself a true artist, sensitive to every perfection of both sequence and quality of sound.'

Later that spring, Samsara Chand invited the couple to his own house, where he introduced Richardson to his female relatives and their friends, who had gathered with a group of babies. The women blushed at the foreign couple, but at Chand's exhortation, began singing a set of lullabies. Richardson, after some time, tried to join in, and later on, Chand proudly transcribed each one of the songs for them as a gift. For Richardson, it was a subtle but sweet victory – Abdul Rahim had balked at the idea of passing on folk songs, owing to his noble lineage, and had only rarely and reluctantly consented to even sharing them.

But if the season was indeed hers, there is little record of Richardson's estimation of the gathering, and the book that the couple would pen together bears no trace of her remembrances – Coomaraswamy having expropriated the narrative with his own characteristically sober exegesis. Those lessons in Kashmir are like so much of the singer's life: chronicled and celebrated, yet fundamentally lost, remembered only in their broadest contours. It remains ours to imagine her singular mix of wonder and fear, thousands of miles away from her Yorkshire home.

It was sometime during their ten weeks together that Abdul Rahim gave Alice Richardson a new name, one more befitting her rising star. Thousands of miles away from Yorkshire, Ratan Devi – the jewel of God – was born. Several years after the pair's Kashmiri spring, it was a name that would grace countless playbills and awnings half a world away.

• • •

The conclave came to an abrupt halt in late spring. Abdul Rahim announced that he had been recalled to his post as a bureaucrat in the Punjabi city of Kapurthala, and the lessons ended a few weeks before the tourist high season dawned on Kashmir. The houseboat emptied out, the musicians dispersed, and Richardson ferried off her heavy tanpura. The couple returned to England in 1911, and Coomaraswamy set to work on a slim art monograph – *Indian Drawings: Second Series, Chiefly Rajput* – which he quickly published and dedicated to Ratan Devi, by then pregnant with their first child, Narada. Increasingly enmeshed in the London arts scene, and dreaming of her time in Kashmir, Ratan Devi began to put together a programme of Indian songs, trying out their unfamiliar melodies all over the city.

Recognition came quickly. In October, Coomaraswamy and Devi appeared on stage together at the Royal Albert Hall, delivering a lecture and a recital of Indian songs before the premiere of *The*

Maharani of Arakan. *Maharani* was a one-act play adapted from a story by Tagore, who had recently arrived in London. The play was dismissed by the London evening papers as overly simple and strange – 'not unlike an Irish drama' – but the performance was not lost on Tagore's friends, Yeats and Shaw, who sat teary-eyed in the audience.

Tagore had grown smitten with Ratan Devi since their meeting in a London parlour on her return from India. Devi had begun the evening at the piano, singing Irish and English folk tunes that Tagore had found charming. 'They were delightful,' he would write later, 'and I prayed in my mind that she should end the evening as she had begun, with the music familiar to her.' Yet Devi moved from the piano to the floor, pulling out the mother-of-pearl-inlaid tanpura that she had shipped back from Kashmir.

The poet squirmed in his chair. 'I felt uneasy in my mind,' he recalled. 'I never could believe it possible for an Englishman to give us any music that could be hailed as Indian. I was almost certain that it was going to be something that defies all definitions, and that I was expected to sit listening to some of those contemptible tunes that a foreigner, without the power to discriminate and the patience to learn, usually picks up in India.'

Devi started to strum the tanpura, its drone flooding the drawing room. The song was an ornate dirge, a wrenching complaint of love grown cold. 'After the first few notes,' Tagore confessed, 'my misgivings were completely dispelled. Neither tunes nor times were the least modified to make them simpler or to suit them to the European training of the singer. There was not a sign of effort in her beautiful voice, and not the least suggestion of the uncouthness we are accustomed to in our singers. The casket was as perfect as the gem.'

'I forgot for a moment,' he would later recall, 'that I was in a London drawing room. My mind got itself transported in the magnificence of an eastern night, with its darkness, transparent, yet unfathomable, like the eyes of an Indian maiden, and I seemed to be standing alone in the depth of its stillness and stars.'

Others were less enamoured. The Sufi mystic Inayat Khan, also in London before the war, was harsher in his assessment. 'I also saw Mrs. Kumar Swami,' he recalled in his autobiography, 'about whom so much has been spoken, and who professed to be the first European artist who performed Indian music. But in her case it was an imitation of the Eastern art rather than real.'

Despite Khan's barbs, Devi was eagerly and imaginatively received throughout London. Two months after performing at the Royal Albert Hall, Devi delivered her recital before the Musical Association of London, who fawned over the performance and argued furiously over the disparate natures of sensitivity and emotion in Eastern and Western musical forms. By 1913, Coomaraswamy and Devi had garnered enough support to publish *Thirty Songs from the Panjab and Kashmir*, an orientalist curio with transcriptions of and notations for Devi's modest repertoire, jewelled with glossy plates of Abdul Rahim, Abdulla Dar, and other Kashmiri musicians. Tagore contributed a gushing Foreword, and Coomaraswamy commissioned four hundred and five copies, set in vermillion and black, from the Old Bourne Press, a London publisher specializing in books of magic and the East.

In 1914, Devi gave birth to the couple's second child, Rohini, pausing briefly before resuming her performances. But as the First World War broke, Coomaraswamy's position in London had grown increasingly precarious. While his scholarship had always been implicitly political – the reappropriation of a colonial art, a tacit undermining of imperial cultural authority – Coomaraswamy's nationalist sentiments crested in 1916, when he registered as a conscientious objector in response to the British enactment of universal conscription. The couple made plans to leave for the States. While Devi found ready permission, Coomaraswamy's political sentiments meant that he had to have a close friend (art historian and poet Lawrence Binyon) attest to his political neutrality before securing leave. By the beginning of 1916, the two were en route to the States, leaving Narada and Rohini behind.

• • •

The couple arrived in New York on 24 February after weeks at sea. Coomaraswamy spent the voyage itching for the opportunity to teach and lecture in freer climes, while Ratan Devi battled ferocious seasickness and dreamed of new theatres. The two arrived in New York and settled into the Hotel Seville on Madison Avenue and 29th Street. Coomaraswamy set to work drafting letters to potential patrons and sponsors, in the hope of selling books and securing lectures, and, with luck, rendering their stay in the States a permanent one. The couple travelled north to Boston, where Coomaraswamy began angling for the curatorial position that he would eventually take at the Boston Museum of Fine Arts.

Back in New York, as the snow began to thaw, the couple met Aleister Crowley. The British occultist had taken up residence in New York, living up to his moniker of 'Wickedest Man in the World' by serially seducing women and men as he prognosticated through a fog of ether and heroin. Crowley's notoriety made him an unlikely confidant: his American days were spent expounding upon mystical cosmology, conducting investigations of the occult, and positing a philosophy of the spiritualist potentialities of sexual climax.

Crowley remained, however, well-connected with an avant-garde arts world increasingly drawn to the East. Crowley reviled Asians – the only thing he despised more were 'Eurasians' like Coomaraswamy, whom he dismissed in his *Confessions* as 'the worm' – but he was all too happy to sell Eastern mystique to an increasingly curious Western audience. He thus found a strange and temporary ally in Coomaraswamy, who introduced himself in March, 'knowing', Crowley recalled, 'my reputation on Asiatic religions and Magick'.

The three met over dinner in Crowley's apartment, where Devi gave her usual recital. Crowley nodded approvingly throughout the evening, and the couple parted with a promise from the occultist to leverage his influence towards the success of Devi's New York premiere. Crowley held true to his word, publishing a brief poem about Devi in *Vanity Fair*, and later that month, Coomaraswamy received an offer for the couple to deliver a lecture and concert at the Princess Theatre.

The two passed the next several weeks entertaining journalists and writers in their room at the Seville, Coomaraswamy pontificating as Devi spoke occasionally and served tea. 'Intensity,' Devi told one reporter a week before her debut, warming to the attention, 'is the chief thing which distinguishes the poetry of East from the poetry of the West.' Meanwhile, Coomaraswamy posited, as he would repeatedly throughout America, a fundamental sameness in the East and the West. 'Sometimes,' he mused, 'John Skelton reminds me of the Hindus. Of all European and American writers, Walt Whitman, William Blake, and Nietzsche are the most Oriental, and they are almost identical in thought. Whitman is not akin to the Oriental poets in the form of his work, but in its spirit he is. In Blake, I find much that reminds me of the poets of the East.'

The long-awaited concert began at 3:30 in the afternoon on 13 April, and glowing write-ups appeared throughout the city in the days that followed. Picking up cues from Coomaraswamy's pedagogical lectures, the *New York Times* sombrely noted that Indian singing 'is not just an entertainment, but a magical ceremony, and the singer's art is not one of self-expression, but the means through which a god or goddess influences humanity.' Devi's performance, accordingly, was met 'with great interest and pleasure: with something quite beyond curiosity'. The couple, *Outlook* predicted, 'ought to find in America an eager public. If attendance at their recital should become a fad, it would be as wholesome and useful a fad as any that ever found favor among Americans. Is it too much to hope for that they will, however, find an adequate response in a growing public appreciation of real art?'

• • •

Two nights after Devi's Princess Theatre concert, Devi and Crowley slept together. For Devi, it was bitter relief from a husband who had grown increasingly distant since their marriage, obsessed with his scholarship and all too eager to latch his didactic speeches onto her entrancing performances. For Crowley, high on ether, it was just another Eastern conquest. 'The Operation,' he wrote triumphantly, was 'the most magnificent in all ways since I can remember'. After his orgasm, the bald and moustached Crowley collapsed onto the bed, muttering a Sanskrit invocation to Shiva that he had learned during his own time in Ceylon, many years before.

Coomaraswamy was wise to Crowley and Devi's liaison, but was loathe to taint their auspicious rise, particularly as he had begun a liaison of his own. Devi and he prepared for a string of concerts in New York, securing critical applause and a guarantee for future engagements from veteran publicist J.B. Pond. It was at one of Devi's concerts that he began to flirt with the eighteen-year-old Stella Bloch, two decades his junior, who would emerge as an art and dance critic in her own right – and Coomaraswamy's next lover.

Meanwhile, however, there was a tour to undertake. As Crowley retreated to his lake cottage in New Hampshire, Devi and Coomaraswamy rode up to Boston to perform at the Twentieth Century Club before heading to Chicago, where they would spend the month of May. The increasingly obstreperous couple perched themselves at the house of Harriet Moody, a welcoming heiress who would shelter a host of poets in her sprawling mansion, from Rabindranath Tagore to Robert Frost and Carl Sandburg.

Coomaraswamy dashed off letters to patrons, buyers, and potential employers, hoping to secure his position in the States before their scheduled return to England at the beginning of July. In the evenings, the couple jostled for the attention of their host's many guests, Devi performing European melodies alongside her Indian repertoire, and Coomaraswamy repeatedly declaring that India was 'finished', and that – as Harriet Moody recalled in her memoir – 'the only soil upon which ancient Indian artistic ideals can flourish and develop is the soil of the west.'

Chilly towards one another in private, Devi and Coomaraswamy nonetheless delivered their performance to four increasingly full houses at Chicago's Little Theatre. Ushers shooed away dozens of extra spectators at each show, and the city's newspapers cooed over the performances. Each show was lit in incandescent blue, to complement, as the Chicago *Daily Tribune* noted, 'the uncanny, hypnotic effect so often found in eastern scenes and eastern music with its benumbing iteration, reiteration, and minor cadences'. But as Chicago raved, the couple fumed – and it was in June that the two realized that Ratan Devi was pregnant.

Coomaraswamy furiously swept Devi back to New York. The child was undoubtedly Crowley's, and the couple teetered on the edge of divorce. A smug Crowley met Devi before he left for his New Hampshire cottage, and later wrote of their meeting with typical hyperbole. 'She was now too far advanced in gestation to appear in public,' he recalled contemptuously, 'so her husband had persuaded her to go to England for the confinement, and also to make various necessary arrangements with regard to the future. He had now cunningly pretended to give way about the divorce, admitting my right to the child and its mother.'

'His real motive,' Crowley claimed, 'was very different. She was a particularly bad sailor. During a previous pregnancy, she had been obliged to break the journey to save her life. She was in fact on the brink of death when they carried her ashore and she lay for weeks so ill that a breath of wind might have blown her away. It was, at least, not a bad bet that the Atlantic voyage would end in the same or even more fortunate way.'

If Coomaraswamy had indeed held hope for a miscarriage, his prediction came true. Devi left for England on the *MS Noordam* on 28 June, and lost the child while still on the steamer, 'hovering', as Crowley gloated, 'between life and death for over six weeks'. Coomaraswamy finished up his business in New York, and reluctantly headed back home to London.

• • •

The pair disappeared into a black and claustrophobic London as Britain's troops plunged into the Somme offensive. Devi spent the rest of the year in convalescence, silent as her husband published a stream of wartime monographs – including, perhaps to Devi's chagrin, the survey of Rajput painting first conceived during their Indian spring. Estranged from Coomaraswamy and subsumed in grief, Devi's singing ceased for the remainder of that tempestuous year.

But back in New York, Tagore had arrived once more for a series of lectures and conversations, during which he began speaking knowingly about Ratan Devi and her 'immaculately Indian' performances, with hints of her imminent return to the States. On 11 January 1917, Devi reappeared at the Princess Theatre, flanked by the familiar poinsettias and incense, and delivering 'in costume, many of the dirge-like India classics and the gay Kashmir dance songs, lullabies', and 'patriotic airs'. J.B. Pond, thrilled at his starlet's return, postered the city in woodcut advertisements, and on 4 March, Devi delivered another recital at the Punch and Judy Theatre, written up glowingly in the *New York Times*.

With the stages and halls of New York as their entrepot, the two again ingratiated themselves to the East Coast elite. Devi returned excitedly to the stage, tearing away from the connubial spats that boomed in their hotel room at the Southern; Coomaraswamy darted to Boston, where he would take his long-awaited position as curator of the Indian exhibition at the Museum of Fine Arts. It was during that spring that Devi and Coomaraswamy met Ruth St Denis, the dancer, at a dinner party in Gramercy Park where Devi had been asked to sing. 'We predicted for her,' the dancer would recall, 'the great success in the concert field which she more than fulfilled.'

St Denis knew well the powerful pull that India had on the American stage imagination: her 1906 dance performance, *Radha*, had drawn upon music from Delibes's nineteenth-century opera, *Lakmé*, and extras from the Indian immigrant community in New York City, to stage the story of Krishna's paramour. Yet St Denis's performance had been an art-house production, its audience the

American avant-garde toying with Eastern esoterica. Twenty years on, even popular audiences were imagining India, proof of which lay in the ecstatic charge of Devi's early performances. St Denis began to plan excitedly for an Indian stage collaboration.

That production would have to wait: in July, Devi received an invitation from dancer Adolph Bolm to join his summertime benefit for the American Ambulance Corps in Russia. Alongside dancers culled from the Ballet Ruse, Devi joined a pageant that would play to the rafters. On 5 August, the production opened to an eager audience in Atlantic City, then moved to New York City, Newport, Long Island and Washington DC, where President Woodrow Wilson took in Devi's raags. That summer, modernist painter Florence Stettheimer had Devi and Bolm pose for 'Sunday Afternoon in the Country', a harlequin tableau featuring Devi aside a tanpura and Bolm balancing a parasol.

As the tour wound down, Devi found herself finally working with Ruth St Denis, under the direction of Shakespearean actor and playwright Walter Hampden, backed by a company of seventy-five and an eighteen-piece orchestra. *The Light of Asia* was a son et lumière retelling of Prince Siddhartha's life. Devi's repertoire was reappropriated for the narrative, with the Buddha's apotheosis lit by crimson gels and backed by a cresting raag.

'What was the result?' moaned a sympathetic critic after the shutters closed. 'The play closed after three weeks of public indifference, due largely to the most stupidly unfair reviews by the dramatic critics. They can, apparently, sit night after night viewing the crime dramas, sex plays and burlesque shows on Broadway without tiring, but lack appreciation for a work of art like Mr. Hampden's production.'

The play's failure marked the start of a difficult year, with public indifference testimony to a waning of the Indian moment. The novelty of Devi's Indian recitals had begun to fade as well. In February of 1918, she made hasty plans for a concert of European songs at the Aeolian Hall in New York. 'It means a great deal to me if it is successful,' she wrote worriedly to the New York lawyer John Quinn, who had long been Coomaraswamy's patron. 'I should of course appreciate it very much if you would be a box-holder for that occasion.' Boxes were sold at a princely $16.50, including war tax. The concert on 7 March began with the nostalgic English folk songs that Devi had been studying before meeting her estranged husband, moving on to Mussorgsky and Brahms, before concluding with 'Sometimes I feel like a Motherless Child'. The concert garnered little attention, and Devi was left reeling.

The spring was silent, save for a small performance at Harvard's Fogg Museum in May. Shortly thereafter, Devi and St Denis received word from Christine Wetherill Stevenson, a Philadelphia philanthropist and theosophist, who sought to reprise *The Light of Asia* in far-off California, where a band of progressives and theosophists were ushering in the New Age at Krotona, a few mountains away from that upon which the Hollywood sign would be erected five years later. Devi and St Denis, drawn to the West Coast, readily agreed, and Devi arrived in Los Angeles in early July.

If the East Coast had begun to tire of Devi's performances, the burgeoning mysticism and theosophism in California meant that she found an eager welcome. 'The art Mme. Devi acquired at the feet of Abdul Rahim, singer in the court of Kapurthala,' gushed a critic from the *Los Angeles Times*, 'has not this in itself the sound of silver water splashing in the fountains in the tiled courts of an Indian palace to the voice of the bulbul?'

Away from Coomaraswamy, Devi took up residence at Krotona, moving her trunk of saris into a domed room with windows open to the resort's gardens and the mountains and valleys beyond. 'It is nearer to the East than any place I have yet visited in this country,' Devi told one interviewer. With Rohini at a girl's camp in the Sierra Mountains, and a copy of Coomaraswamy's *Rajput Painting* in hand for reference, Devi set to work advising the production. California was a far better match for the performance than New York had been: *The Light of Asia* ran in the garden stadium at Krotona and in a theatre in Beachwood Canyon for thirty-five well-received performances.

• • •

It was perhaps too much to ask that Aleister Crowley remain silent as Devi enjoyed her California success. In 1918 the occultist's venom flared up once more, furious at a sanctimonious digression on Western romance and physical passion in Coomaraswamy's newest monograph, *The Dance of Shiva*. Crowley, ever ready to eviscerate 'the Worm', fired back with a spiteful review of the book in his occultists' bulletin, the *Equinox*.

'There is certainly no one equal to Dr. Coomaraswamy for tangling up situations,' Crowley begins, 'perhaps not always too pleasantly. Consider the first child, Narada, who is a bastard. Was the father the "worm" after all? We have nothing for it but the unsupported statement of its mother, the "worm's" second wife. This may be doubted. Even the colour tells us nothing, for there were plenty of pigmented people in London at the date of the story.'

The spurned lover digs his talons into Devi. 'The first time he leaves her alone, he sets up a harem in India, while she, traveling thither to join him under the charge of his best friend, Dr. Paira Mull, immediately begins an intrigue with this fascinating Panjabi. The "worm" seems rather to have welcomed this domestic tangle, as Paira Mull is very well off.' The result of that purported liaison, Crowley alleges, was Rohini.

'About this time,' he continues, Coomaraswamy 'is getting out a book of Indian folk songs, and he actually tries to include a number of translations made by his wife's lover as his own. However, he is forced by her (after a stormy scene) to make a very inadequate acknowledgment [that he doesn't know] ten words of the language from which he is supposed to be translating. Isn't this complex enough for anybody?'

Apparently not. Writing himself entirely out of the couple's fractured domestic tableau, Crowley weaves a tale of Devi and a lover by whom she becomes pregnant, a series of German concubines for an egomaniacal and shrewd Coomaraswamy, and most cuttingly, the very real tale of her summer miscarriage on board the *Noordam*. 'The "worm",' he concludes bitterly, 'gets a job as curator of the Oriental Department of some Art Museum in Boston, and settles down with his wife to live happy ever after. I feel that this may be life, but it is not art.'

Lest he needlessly curtail his barbs, Crowley lampooned Coomaraswamy – or as he would dub him in a show of vulgar Hindi, Haramzada Swamy – in 'Not Good Enough', a short and invective instalment of his popular 'Simon Iff' mystery stories. The coarse name wasn't, of course, meant to protect Coomaraswamy: in the story, Haramzada Swamy is introduced with Coomaraswamy's full street address. 'Curiously enough,' the story's assistant commissioner of police notes of the 'Eurasian' murderer, 'it is his father that was black, a Tamil. The mother was an Englishwoman.'

Littered with references to Coomaraswamy and Crowley's version of his various infidelities, real and imagined, the salacious episode chronicles the murder of a bed-hopping socialite in Haramzada Swamy's apartment, with evidence of the scholar's own loose morals garnered from one of his hagiographic volumes on Buddhism. In a dialogical manner – in the spirit of a more lurid Conan Doyle – Crowley's police officers unravel a tale of greed, harems, and a forced seaborne miscarriage, ultimately implicating the scholar's wife in a dalliance with her Indian music teacher.

Tried and found guilty of murder, Coomaraswamy's doppelgänger is received into the Catholic Church, before 'Ananda Haramzada Swamy, Doctor of Philosophy, [suffers] the extreme penalty of the law'.

• • •

If Coomaraswamy or Devi were affected by Crowley's blows, they fumed privately. Devi returned to England shortly after Crowley's allegations appeared in print, and her next appearance was not until 1920, when she performed at a small staging of several plays written by Tagore's father, singing between two potted plants on stage during the intermissions. 'Though at times she was monotonous,' one reviewer noted, 'her voice was much appreciated.'

However much appreciated, Ratan Devi's wane had begun. She sailed once more to the States late in 1921 on the liner *America*, playing a small show at the familiar Princess Theatre before making her way to California. There were no concerts or shows, save for a performance in 1924 at Henry Miller's Theatre in New York. The Indian moment had dimmed, and in the absence of a diary, a set of letters, a desperate communication, there is little by which to measure the depths of Devi's frustration.

In 1926, Ratan Devi and Ananda Coomaraswamy divorced unceremoniously, drawing to an end a decade of public partnership and private sparring. The marriage had outlived most others' expectations – certainly Aleister Crowley's. But the long-awaited divorce came with its price: without Coomaraswamy, Devi found her access to the stage choked off by her former husband, at least by his absence. With the country deep in depression, the audiences and socialites who had flocked to Ratan Devi's appearances found little patience for her Indian recitals, wary of the Eastern ornament and subtle raags that had so thoroughly enthralled them before.

Devi found herself alone with Rohini and Narada in New York City. She enrolled her children in the experimental City and Country School, where a progressive curriculum and a regular music teacher's illness allowed Devi to step in as a twice-a-week elementary school music teacher. Half her lessons were structured pedagogical exercises, the other half given over to raucous folk singing and pantomime. A year after her divorce, Devi gave a recital to her primary school audience, clad in a sari, wistfully recounting stories and customs from her time in Kashmir.

In 1928, Devi was invited to perform at the Arts Club of Chicago. Now nearly forty, her voice had grown less pliant, but against the 'continuous, unchanging, gentle hum' of the tanpura, Devi's voice, it was said, still 'glided through arabesqued ornamentations, making great leaps from low to high and back again.' The review of her last performance appeared in the *Tribune* next to a tally of the 13,000 Boy Scout badges awarded in Chicago that year.

Several months later, Devi – who had since reverted to being Alice Richardson – married Francis Bitter, a physicist twelve years her junior and a freshly minted PhD from Columbia. In love,

Richardson followed Bitter to Cambridge, Massachusetts, and then to Cambridge, England, before the pair returned home in 1934, when Bitter joined the MIT faculty. As Bitter's career blossomed – in time, he would quietly and confidently revive the study of magnetism for the modern era and become one of the century's most respected physicists – Richardson's tanpura case gathered dust, its strings growing lax next to her long-forgotten saris.

• • •

Alice Richardson – the professional name under which she spent half a lifetime had been reduced to a mere footnote in her obituary – died at a Cambridge hospital in 1958, a decade before her magnetist husband, and a decade after the man with whom she had embarked on her Indian journey.

I've looked long and hard for any tangible trace of her: for a tombstone in some Massachusetts graveyard, or a pile of letters tucked away in some attic or archive – even for that mother-of-pearl-inlaid tanpura. All I've managed to find is a crinkly letter in New York, a few playbills and posters, and the hard pages and glossy plates of her book. Tucked inside the poetry library at Harvard, there is a tinny reel of her singing, a memento recorded a few years before her death. For all her accolades and successes, there is precious little by which to recompose her strange life – even the Princess Theatre is gone, its stucco felled by a wrecking ball in the mid-1950s.

Her daughter, Rohini, a talented cellist, grew friendly with the composer Samuel Barber; his generous biographer told me of her home on the tip of Manhattan and her migration down to Guadalajara, where she played in the symphony orchestra. But the search for Rohini proved fruitless, and with Narada having died young, there are no descendents to grill, no attics to probe, no memories of Ratan Devi as mother, friend, or wife.

Her absence remains oddly troubling – though not for the paucity of sources, since that very reconstruction from tenuous strands is a historian's quiet joy. Rather, it is the seeming exigency with which she has been removed from all memory that is vexing, her erasure in official record and biography that fills me with both sadness and indignation. Ananda Coomaraswamy's papers in Princeton and Bitter's lot in Cambridge bear no mark of her presence, and while her star in many ways eclipsed those of both of her husbands, she has been summarily excised from their biographies. The meticulous and doting Ceylonese–Malaysian who served as Ananda Coomaraswamy's biographer made scant reference to the woman with whom he spent a tumultuous sixteen years, and Bitter's correspondence gives no clue as to the origins of his romance with a woman a dozen years his senior.

The lilting reviews imbued with orientalist imagination provide one story. But the traces of Ratan Devi scattered across archives are still dishearteningly far from an index of her emotional life. There's nothing by which to cull up the mix of excitement and apprehension of that Indian spring, the crest of ambition and the highs of stardom during her first wartime tour, the humiliation of her affair with Crowley, or the depths of depression as her star faded. And while her tours' trajectories speak to a curious America, and the fawning, romantic reviews suggest a country deeply caught up in its Indian moment, it still remains unclear as to what a woman from Yorkshire felt through her celebration as the jewel of the East amidst an avalanching private life. Without a redemptive set of letters, without any sign of tenderness, it remains too easy to seethe with anger at Coomaraswamy's womanizing and his own unctuous celebrity.

There is a series of photographs taken of Ratan Devi in 1917 by the photographer Arnold Genthe, a year after her arrival in the States. In hazy monotone, Devi is seated before a velvet curtain, reverentially, if absently, cradling her tanpura, which appears so tall as if to dwarf her. In one photo, her fingers pull at the taut strings; in another, the plucking hand sits idly on her knee. In both photos she wears the same glinting bangles on her wrists and the same salwar-kameez, its oversized dupatta pulled over her hair to rest on her shoulders. Her eyes are held half-closed in each shot, glaring impassively past her long nose to survey the paisley curls of the rug beneath her: a strangely disconsolate tableau with its star's frown caught indelibly on glass plate.

It is perhaps overly simple to suggest that those wistful, narrowed eyes reveal anything other than an artful pose, a momentary set of distractions, or irritation at the photographer's set-up. But in the absence of any written record of her thoughts, these are the images of Ratan Devi that remain; the quiet performer, perhaps more alive on stage than off it, her eyes hinting at the premonition of her own passing fame.

Works Consulted

'A Concert of Indian Music', *New York Times*, 14 April 1916, p.7.

'A Line O' Type or Two', *Chicago Daily Tribune,* 9 May 1916, p.8.

'An Artistic Triumph', *East-West Magazine,* date unknown.

Anderson, Anthony, 'Musical. Mystical. Mme. Ratan Devi', *Los Angeles Times,* 7 July 1918, p.III2.

Antliff, Allan, *Anarchist Modernism: Art, Politics, and the First American Avant-Garde*, Chicago: University of Chicago Press, 2001.

'Chamber Music in Many Halls', *New York Times*, 9 November 1924, p.X6.

Clayton, Martin, and Bennett Zon, *Music and Orientalism in the British Empire, 1780s–1940s: Portrayal of the East,* Hampshire: Ashgate Publishing, 2007.

Coomaraswamy, Ananda K., *The Dance of Siva,* New York: Sunwise Turn Press, 1918.

Coomaraswamy, Ananda K., and Ratan Devi, *Thirty Songs from the Panjab and Kashmir,* 1st ed., London: Old Bourne Press, 1913.

Coomaraswamy, Ananda Kentish, *Rajput Painting*, London: Oxford University Press, 1916.

Coomaraswamy, Ananda, 'Letter to John Quinn', 29 June 1916, John Quinn Papers: Manuscripts and Archives, New York Public Library, New York City.

_____, 'Letter to John Quinn', 6 June 1916, John Quinn Papers: Manuscripts and Archives, New York Public Library, New York City.

_____, 'Letter to John Quinn', 26 March 1916, John Quinn Papers: Manuscripts and Archives, New York Public Library, New York City.

Crouch, James S., *A Bibliography of Ananda Kentish Coomaraswamy*, New Delhi: Manohar, 2002.

Crowley, Aleister, 'The Dance of Shiva', *The Equinox* III, no. 1 (1919), pp.292–4.

_____, *The Confessions of Aleister Crowley: An Autohagiography*, London: Routledge & Kegan Paul, 1979.

_____, *The Scrutinies of Simon Iff*, Chicago: The Teitan Press Inc., 1987.

'Dances of the East: Bolm, Itow, Ratan Devi, Roshanara, Start Extraordinary Tour', *New York Times*, 5 August 1917, p.X5.

Devi, Ratan, 'Letter to John Quinn', 2 February 1918, John Quinn Papers: Manuscripts and Archives, New York Public Library, New York City.

_____, *Songs of India and English Ballads* (sound recording), Cambridge, Massachusetts.: Woodberry Poetry Room at Harvard, 1953.

Dunbar, Olivia Howard, *A House in Chicago*, Chicago: University of Chicago Press, 1947.

'First European Song Recital: Ratan Devi', Playbill, March 1918, John Quinn Papers: Manuscripts and Archives, New York Public Library, New York City.

'Francis Bitter, 65, of M.I.T. Is Dead', *New York Times*, 27 July 1967.

'Give Talks on India', *Boston Daily Globe*, 21 May 1916, p.31.

'Guggenheim Fund Gives 38 Awards', *New York Times*, 27 Mar 1993, p.19.

Gupta, Charu, *Sexuality, Obscenity, Community: Women, Muslims, and the Hindu Public in Colonial India*, New York: Macmillan, 2002.

Hadland, F.A. 'Indian Music: Ratan Devi's Recital', *Musical Times [London]*, 1 January 1916, p.27.

Harvard University, *Report of the President of Harvard College and Reports of Departments*, Cambridge, Massachusetts: Harvard University Press, 1919.

Heyman, Barbara B., 'Samuel Barber', Email to author, 16 October 2007.

_____, *Samuel Barber: The Composer and His Music*, New York: Oxford University Press, 1994.

'Interpreters of the Soul of Hindu Music to the Western World: Photograph by Arnold Genthe & Photograph by Alvin Langdon Cobumm', *Outlook [London]*, 26 April 1916, p.962.

Jayawardena, Kumari, *The White Woman's Other Burden: Western Women and South Asia During British Colonial Rule*, New York: Routledge, 1995.

Jenkins, Edith A., *Against a Field Sinister: Memoirs and Stories*, San Francisco: City Lights Books, 1991.

Khan, Inayat, *Biography of Pir-o-Murshid Inayat Khan*, Rotterdam: East-West Publications, 1979.

Kilmer, Joyce, 'Oriental Poetry More Realistic Than Ours', *New York Times*, 2 April 1916. p.SM12.

Lipsey, Roger, *Coomaraswamy: His Life and Work*, Princeton: Princeton University Press, 1977.

Lubach, Kaye Leora, 'Tradition, Ideology, and the History of Hindustani Music in the United States in the 20th Century', PhD dissertation, UCLA, 2006.

'M.I.T. Adds 3 to Faculty', *New York Times*, 31 March 1934, p.12.

Moore, Edward, 'Chicago Again Hears Wailing Songs of India', *Chicago Daily Tribune*, 3 February 1928, p.27.

'Music of Hindustan', *Outlook*, 26 April 1916, p.941.

'News of Chicago Society', *Chicago Daily Tribune*, 4 June 1916, p.D2.

'Our First Actual Contact with the Music of India', *Current Opinion*, June 1916, p.29.

'Queries from Times Readers and Answers to Them', *New York Times*, 21 May 1916, p.X5.

'Ratan Devi Back From Europe', *New York Times*, 27 November 1921, p.14.

'Ratan Devi Is Dead', *New York Times*, 15 July 1958, p.25.

'Ratan Devi Reappears', *New York Times*, 12 January 1917, p.11.

'Ratan Devi Sings', *New York Times*, 4 March 1917, p.9.

'Ratan Devi: Costume Recital of Classical East Indian Raags and Kashmiri Folk Songs', Poster, March 1917, John Quinn Papers, Manuscripts and Archives, New York Public Library, New York City.

Sedgwick, Mark J., *Against the Modern World: Traditionalism and the Secret Intellectual History of the Twentieth Century*, Oxford: Oxford University Press, 2004.

'Singer of Indian Raags: Heard in "The Light of Asia" at Krotona', *Los Angeles Times*, 7 July 1918, p.III14.

Singham, S. Durai Raja, *Ananda Coomaraswamy: Remembering and Remembering Again and Again*, Kuala Lumpur: privately published, 1974.

St Denis, Ruth, *An Unfinished Life: An Autobiography*, New York: Harper & Brothers Publishers, 1939.

Stettheimer, Florine, 'Sunday Afternoon in the Country', Cleveland Museum of Art, Cleveland.

Stott, Leila, *Adventuring with Twelve Year Olds (Experimental Practice in the City and Country School Series)*, New York: Greenberg, Publisher Inc., 1927.

———, *Eight Year Old Merchants (Experimental Practice in the City and Country School Series)*, New York: Greenberg, Publisher Inc, 1928.

Sutin, Lawrence, *Do What Thou Wilt: A Life of Aleister Crowley*, New York: Macmillan, 2007.

Tagore, Rabindranath, *Selected Letters of Rabindranath Tagore*, Cambridge: Cambridge University Press, 1997.

———, *On the Edges of Time*, Bombay: Orient Longmans, 1958.

'Tour of Resorts for War Charities', *New York Times*, 10 July 1917, p.12.

Westharp, Alfred, 'Education of Musical Sensitiveness', *Proceedings of the Musical Association*, 39th Session (1912–1913), pp.27–44.

Willis, Jeffrey R., 'Rohini Coomara', Email to author, 17 September 2007.

NIZAMUDDIN AT NIGHT

Gauri Gill

I started to photograph my neighbourhood in the year 2005. Returning home late at night, I would notice things that I didn't in the day. Lit up by streetlights, house lights and moonlight, sometimes diffused by the rain and fog, or smog, Nizamuddin became another place. One of the first pictures I took was of a white van. Its precise location on the road, its mysterious alignment with the shadows imprinted on it, transformed it from an ordinary van into another creature altogether. It was as if I had passed through a door into another world. Within it lay everything. Sometimes, I imagined a conversation between the two halves of Nizamuddin: the West side which houses Auliya's shrine – a piece of old Delhi in New Delhi, alive with qawwali singing, pilgrims, Sufis, fake Sufis, poets, beggars, tourists, hakims, people gathered around fires, guesthouse owners asleep in courtyards with cats in the razai, butchers' shops, garbage warehouses, restaurants... and people at all hours; and the more genteel East side – Humayun's tomb overlooking its empty parks, gates and guards; the Saint and the Emperor. Their audience might include the ghosts of the Dayanand Muktidham Electric Crematorium and Cremation ground on the Western fringe, and the just arrived travellers of the Hazrat Nizamuddin railway station on the Eastern edge. They alight from trains at all hours, many of them coming from villages and small towns, then fanning out across the neighbourhood in the early hours, looking for buses and auto rickshaws to the Dargah, and to Delhi.

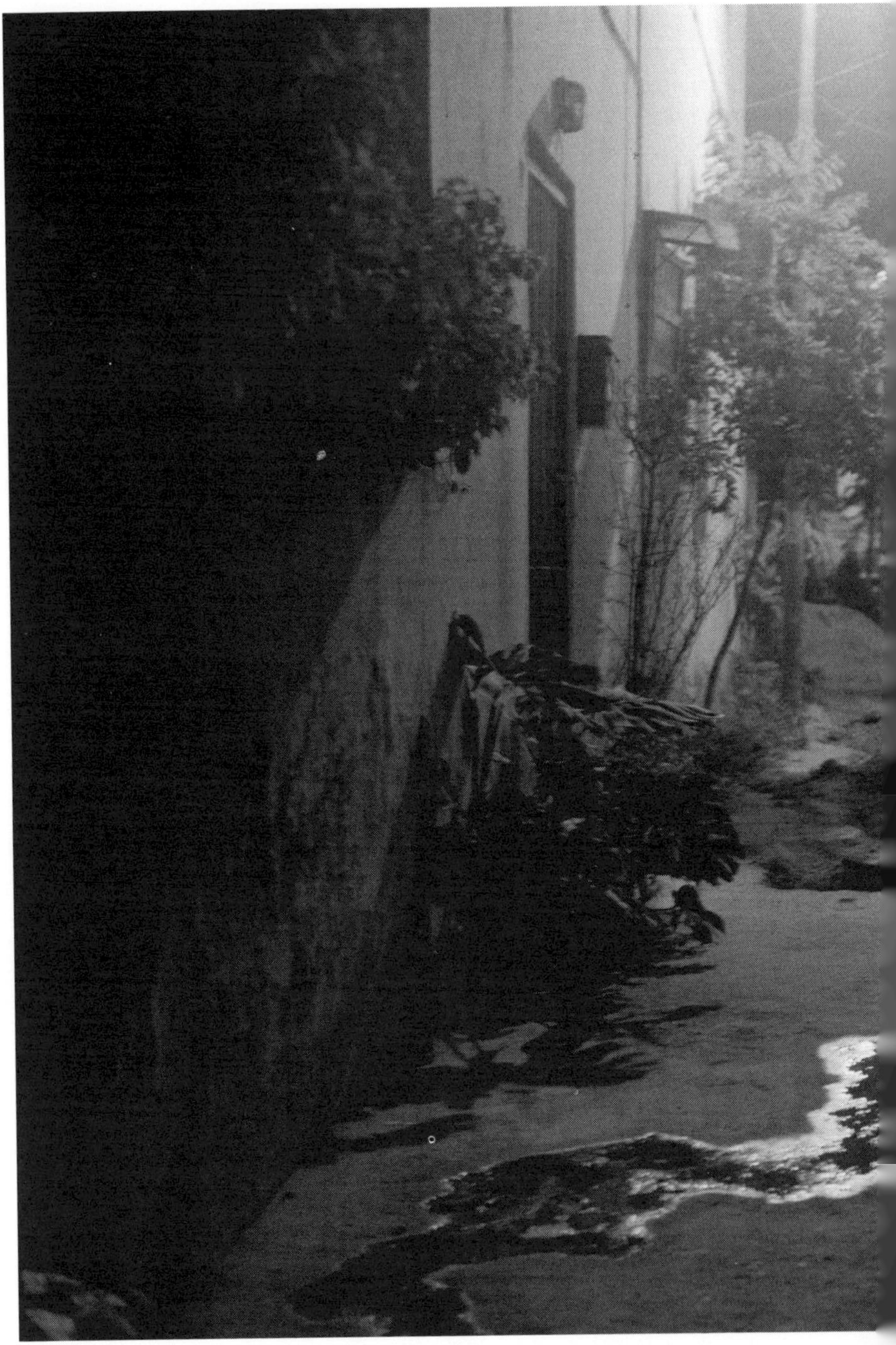

Nizamuddin at Night | 229

230 | Gauri Gill

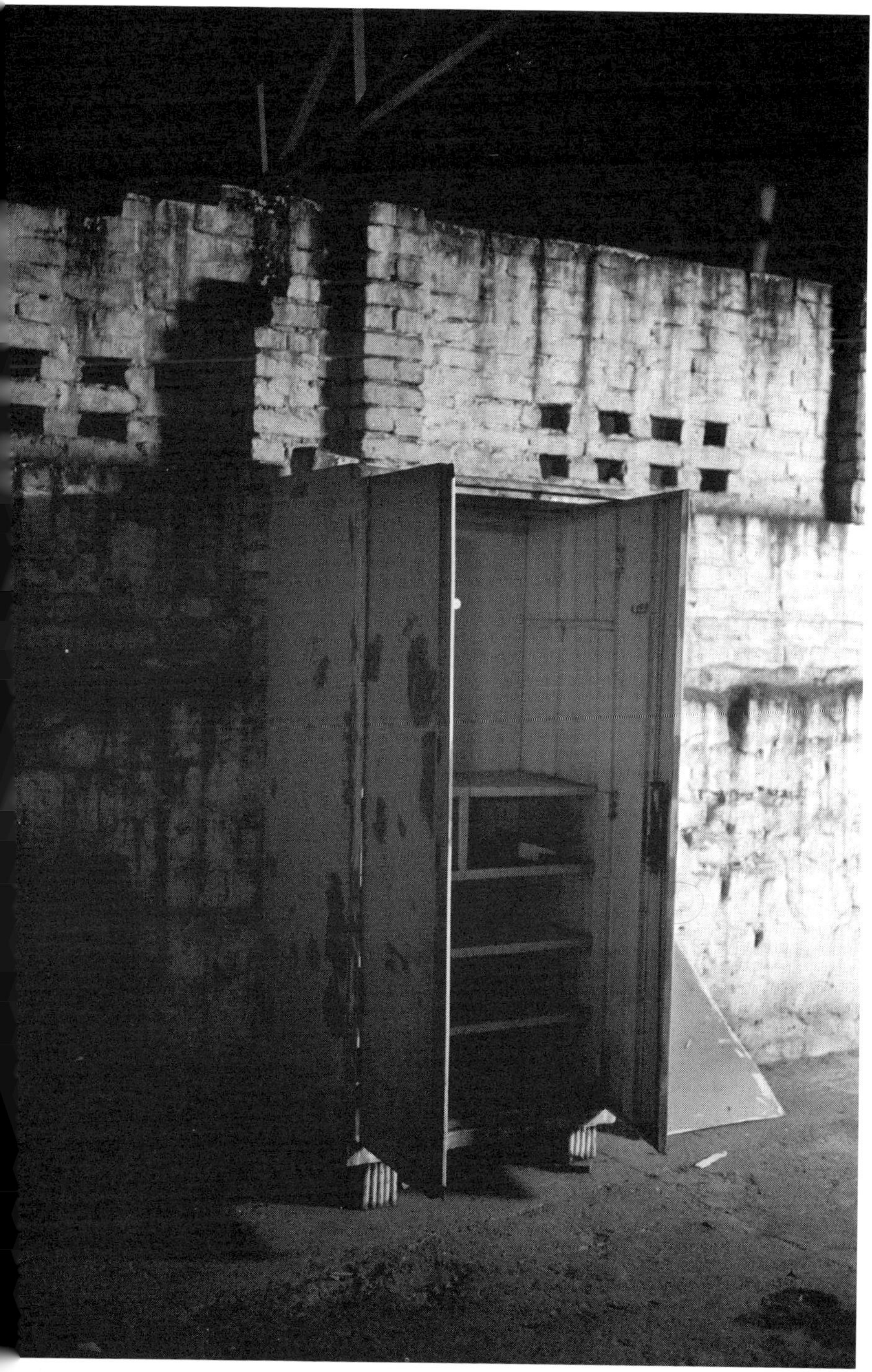

Gauri Gill

Nizamuddin at Night | 233

234 | Gauri Gill

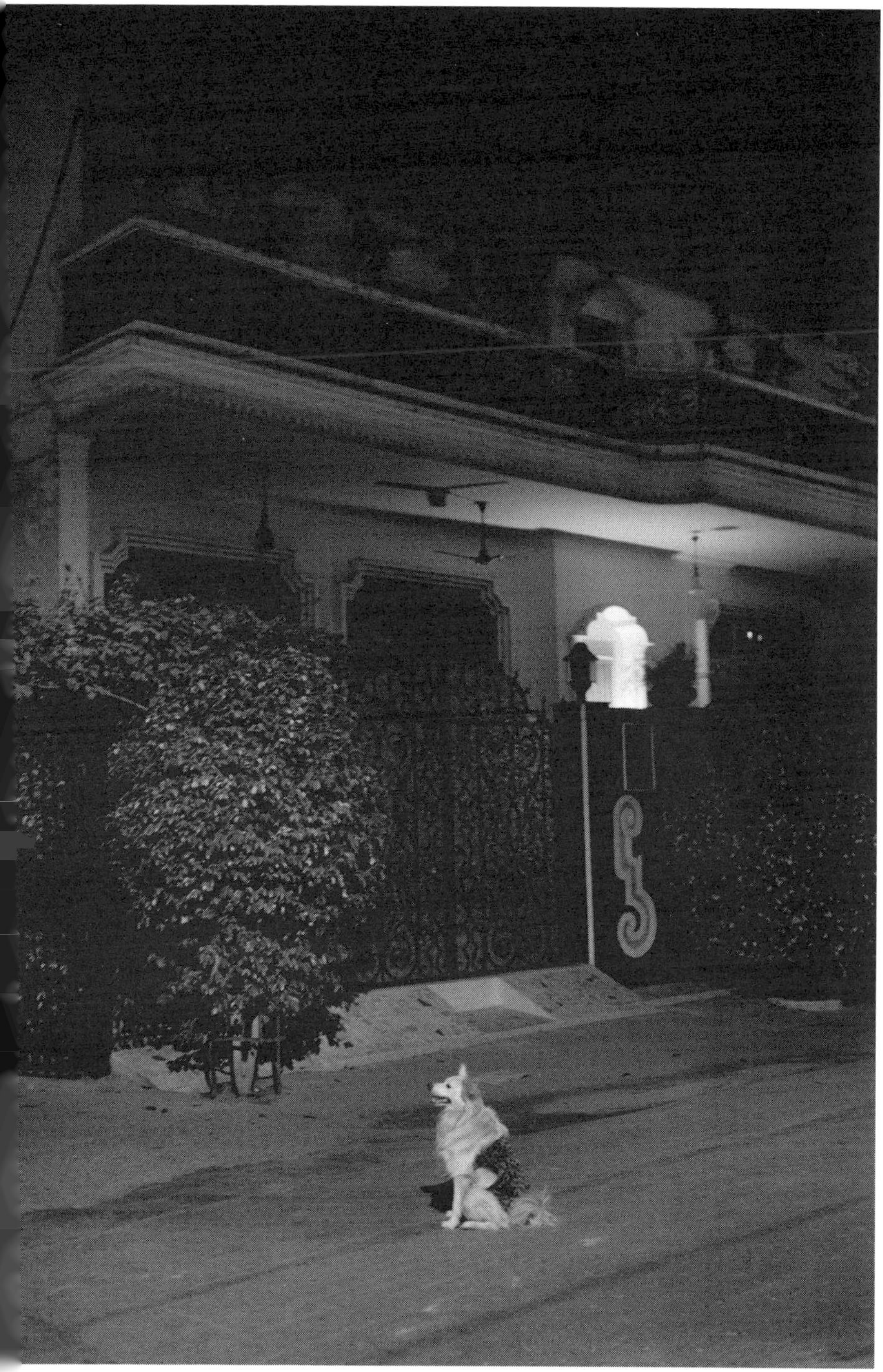

236 | Gauri Gill

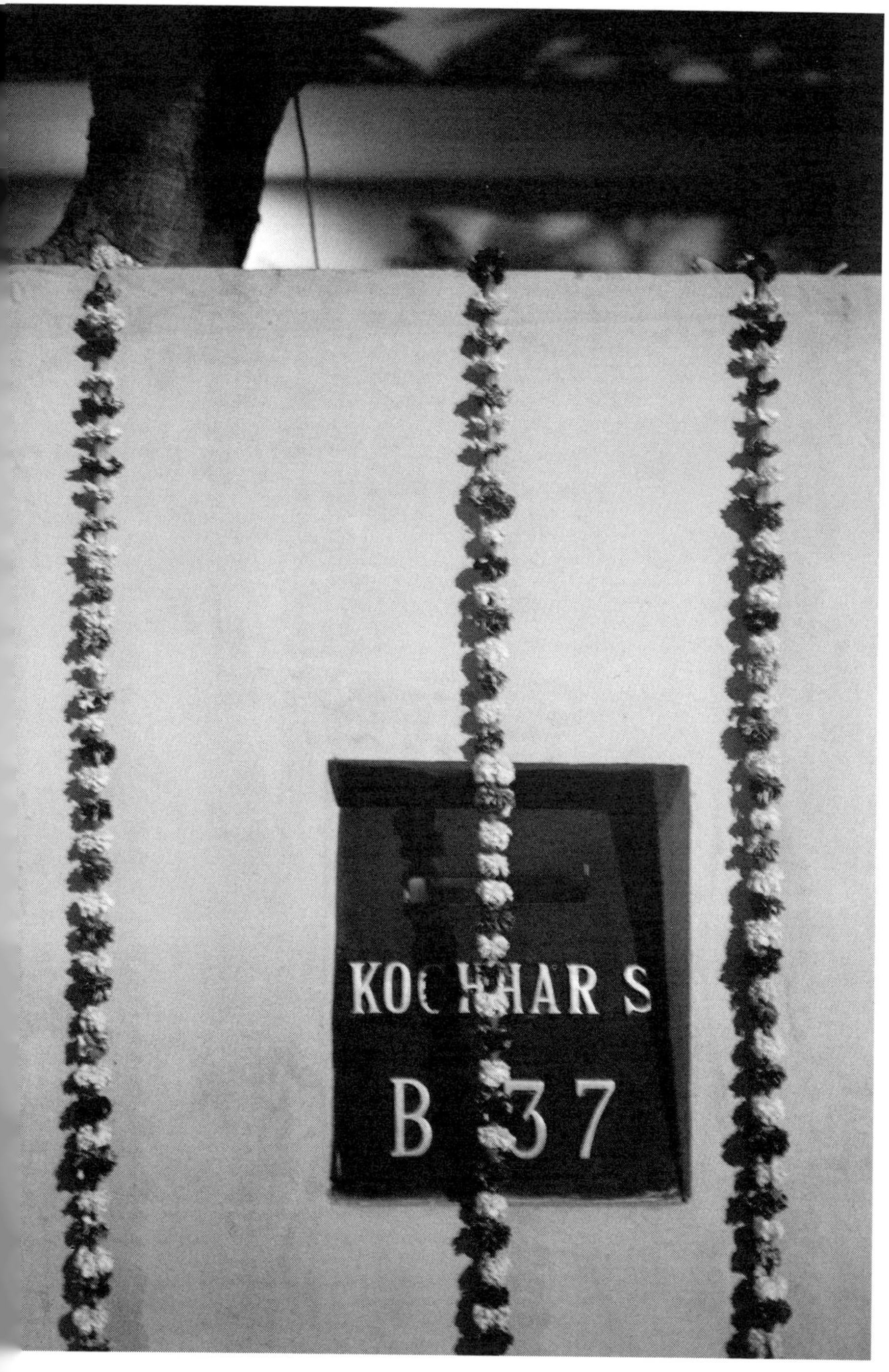
KOC HAR S
B 37

Gauri Gill

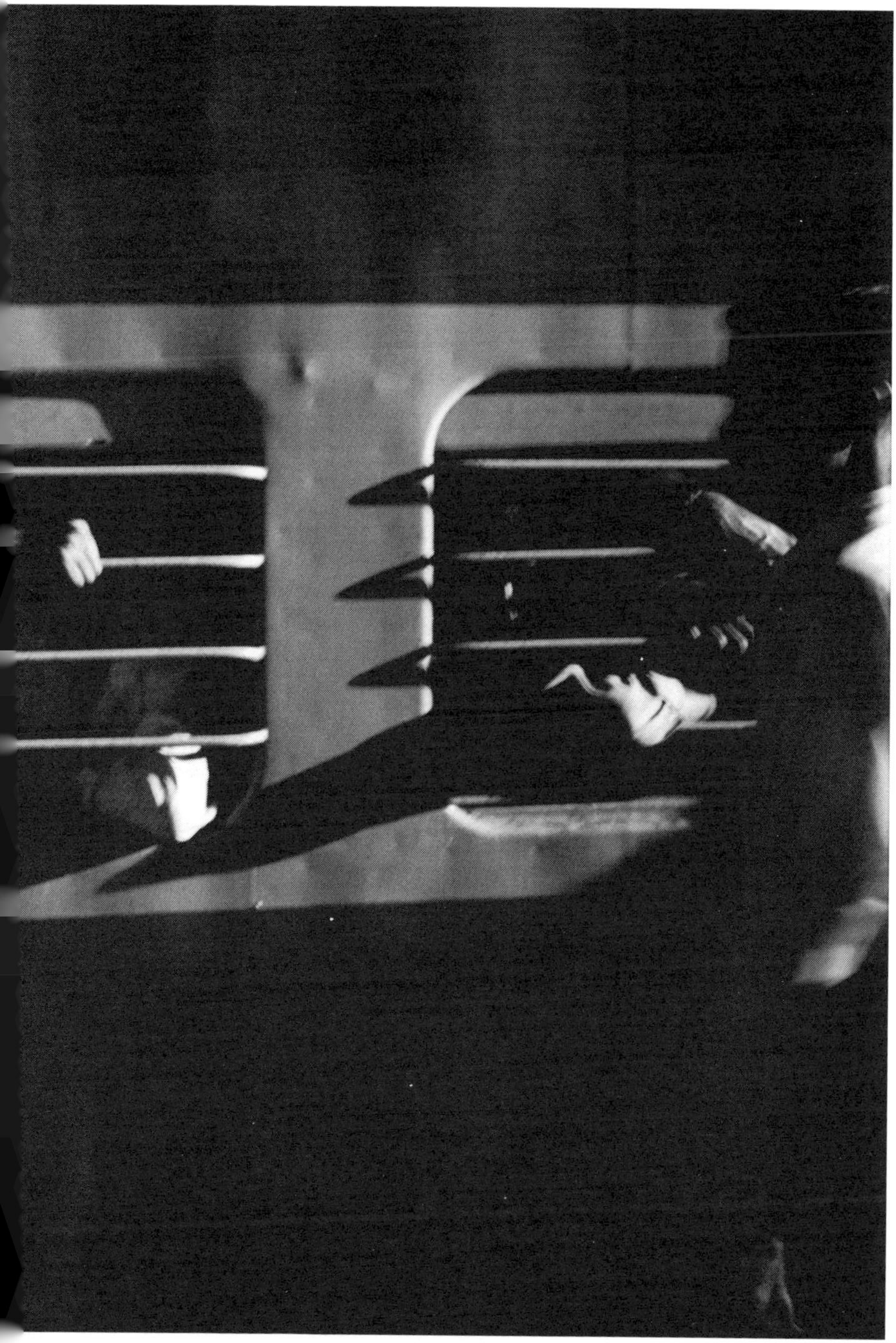

Gauri Gill

Nizamuddin at Night

242 | Gauri Gill

Nizamuddin at Night | 243

244 | Gauri Gill

Nizamuddin at Night | 245

CONTRIBUTORS

(In order of appearance)

Ruchir Joshi is a film-maker and writer based in Calcutta. His first novel *The Last Jet-Engine Laugh* was published by HarperCollins in India and Flamingo in the UK. This is an extract from a work in progress, a second novel: *Great Eastern Hotel*, which is set in Calcutta during the Second World War.

Itu Chaudhuri practises design in New Delhi in the blinks between watching cricket, listening to Hindustani music and other obsessions.

Achal Prabhala is a writer and researcher in Bangalore.

U.R. Ananthamurthy is a leading writer and critic whose body of work is primarily in Kannada. He is the author of *Samskara* among other novels, and several plays, poems and essays. He is a recipient of numerous literary honours, among them the Sahitya Akademi fellowhsip, the Jnanpith, and the Padma Bhushan. His piece in this issue is adapted from an interview with Archana Rai in *Outlook Traveller*.

Ananya Vajpeyi grew up in Mexico City and New Delhi. She was educated at the Jawaharlal Nehru University, at Oxford University, where she read as a Rhodes Scholar, and at the University of Chicago. She has taught at Columbia University in New York, and at the University of Massachusetts in Boston. In 2011–12, she is at the Centre for the Study of Developing Societies, New Delhi. Her first book, *Righteous Republic: The Political Foundations of Modern India*, is forthcoming from Harvard University Press in 2012. She writes regularly for newspapers and magazines in India and abroad. This is her first published piece of fiction; it was written in 2002. She dedicates it to Dilip Chitre, 1938–2009: a friend in the field.

Contributors

Shougat Dasgupta lives, temporarily as always, in Washington DC. In the midst of Washington's wide, empty avenues, among its self-aggrandizing monoliths, he often thinks of the shami kebabs, large as a fist, at Wenger's in Delhi.

Naresh Fernandes is consulting editor at *Time Out* India, which has editions in Bombay, Delhi and Bangalore. He has previously worked with the Associated Press and the *Times of India* in Bombay, and the *Wall Street Journal* in New York. He is the editor (with Jerry Pinto) of *Bombay Meri Jaan*, an anthology of writing about India's commercial capital and the co-author, with Jim Masselos, of *Bombay Then, Mumbai Now*. His non-fiction book, *Taj Mahal Foxtrot: The Story of Bombay's Jazz Age* (Roli Books) will be published in October, 2011.

Nilanjana Roy is a Delhi-based columnist who writes on books for the *Business Standard* and on gender for the *International Herald Tribune*. She is the editor of an anthology of food writing for Penguin India, *A Matter of Taste* (2004) and is working on a collection of essays on reading, *How To Read In Indian*, for HarperCollins India.

Anand Balakrishnan is an all-time lawyer who used to live in the Middle East. His piece in this issue is adapted from an essay that originally appeared in *Bidoun*.

Binyavanga Wainaina is the winner of the 2002 Caine Prize for African writing, founder of the Kenyan literary magazine *Kwani?* and director of the Chinua Achebe Centre at Bard College. His iconic essay, *How to write about Africa*, appeared in *Granta* in 2005. His first book, *One day I Will Write About This Place*, is forthcoming from Graywolf Press and Granta Books in 2011.

Rimli Sengupta is a willing refugee from engineering academia. She has lately been entertaining herself with various experiments in writing. She writes in both Bengali and English.

Manu Herbstein is a citizen of both South Africa, the country of his birth, and Ghana, his adopted home. After a career in civil engineering, he started writing at the age of sixty. His novel, *Ama, a Story of the Atlantic Slave Trade*, won the 2002 Commonwealth Writers' Prize for the Best First Book. Bookman India re-published it in 2009. The novel's prize-winning companion website is at www.ama.africatoday.com. A sequel, *Brave Music of a Distant Drum*, is being published in Canada in 2011. His piece in this issue is adapted from an essay that originally appeared in *Chimurenga 14: Everyone has their Indian*.

Benjamin Siegel is a Ph.D candidate in history at Harvard University. He was formerly a Yale University Fox International Fellow at Jawaharlal Nehru University, New Delhi, and a contributor to *Time* magazine and other publications based in New Delhi and Hong Kong. He is currently working on his first book.

Gauri Gill is a Delhi based photographer. She studied at the Delhi College of Art (BFA 1992), Parsons' School of Design, New York (BFA 1994) and Stanford University (MFA 2002). Gill's practice is complex because it contains several, seemingly discrete lines of pursuit. These include her more than a decade long study of marginalized communities in Rajasthan, and their often difficult encounter with modernity (*Notes from the Desert*). She has also investigated and recorded issues around migrancy, memory and cities *(The Americans, What Remains, Rememory)*. Working in both black and white and colour, Gill's work addresses the twinned Indian identity markers of class and community as determinants of mobility and social behaviour. In her work there is empathy, surprise, subversive humour, and a human concern over issues of survival. She received the Grange Prize for contemporary photography in 2011.